THE HAILONA PROPHECY

THE HAILONA PROPHECY

J. LANCE SANDERS

SAND PRESS

PROLOGUE

◆ I ◆

The old monk donned a white tunic and a dark pair of sunglasses. He ran his fingers through his long, flowing gray beard (he was making sure all his whiskers were in order). A gentle island breeze blew through his temple, causing several wind chimes to tinkle softly. As the old monk lit a votive candle and sat down to start his morning prayers and meditations, he listened intently to the surf as it pounded the nearby beach. He looked apprehensively at a Victorian door in the corner of his temple's central meditation room and squeezed several purple crystals tightly. Then he looked at the giant statue of Buddha in front of him. He prayed deeply.

The old monk stood up and walked across the wood floor toward the Victorian door. He was still squeezing his purple crystals, certain they were casting a glowing shield of protection around him.

The door, made of polished Hawaiian koa wood, was large and grand. The old monk slowly opened it. Immediately, a blinding white light washed over him, illuminating the entire meditation room. He stepped over the threshold, adjusted his sunglasses, and closed the door behind him. The flame in the votive candle in front of the statue of Buddha flickered and died.

CHAPTER 1

◆ I ◆

Zach sat at his desk in Mrs. Hildebrand's seventh grade English class. He was not paying attention to the lesson about a book written by Charles Dickens; he had not even started it and was hoping Mrs. Hildebrand would not ask him a question. Zach just wanted the class to end so he could go to the beach to do some body boarding. Or, perhaps, he would organize a game of touch football with his friends.

"Pay attention, Zach," whispered Amanda. She noticed he had been staring out the window, daydreaming. "You don't want Mrs. Hildebrand to call on you, do you?"

"Amanda!" shouted Mrs. Hildebrand. "Would you like to share with the rest of the class what you just whispered to Zach?"

Mortified, Amanda was unable to respond. Not the confrontational type, she was unlikely to come up with a witty rejoinder to test Mrs. Hildebrand. Amanda had wavy, shoulder-length blonde hair, hazel eyes, and fair skin (though her face had just turned several shades of red). Amanda loved animals and wanted to become a veterinarian when she got older. She could not stand to see any animal in pain.

"Well, Amanda?" Mrs. Hildebrand's tone was tough and domineering. She crossed her arms and began tapping her foot rapidly against the floor. "Let's have it. What is so pressing, so important, that it cannot wait until after my lesson?"

Amanda decided to fib. "Um . . . I was just asking Zach about his plans for after school today."

"Is that so? Well, missy, save it for later. The classroom is a place for learning, not socializing. Got it? There will be no socializing in my classroom."

"Yes, Mrs. Hildebrand," Amanda said softly.

The school bell rang, signaling the end of the class. The students started shuffling papers and gathering books. Mrs. Hildebrand's class was the last one of the day, and they were eager to go home.

Mrs. Hildebrand announced, "Remember class, you are responsible for the next chapter tomorrow. There will be a quiz. And you had better prepare well. Dismissed!"

◆ II ◆

Zach and Amanda were walking home together from school when two of their friends—Kalani and Glen—caught up to them from behind.

"Wow, Amanda, you really got it from Mrs. Hildebrand today," remarked Kalani.

Amanda sighed. "Yeah, I guess so. She's really strict, isn't she? I wonder why she's so serious all the time. She needs to get a life."

"So, Zach, have you even started the book yet?" asked Kalani.

"No." Zach looked at Kalani and Glen earnestly. "I don't know how I'm going to pass tomorrow's quiz. I'm in big trouble."

Zach stared out across a nearby beach at the frothy ocean. He bent over, picked up a lava rock, and threw it into the surf. Zach was tall for his age. In fact, he towered over most of his classmates. Everybody seemed to like him; he was very popular at school and excelled at almost every sport he tried. He was a natural, gifted athlete. In the classroom, Zach did reasonably well; he was not stupid. Sometimes, however, he neglected his studies—such as reading books by Charles Dickens—when he was not particularly interested in the lesson.

Glen and Zach were complete opposites. Glen was studious, scientific, extremely intelligent, shy, and not particularly tall. Moreover, he wore thick glasses and was uncoordinated (though he liked to try different kinds of sports). Nonetheless, Glen and Zach had been friends for as long as either of them could remember. They always tried to help each other in their own way. Zach would give pointers to Glen on the athletic field, while Glen would help Zach whenever he had neglected his studies for too long and found himself in a jam.

"Hey Glen—" started Zach.

"Yeah, yeah. I'll help you with tomorrow's quiz. But you have to do something for me. Something really important."

"You want me to give you some basketball pointers? Or help you with your wiffle-ball swing?"

"No, nothing like that."

"Well, what then?"

Glen glanced at Kalani. She had long black hair and flawless, sun-kissed skin. Charismatic and pretty, she was very popular. Kalani liked to tell people she was going to be the first female president. Glen often thought she just might pull it off.

"Zach, could you . . . oh, never mind," said Glen. "It's not important. Let's just say that if I help you pass tomorrow's quiz . . . well, you'll owe me one."

"Okay," said Zach with a big grin. "That works for me."

"Hey Zach," said Amanda.

"What?"

She pointed at a small temple in the near distance. "I dare you to go over there and peek inside."

The temple, an odd-looking structure, was located about fifty yards ahead of the kids, next to the white-sand beach. Its base was fashioned out of a combination of black, tan, and rust-colored lava rocks. At shoulder level, however, the material changed to stained wood and Japanese-style shoji screens. A staircase of stone led up to the main entrance. Curiously, there was a Victorian door on the temple's side. Although at the same level as the main entrance, no stairs led up to it. Overall, the building looked like a cross between a heiau—a Hawaiian religious structure—and a Japanese Buddhist temple.

"Are you kidding me? I'm not going anywhere near that temple," said Zach. "Not after what Kevin told me."

"Who's Kevin?" asked Kalani. "And what did he tell you?"

"He's the temple gardener." Zach pointed at a spot about twenty yards away from the temple. "One day I was body boarding at that beach. The surf was really up that day and there was a wicked under-tow. So it wasn't long before I caught a really big wave and almost crashed into the temple garden. Of course, it also happened to be the day Kevin was working. 'You better not mess up my garden,' he snapped at me. But Kevin's cool. After yelling at me, he asked if I wanted to have a soda with him. I said, 'Fer sure, dude,' and Kevin grabbed a couple from his cooler. We sat down and started chatting about, you know, the usual guy things."

"And what might those be?" Kalani teased.

"I don't know," Zach said irritably. "Girls, cars, sports. That's not important. Anyway, Kevin asked what I know about the temple. I said an old monk who's been there for years maintains it. But nobody really knows the monk. He's aloof. Kind of a hermit. End of story. Nothing to get excited about."

"Right," said Glen.

Zach continued, "Yeah, well, Kevin told me that one day he saw something unbelievable. Something that completely floored him. Something that often keeps him up at night in a cold, terror-stricken sweat. Something that—"

"We get it!" exclaimed Kalani.

"Okay, okay," said Zach. "Where was I? Oh, yeah. One day, while Kevin was tending the garden, he needed to ask the monk a question. So he walked up the stone stairs to the temple's entrance and poked his head inside. He saw the monk walking toward that door on the other side of the temple. You know, the one that leads outside but doesn't have any stairs."

"Go on," said Kalani.

"According to Kevin, the monk opened that door and a blinding light filled the room," explained Zach. "Kevin said if he hadn't been wearing his sunglasses, he wouldn't have been able to see what happened next. You see, the monk actually stepped through the door, into the blinding light. He disappeared and the door slammed shut behind him!"

"So?" exclaimed Kalani. "The monk just opened the door and jumped down onto the sand below. The blinding light was sunlight."

"At his age? At that height? He'd have broken both his legs!" exclaimed Amanda.

"Well, I don't know." Kalani shrugged her shoulders. "What do you want from me?"

"At any rate," continued Zach, "Kevin claimed he didn't see the beach, palm trees, or anything like that when he was looking through the open door. All he saw was pure white light. He also said the monk didn't jump or suddenly drop. The monk just walked calmly in a straight line through the open door and vanished."

"Oh, come on!" exclaimed Kalani. "Kevin was just pulling your leg. Don't be so gullible."

"But why would he make up such a story?" asked Zach.

"Who knows?" Kalani scrunched her face. "Some guys are just jerks."

"Zach, I know how to find out if Kevin was telling the truth," said Amanda.

"How?"

"Stakeout the temple. You know, to see with our own eyes if the monk disappears."

"That's not a bad idea," responded Zach. He grinned. "In fact, it could be fun!"

"It might take some time, though," Amanda cautioned. "I doubt we'll see him disappear right away."

"Well, we won't know if we don't try," said Zach. "I'm game. Who's with me?"

"You guys must be crazy. Kevin was just playing with you, Zach." Kalani flipped her hair. "I have better things to do."

"Come on Kalani, it'll be fun!" insisted Amanda.

"Forget it!"

"Tell you what," Zach said to Kalani. "If we don't see the monk disappear on our first couple tries, I'll carry your books home for you for an entire week."

Kalani raised an eyebrow. "Two weeks."

"Okay, two weeks. Are you in?"

Kalani smiled. "I'm in."

"Great." Zach turned to Glen. "What about you?"

"Will you carry my books too?"

"Of course not! What's the matter with you?"

Glen chuckled. "Oh well, it was worth a try."

"So, are you in?" pressed Zach.

"I highly doubt we'll see a vanishing monk." Glen glanced at Kalani. "But yeah, sure, I'm in."

◆ III ◆

Mrs. Hildebrand paced up and down the classroom aisle. She peered menacingly over horned-rim glasses at her pupils, who were taking a quiz on one of the chapters in Charles Dickens' book *A Tale of Two Cities*. She brandished a long, metallic pointer. Mrs. Hildebrand was making sure nobody was cheating. She knew her quiz was tough and fully expected some students to fail. She enjoyed it when her quizzes caused fear. She also relished meting out punishment; it ensured that she was taken seriously. Mrs. Hildebrand hated not being taken seriously.

She glanced conspicuously at a clock on the wall. "Time is up! Pass your papers to the front of the room. Only after I have received *all* quizzes may you leave the classroom. Make sure your name is at the top. Any student who forgets will automatically receive an *F*. No exceptions. Absolutely no exceptions!"

"No exceptions," Zach whispered to Amanda in a mocking tone.

"Are you crazy?" Amanda whispered back. "Don't do that again!"

Zach looked at her and laughed uneasily.

♦ IV ♦

Zach, Amanda, Kalani, and Glen were walking toward the old monk's temple. A car sped by and came to a screeching halt just ahead, at a red stoplight. The driver spewed a torrent of curse words. The light turned green. The driver—an old lady—leaned out the window, spat out a wad of phlegm, and flicked a still-glowing cigarette butt onto the asphalt road. Grimacing, she looked back at the four students, shook her fist in the air, and uttered a few more curses.

Glen said, "Hey, wasn't that—"

"Mrs. Hildebrand!" the others shouted in unison.

Kalani exclaimed, "Oh-my-God!"

The car peeled out and sped off, leaving in its wake the acrid stench of burned rubber and exhaust fumes.

◆V◆

After walking about a half mile further, the kids stealthily approached the side of the stone and wood temple.

Kalani whispered, "Can you smell it?"

"Yeah," replied Glen. "Incense."

"He must be inside," Zach commented.

Amanda said, "Or *was* recently inside."

"Can you hear anything?" asked Glen.

They fell silent and listened intently for a few moments.

"Nothing," whispered Zach. "I don't hear anything but the ocean. Did you guys hear anything?"

Glen shook his head.

Kalani said, "No, nothing."

"Just the waves," whispered Amanda.

"Let's sneak around front and see if the door's open," suggested Zach.

They scrambled around the side of the temple to the stone staircase leading up to the front entrance. The door—on which a fluttering piece of paper had been tacked—was slightly ajar. Zach climbed the stone stairs. He bent over slightly and examined the piece of paper. It was a square sheet of parchment, on which the following verses had been neatly inscribed (in calligraphic letters):

I saw their sagging, unsmiling faces
Etched and burned by unkind places.

I smelled their sweat and quiet despair
As I hurtled through the humid Tokyo air.

I heard the strained and artificial voices
Of those unhappy with most of their choices.

◆ ◆ ◆

But, you see, I know a little something
They won't ever know.

Welcome, my four curious children.
Welcome to the sanctuary of my temple.

"Wow!" exclaimed Zach.

"Shhhhhh! He might hear you," said Amanda. "What does it say?"

Zach did not reply. He opened the door slightly and poked his head inside the temple. He entered it and disappeared from sight.

"I guess the monk isn't home," commented Kalani.

"Anybody want to go up there and take a look at that note?" asked Amanda.

Silence.

They waited. Several minutes later, Zach re-appeared. "The temple's completely empty. No monk. But the smell of incense is really strong and some fresh candles are still burning. Oh, and about that note? It seems he knew we were coming."

"What!" exclaimed Kalani. "Come on, Zach. Stop playing."

"I'm serious!"

"Really? Let me see it." Kalani scrambled up the stone steps, removed the note from the door, and read it. "Zach's right, guys. Take a look."

Amanda and Glen ascended the stairs and read the note.

"How did he know we were coming?" asked Amanda. "How did he know there'd be four of us? Where is he?"

"I'm sure there's some logical explanation for all this." Glen wiped his brow. "Maybe he saw us coming, dashed off this note just before we arrived, and—"

15

"It's handwritten in a fancy calligraphic script, stupid," Kalani interrupted sharply. "There's no way that monk dashed off this note in just a few minutes."

"Don't call me stupid."

Zach added, "Glen, even if the monk did dash off the note like you said, how could he do that *and* disappear so quickly? We'd have seen him leave."

"I don't have an answer for that," admitted Glen.

"Okay, so what's our next move?" asked Zach.

"We could wait around to see if he comes back," suggested Kalani. "Or we could try again tomorrow, after Mrs. Hildebrand's class. He seems to know what we're up to. Maybe he'll make the next move."

"Makes sense to me," said Zach. "I really don't feel like hanging around here. Who knows how long it'll be before he returns."

"One thing's for sure," said Amanda. "I'm not lurking around this place after dark."

"Hey Glen, what do you think?" asked Zach.

"I don't have an answer for any of this."

◆VI◆

Mrs. Hildebrand was in an especially foul mood. Her grimace was more pronounced than usual, and her horn-rimmed spectacles were riding low on her nose. She paced around the room, thwacking the tip of her metallic pointer against her outstretched palm.

Zach thought, "This isn't good."

When Mrs. Hildebrand turned her back, Amanda leaned over to Zach and whispered, "Wow, she's really crabby today. I guess we didn't do so well on that quiz."

Mrs. Hildebrand spun around and shrieked, "Who said that?"

Silence.

"Fess up this instant!"

More silence, save for the sound of Mrs. Hildebrand's right foot. It was tapping the floor wildly.

"If somebody does not tell me this instant, each and every one of you will get detention for an entire month! Now who was it?"

Zach asked, "What'll happen to the confessor?"

Mrs. Hildebrand peered at Zach suspiciously. "That is for the miscreant to find out himself. There will be consequences, naturally."

Amanda said, "It was—"

"Me," interrupted Zach. "I was whispering in your class, Mrs. Hildebrand."

Amanda said, "No, no, it wasn't—"

Zach glanced at Amanda. "Yes, it was. She's just trying to protect me."

Kalani glanced at Zach and arched her eyebrow.

Mrs. Hildebrand smiled tightly. "Well, well, well, Zachary. I should have known it was you. Judging from your performance on yesterday's quiz, you do not take my class seriously. Not seriously at all."

Zach hated it when she used his full name. "Did I fail?"

"No, you passed," replied Mrs. Hildebrand. She looked disappointed. "Barely. In fact, everybody passed. That shocked me. Hmm. Perhaps I should make my next quiz even tougher."

Zach sighed.

"Zachary, starting tomorrow, you will have detention every day for the next two months," announced Mrs. Hildebrand. "Furthermore, given your poor performance on yesterday's quiz, I will be assigning you supplementary homework assignments."

"Supplementary homework assignments?"

"Yes. Short essays—on topics of my choosing—to be handed in each and every week until we finish the book. And you had better do a good job."

"But Mrs. Hildebrand," said Zach in a pleading tone. "You—"

Amanda, sitting next to Zach, kicked his leg sharply to silence him.

Mrs. Hildebrand appeared smug. "Yes, Zachary? You have something to say?"

"No, Mrs. Hildebrand."

"I didn't think so."

◆VII◆

"Thanks, Zach. I really appreciate your taking the fall for me earlier. You know, in Mrs. Hildebrand's class," said Amanda. The kids were walking back to the old monk's temple. "You didn't have to do that."

"Sure I did," replied Zach. "You actually have a chance at getting a good grade in that class. My case is hopeless. I'll be lucky if I get a *D!*"

Amanda leaned over and kissed Zach lightly on his cheek. Kalani and Glen exchanged glances. Zach blushed and quickly changed the subject. "Um . . . do you think the monk will be home today?"

Glen shrugged his shoulders. "Your guess is as good as mine."

Zach said, "I wonder if he knows we're coming again. Wouldn't that be something?"

A car rapidly approached from behind. Kalani said, "Wait, isn't that—"

"Mrs. Hildebrand's car!" interjected Glen.

Zach frowned.

The car passed by rapidly and screeched to a halt about twenty yards ahead of the kids. Mrs. Hildebrand leaned out the window—no cigarette was visible today—and shouted, "Remember, Zachary, two months of detention! And extra homework assignments!" She popped her head back inside the car. Moments later, she leaned out again. Shaking her fist, she shouted, "Nobody whispers behind my back and gets away with it! Nobody!"

Mrs. Hildebrand gunned the engine and sped off.

Silence.

"What a witch," declared Kalani.

"No arguments here," said Zach.

◆VIII◆

The kids gingerly approached the temple. As before, they crept up to its side and listened intently to see if they could hear anyone stirring within.

"I don't smell any incense today," said Amanda. "Does anyone smell any incense burning?"

Nobody responded.

Kalani started to walk around the side of the temple toward the main entrance. "Hey guys, let's go around front. We're not going to hear anything here."

The others quickly followed her.

Kalani pointed at the front door, which was closed. "Look, another note for us!"

"Isn't it just the same one from yesterday?" asked Zach.

"No. I took that one home with me," answered Kalani.

Glen said, "Wait a minute. We don't know if that note's for us. For all we know, it could be a message for the local pizza delivery guy."

"Go take a look then," said Zach

"Fine. I will."

Glen brushed past Zach, climbed the stone stairs, and peered at the parchment:

> *I know a little something*
> *You won't ever know.*
>
> *Unless you—Glen—and your friends*
> *Four curious travelers*
> *Enter the sanctuary of my temple.*

"Well?" called out Kalani.

Glen turned around very slowly. His eyes were bulging. "I . . . I . . . I don't know how to explain it."

Kalani scrambled up the steps, pushed Glen aside, and read the note for herself.

"Is the note for us?" asked Zach.

"You better come up here and read this for yourself," Kalani replied. "It's amazing! The monk knew we were coming again, and he mentioned Glen."

"Are you kidding me?" asked Zach.

"It's true," responded Glen.

Kalani removed the note and showed it to Amanda and Zach. The four kids huddled at the base of the stone staircase to decide what to do next.

Zach said, "The note sounds like an invitation to enter his temple."

"Do you think he's inside?" asked Amanda. "Do you think it's safe?"

"He's a monk, not an axe murderer." Zach glanced at the entrance. "Of course it's safe. I'm going in. Who's with me?"

"I am," announced Kalani.

"Okay," Amanda said tentatively.

Zach smiled. "What about you, Glen? He seems to know you best."

"Yeah, yeah. I'm with you."

"Good."

Zach ascended the stairs, followed closely by his friends. After reaching the top, he took a deep breath and slid open the temple door.

CHAPTER 2

◆|◆

The kids shuffled toward the middle of the temple's central meditation room. A giant statue of Buddha in the altar transfixed them. It was carved completely out of sandstone and was ringed by a semi-circle of flickering candles. The light gave the stone a soft, textured glow. A shoji door that led to an adjoining room slid open, revealing an old man dressed in a white tunic.

Kalani gasped.

The figure stepped out silently into the dancing candlelight, toward the kids. He had a long, flowing gray beard and sparkling blue eyes. He looked very distinguished. Smiling subtly (he was enjoying his dramatic entry immensely), he lowered his hood to reveal a mane of thick white hair, parted neatly on the side. In his left hand, he clutched a pair of sunglasses.

"Welcome, my four curious travelers!" exclaimed the old monk. "Welcome to the sanctuary of my temple. I'm heartened you made the wise and brave decision to join me this fine afternoon." He pointed at the statue. "I noticed you were staring at my Buddha statue. Do you like it? I carved it myself out of sandstone. It is . . . unique. I thought it only fitting to have such a statue, since I'm . . . the Sand Monk!"

"Sand Monk? What's that?" asked Kalani. She chuckled. "Do you like to play in the sand?"

"Kalani!" admonished Amanda.

"No, no. It's quite alright," said the Sand Monk. He looked at Kalani. "This one is quite mischievous and clever with words. Authority doesn't intimidate her easily. That will serve her well for upcoming events."

Kalani raised an eyebrow. "Huh?"

"All in good time," the Sand Monk said knowingly. He pointed at several cushions on the wood floor in front of the altar. "Please, have a seat in front of the sandstone Buddha. I'll be back."

The Sand Monk disappeared through the door from which he had emerged moments earlier. The kids followed his instructions and sat on the cushions.

Kalani said, "What did he mean by that comment?"

"About upcoming events?" asked Zach.

Kalani nodded.

Zach shrugged his shoulders. "Who knows? But he does seem to be able to see into the future."

"Hmm . . . " responded Kalani.

The Sand Monk re-emerged carrying a tray of small porcelain cups filled with steaming green tea. He walked over to the kids and handed a cup to each of them and said, "Please have some green tea while we chat. It's fresh; I brewed it just before you arrived."

Glen, Zach, and Amanda started to drink. Kalani, unable to contain herself any longer, blurted out, "Mr. Sand Monk, how did you know we were coming to your temple? And what exactly did you mean by that comment about me earlier?"

The Sand Monk smiled softly, glanced at the sandstone Buddha, and took a sip of green tea. "You are correct, I did have foreknowledge of your arrival—"

"But how is that possible?" interrupted Glen. "I don't understand."

The Sand Monk leaned back and raised his eyebrow. He looked at Glen intently. "Yes, I can see how it troubles you. Yes."

"You didn't answer my question, Mr. Sand Monk," said Kalani.

"Take a look around this room. Is there anything particularly out of place?" asked the Sand Monk.

"You mean besides the four of us?"

The Sand Monk laughed. "Look closely. What *object* is out of place?"

Kalani scanned the room. "That big door over there. Every other door in this joint is Japanese."

"Indeed!" exclaimed the Sand Monk. "Now why do you suppose a big Victorian door is in the middle of a Japanese-style Buddhist temple?"

Kalani shrugged her shoulders. "How should I know?"

The Sand Monk continued, "Before I explain the door, I need to tell you something you may not already know about Hawaii."

"I'm listening," said Kalani.

"This island—the Big Island of Hawaii—is sometimes referred to as the land of fire and ice," explained the Sand Monk. "Why?"

Glen smiled. "That's easy. The Big Island is the land of fire because there's an active volcano here. It's also the land of ice because there's snow on the peaks of Mauna Loa and Mauna Kea."

"Yes!" exclaimed the Sand Monk. "The Big Island has a tremendous amount of energy. The earth actually liquefies inside the volcanoes!"

"Magma," commented Amanda.

The Sand Monk continued, "Some consider this island to be a place of purification, of new beginnings. But there's something else. Certain places on the Big Island are especially potent, energetically speaking. So potent, in fact, that one can actually cross over—physically—into alternate realities. In other words, the Big Island is a doorway. A gateway between dimensions, between realities."

Glen started to fidget. "Hmm . . . "

The Sand Monk gazed at him. "Yes. This kind of talk troubles you."

"It's just really hard for me to believe something without concrete proof," explained Glen. "If you can prove that different dimensions exist, I'd be more than happy to believe it. But as far as I know, nobody's ever been able to prove it."

The Sand Monk chuckled. "You require proof? That Victorian door is a portal to the strongest and most stable energy vortex on this entire island!"

"Wow! So you can cross over to an alternate reality simply by walking through that door?" asked Kalani.

"Indeed you can," replied the Sand Monk. "Indeed you can."

"How did you find it?" asked Amanda.

"That's quite a story." The Sand Monk paused. "I should probably begin by informing you that I'm not originally from this reality."

Glen dropped his cup, spilling a bit of tea onto the temple floor. He quickly fished a handkerchief out of his pocket and wiped it up.

"I'm from a place called Sandtopia," continued the Sand Monk. "Much like the Big Island, Sandtopia is surrounded by a vast ocean, has a pleasant climate, and is blessed with gorgeous, pristine beaches."

"Where is it?" asked Zach.

"It's located on another planet in a completely different dimension of the universe. Things are quite different over there."

Kalani inquired, "Are you a monk over there too?"

"Indeed. In fact, at one time I was the head priest."

"You *were* the head priest? Did something bad happen?"

"Yes. In fact, something terrible *is* happening on Sandtopia. There are two kinds of inhabitants on the island. The rulers are called sandroids. Although they're humanoid in form, and they walk around just like humans, they're actually made of sand."

"Sand?" asked Glen. "Are you kidding me?"

29

"No, I'm not," replied the Sand Monk. "As you can see, I'm not constructed out of sand. As far as I can tell, I'm fully human. I have no trouble surviving here on Earth. Nobody would ever suspect that I'm originally from a different dimension."

Amanda asked, "Are humans the other type of inhabitant on Sandtopia?"

"Yes. Though there are some other entities."

Zach asked, "How the heck did humans get on Sandtopia?"

The Sand Monk pointed at the Victorian door. "Well, most likely they came through some portal, much like the one over there. We don't really know when the first people arrived on Sandtopia, or where they came from. We do know, however, that humans were on Sandtopia before the sandroids. You see, the sandroids started to arrive by means of a portal about a couple hundred years ago. Obviously, they didn't come from Earth."

"Right," said Zach.

The Sand Monk continued, "The humans who came into contact with the first sandroids—there were four—immediately took them to meet their king. Things went well and the four sandroids returned to their home planet."

"Let me guess," said Kalani, "this doesn't turn out well."

The Sand Monk stroked his thick beard and furrowed his brow. "Not well at all. The sandroids soon returned—in force. About a hundred or so heavily armed soldiers. They marched to the king's palace and demanded he abdicate his throne."

"Did he surrender?" asked Zach.

"No, he refused," answered the Sand Monk. "In response, several sandroid soldiers seized the king and started to drag him off. The king's security detail tried to save him by attacking the sandroids. But swords and knives—weapons used by the king's soldiers—were completely ineffective against the sandroids. The sand just absorbed the blow, shifted around the weapon, and refilled the wound as soon as the weapon was withdrawn. The king's soldiers—try as they might—couldn't kill the sandroids. They didn't know how! Unfortunately for the king, the sandroids quickly discovered how easy it is to kill humans. In short order, they dispatched the king's entire security detail and detained the king."

"Oh, no!" exclaimed Amanda. "What happened to him?"

"He was executed."

"How awful!"

The Sand Monk stroked his beard. "It certainly was. After the king was eliminated the sandroids quickly took over. They've been in charge ever since. In fact, they're the ones who renamed the island."

"To Sandtopia?" asked Amanda.

The Sand Monk nodded.

"You never answered my question," said Kalani. "Why aren't you the head priest anymore?"

"To answer that, I first need to explain how things are organized on Sandtopia."

"Okay. Go on."

"The island is ruled by a very diabolical, greedy queen. Her official title is Sand Queen." The Sand Monk chuckled. "Most people call her the evil Sand Queen. Behind her back, of course."

Amanda asked, "If she's the Sand Queen, why are you the Sand Monk? You're not made of sand."

"Sand Monk is the title given to the head priest of Sandtopia's religion."

Zach said, "So you must've been pretty high up there in rank. But how could that be? You're not a sandroid. You're human! Why would the sandroids put a human in charge of their religion?"

The Sand Monk responded, "I wasn't in charge of their religion. I know very little about sandroid religion. Humans aren't allowed to participate. I'm in charge of human religion, called Daijarism. It's a form of Buddhism that became ascendant on Sandtopia."

"How did that happen? Did you bring it to Sandtopia from Hawaii?" asked Kalani.

"No, Daijarism was already well established on Sandtopia long before I was born," answered the Sand Monk. "In the distant past, many different religions flourished on Sandtopia, since people came here through portals from various places on Earth. At some point, however, most of those portals closed or shifted. Few, if any, new humans—with their varied cultures and religions— were able to come to the island. By the time the sandroids arrived on the scene, Daijarism had become the primary religion."

"I don't get it," said Zach. "Why would the sandroids allow you, a human, to hold such a high ranking position?"

"Yeah, why don't they just install a sandroid?" asked Amanda.

"Credibility," answered the Sand Monk. "The sandroids know that humans will never truly accept a sandroid as the head of their religion."

"Couldn't they just do it anyway?" asked Kalani. "The sandroids have all the power. People would just have to accept it."

The Sand Monk replied, "The sandroids already tried that once—not long ago, in fact. It didn't work. The sandroid head priest had no legitimacy. Nobody attended the religious services;

the religion went entirely underground. It soon became a focal point for opposition to the sandroid regime. The sandroids quickly realized their mistake and re-installed a human as head priest. The sandroid leader at the time—the Sand King—concluded that as long as he had control over the head priest, it didn't matter if that priest was sandroid or human."

"So the religion went back above ground," stated Kalani.

"Yes," confirmed the Sand Monk. "And that's where I come into play. I was the one who was re-installed by the Sand King. But he either didn't know, or didn't care that I had strong ties to the opposition—the Resistance. I think he thought I could be controlled easily. At any rate, it became easier and easier for us—the Resistance—to operate above ground as the Sand King aged and grew increasingly senile. But his wretched daughter was waiting in the wings, waiting for him to die so she could take over."

"The Sand Queen?" asked Amanda.

"Yes," replied the Sand Monk. "But at that time, she was known as the Sand Princess. She hated me because she knew exactly what I was up to. But, try as she might, she couldn't get her father to crack down on the Resistance."

"Let me guess," said Kalani, "the Sand King dies and the Sand Princess becomes the Sand Queen. And she comes after you."

The Sand Monk ran his fingers trough his thick mane of hair. "Yes. But it wasn't that simple. The Sand King's death was shrouded in mystery. In fact, many people suspected the Sand Princess killed him. Since she was heir to the throne, she would have benefited the most from his passing."

"Wait a minute," said Zach. "Earlier you said sandroids couldn't be killed. Remember? Way back in the beginning you said the king's soldiers couldn't defeat the sandroids."

"I merely said that swords and knives are ineffective against sandroids," explained the Sand Monk. "They're not immortal."

"So how do you kill them?"

"Older sandroids are quite vulnerable. Their skin, which is transparent, grows increasingly brittle as they age. Cracks develop, through which sand seeps out. Eventually, they start to crumble away. At some point they disintegrate into a pile of used-up sand."

Kalani asked, "What about younger sandroids?"

"When humans try to kill younger sandroids with knives or swords," answered the Sand Monk, "they're foiled by the transparent skin. It's possible to puncture the skin momentarily, but because it's pliable and gelatinous, the skin repairs itself almost instantly. It's much easier to dispatch older sandroids because their protective casing can be shattered quite easily."

"Can younger sandroids even *be* killed?" asked Zach.

"We know very little about sandroid biology. How to kill them when they're young is a tightly guarded secret."

Amanda said, "I imagine the Sand King really had to be protected when he got older."

"He did," confirmed the Sand Monk.

"What happened after the Sand King died?" asked Zach.

"Yes. Back to my story. After the Sand King died, the Sand Princess ascended to the throne. She became the new sovereign—the Sand Queen. Soon after, she accused me of killing her father in an attempt to seize power for myself."

"So she came after you," stated Zach.

"With a vengeance."

"She must've hated you," Amanda remarked.

"Yes, and she still hates me. Remember, the Sand Queen currently rules Sandtopia."

"But why does she hate you so?" asked Kalani. "Because you're part of the Resistance?"

"Yes." The Sand Monk chuckled. "I'm a big thorn in her side. Whenever the Sand Queen hands down an unjust decree, we ignore it as much as possible. Often, we organize a huge, non-violent protest rally."

"Do your tactics work?" asked Kalani.

The Sand Monk sipped some tea. "Not right away. As you can imagine, the Sand Queen doesn't like it when we do such things. She cracks down hard. And, unlike me, she relishes violence."

"I can't believe what I'm hearing!" interjected Glen. "This whole story is nonsense. How can the rest of you be taken in by this fairy tale? I can't—"

"Pipe down, Glen," interrupted Zach. "Don't you remember what the Sand Monk said earlier?"

"Huh?"

"He's got proof." Zach pointed at the imposing Victorian door. "Over there."

"Now, now, there's no need to get confrontational." The Sand Monk smiled at Zach. "Indeed, you're right. That door is my proof, so to speak. Now, back to my story. As soon as the Sand Queen ascended the throne, she came after me, on the pretext that I had murdered her father."

"Which you didn't do," stated Kalani.

"Of course not. And she knew it. One day, I was tipped off that her soldiers were on their way to my temple to arrest me. I fled at once into the island's interior. A manhunt quickly ensued. It wasn't long before they caught up to me. As they were about to apprehend me, I stumbled, unseen, through a portal that instantly deposited me here, at this very spot, on the Big Island. I was saved!"

"Whew!" exclaimed Kalani.

"Why didn't they just follow you through the portal?" asked Amanda.

"Sandroids hate portals. They avoid them like the plague."

"Why?" inquired Kalani.

"I don't know. Probably because the portal connecting them to their home planet suddenly closed down, stranding them on Sandtopia," replied the Sand Monk.

Zach said, "It sounds like they have it pretty good on Sandtopia. Why take the chance of going through a portal when you have no idea where you might end up?"

"Yeah," said Kalani, "and you might not be able to return home."

"That's true." The Sand Monk pointed to the Victorian door. "In fact, I take a similar chance every time I walk through that door. If I become stranded on Sandtopia, unable to return to Hawaii, it'll only be a matter of time before the Sand Queen catches me. She's ruthless and relentless."

"Did you build this temple so you can have easy access to the portal from this side?" asked Kalani.

"Indeed. This temple is my sanctuary, my place of rest and repose. I frequently cross between the two worlds. I enjoy stirring up trouble for the Sand Queen. When the heat gets really intense, when she's hot on my trail and close to capturing me, I slip across realities to Hawaii. The Big Island is where I rest and gather strength before returning to my mission on Sandtopia. I'm quite famous on Sandtopia, actually, for my ability to elude the Sand Queen." The Sand Monk grinned mischievously. "I'm told the Sand Queen's inability to capture me drives her into fits of rage."

"Craziness!" exclaimed Glen. "How can you all believe such fantasy? A world full of sandroids and evil queens. Come on!"

The Sand Monk looked at Glen. "You don't believe me? Well, let me tell you something. There's a reason I've been describing Sandtopia to you and your friends at such length. I would like to offer you all the opportunity to travel there!"

"Really?" blurted Zach.

The Sand Monk waved his arms dramatically. "If it's proof you seek, you'll receive it in spades!"

"But why us?" asked Kalani. "Mr. Sand Monk, of all the people on this island, why are you offering this opportunity to us?"

"Because you've been chosen. You're the chosen ones. Do you accept or decline? In fairness, I must warn you: there's a small chance the portal may close down after you've crossed over to Sandtopia. The possibility is extremely remote, but it does exist."

"Wait a minute chief," responded Kalani. "We've been chosen? What does *that* mean?"

The Sand Monk paused a moment to gather his thoughts. "There's an ancient inscription on some stone tablets. It's called the Hailona Prophecy. It was written many years before the sandroids first came to Sandtopia. In essence, it foretells the hardships the people of Sandtopia will be forced to endure at the hands of strange intruders. And it states that the tyrannical rule of these strange intruders will end when 'the most evil one' comes to power. And 'the most evil one' is identified as being female. A queen."

"So you think it's talking about the Sand Queen?" asked Amanda.

"Yes. But the Prophecy goes on to say that four newcomers to Sandtopia will undo 'the most evil one.' They won't become the new rulers, but they will usher in the transfer of power to the people."

The Sand Monk paused for dramatic effect. "A democracy that will herald the beginning of Sandtopia's golden age!"

Zach asked, "So, who are these newcomers? You know, the ones supposed to topple the Sand Queen?"

Kalani gasped. "You said *four young newcomers*. You also said we're the chosen ones. It's us, isn't it? The four of us!"

The Sand Monk replied, "Yes, that's what I think. The Sand Queen knows all about the Prophecy and will do everything in her power to make sure it's never fulfilled. She's insidious. She'll stop at nothing to make sure she remains in power until the day she dies. Now, once again, I formally offer you the opportunity to join me on a trip through the doorway to Sandtopia. An opportunity to test your mettle and fulfill the Hailona Prophecy!"

Silence.

The Sand Monk continued, "I understand this is a momentous decision, so I'll give you some time to decide. I'll retire to the next room and refresh your cups with some more green tea. When I return, I expect that you will have come to a decision."

The Sand Monk got up, gathered the kids' cups, placed them on a tray, and walked toward a sliding door. As he passed through, he turned around, smiled, and winked. "You know, Sandtopia is a very interesting place!"

The Sand Monk disappeared through the door.

◆ II ◆

"You've got to be kidding me," said Glen. "The man's a kook. He's off his rocker. He's going to open that door, get you to walk through, and have a rollicking laugh when you fall on your faces into the sand below. He's just setting you up for a big laugh. You don't believe any of this, do you? Guys?"

"I'll admit, it's quite a story," responded Zach. "But the Sand Monk claims to have proof. He says if we walk through that door, we'll find ourselves in Sandtopia. I'm willing to see if he can put his money where his mouth is. Because, truth is, if he opens that door and nothing happens, he's going to look like a fool, not us."

Kalani said, "Zach's right. We're the ones with nothing to lose. If the Sand Monk opens that door and nothing happens, we simply thank him for an entertaining story and go home. It's as simple as that."

"I agree," offered Amanda, "but I'm kind of nervous. What if it really is a portal? Aren't you kind of nervous about crossing over? I mean, what if we can't make it back home? What if it messes up our bodies? I don't want to be stranded on Sandtopia for the rest of my life. And I definitely don't want to return to Hawaii with two left arms."

"Dangerous or not, I've made my decision," Zach announced firmly. "I'm going. After all, this temple's been here for as long as I can remember, so the portal must be fairly stable. Odds are it's not going to disappear anytime soon."

"I'm going too," declared Kalani. "If true, it's just too exciting an opportunity to pass up!" She turned toward Glen. "What about you?"

"No. I'll stay right here and laugh while you're all made to look like fools by that nut job." Glen placed his hands onto his hips. "I'm not going anywhere."

Zach said, "Amanda?"

"I think I'll stay back here with Glen. After all, he'll need someone to keep him company while you two are gone, right? Maybe I'll join you on the next trip."

"Are you sure?" asked Kalani.

"Yeah . . . thanks. I'm just not ready right now."

The Sand Monk slid the door open and emerged from the adjoining room. He distributed a cup of steaming green tea to each of the kids and took the fifth one for himself. "So, have you made your decisions?"

Zach answered, "Kalani and I will go with you. But Glen and Amanda have chosen to remain behind."

"I see," the Sand Monk said thoughtfully. "I must respect your decisions." He smiled at Kalani and Zach. "Then it'll be the three of us. Shall we go for about an hour?"

"Okay," replied Zach and Kalani in unison.

"Very well. It's now 4:20. We'll prepare ourselves and cross over at 4:30." The Sand Monk turned to Amanda and Glen. "We'll return at approximately 5:30. I suggest you remain here in the temple until then."

The Sand Monk struck a match and lit some joss sticks. He placed them in several sand-filled porcelain cups. A sweet scent quickly permeated the central meditation room. Next, he walked over to the corner of the room to fetch a leather satchel. He opened it, thrust his hand inside, and removed three purple crystals.

"Please take a purple crystal and squeeze it tightly," the Sand Monk said to Kalani and Zach. He offered one to each of them. "Their soft, protective energy helps immensely during the trip through the doorway."

"Good to know," said Kalani.

The Sand Monk sat on a cushion in front of the sandstone Buddha. He motioned to Kalani and

44

Zach. "Please sit on either side of me and hold my hands." Silently, they followed his instructions. The Sand Monk continued, "Now, please cast your gaze downward and try to empty your mind of all thoughts as I go through a series of silent prayers."

About five minutes later, the Sand Monk finished praying. He released his grip on the kids' hands and stood up. "It is time." He walked over to his satchel and fished out three pairs of sunglasses.

"Cool!" exclaimed Kalani. "Pretty sunny over there on Sandtopia, eh?"

The Sand Monk replied, "Yes, but these are more for your protection during the crossing. The light is quite bright!"

The Sand Monk took Kalani and Zach's hands and walked them slowly toward the Victorian door. He said to Amanda and Glen, "Remember, we'll be back by 5:30." He asked Kalani, "Are you sure you want to go through with this?"

"Yes, I think so."

The Sand Monk looked at Zach and asked the same question.

Zach replied, "Let's do it!"

"Splendid!" said the Sand Monk with a grin.

They approached the door. The Sand Monk opened it slowly. Immediately, a blinding white light washed over them and illuminated the entire meditation room. The Sand Monk stepped over the threshold, followed closely by Zach and Kalani.

◆ III ◆

Amanda and Glen exchanged astonished glances. They ran to the temple's front door (knocking over several cups of green tea in the process), slid it open, dashed down the stone staircase, and scrambled around the side of the temple to see what—if anything—had happened to the Sand Monk and their two friends.

"I don't see them anywhere," said Amanda. "Do you see them?"

Glen stared at the Victorian door. "It can't be true." He looked at Amanda earnestly. "It just can't!"

CHAPTER 3

♦|♦

A tropical forest landscape materialized slowly before Zach's eyes. He looked to his right and saw Kalani. She was dumbstruck. The Sand Monk was several yards in front of him.

"Hey, Mr. Sand Monk, you were right!" said Zach, barely able to contain his excitement. "That door *does* lead to another dimension. I can't believe it!" He turned to Kalani. "Can you believe it?"

Kalani could not say anything in reply; she just stood there, slack jawed.

The Sand Monk turned around and smiled. "Welcome, my children. Welcome to Sandtopia!"

Zach examined his surroundings. They were standing in a small clearing, surrounded by large trees and giant ferns. The soil was dark, and the foliage was a deep, rich shade of green. Nearby, a rocky stream bubbled and gurgled. Zach spotted

47

numerous multi-colored fish swimming with the current, bobbing and weaving playfully.

Suddenly, they heard an odd flapping noise. A giant bird—with black feathers, enormous wings, and a huge, yellow, elongated beak—slowly approached them. Hovering, the bird's massive wings flapped lazily as it looked at them with piercing red eyes. Zach glanced uneasily at its sharp talons.

"Um, Mr. Sand Monk, what's going on here?" asked Kalani. There was a slight tremor in her voice. "I didn't sign up for this!"

"It's okay. It's just a lohapa. He looks menacing, but he's actually quite friendly to humans." The Sand Monk chuckled. "But I don't think he cares much for sandroids."

"Why not?" Kalani asked.

"Sandroids have been known to mistreat them." The Sand Monk, with a tinge of sadness entering his voice, continued, "Lohapas are very intelligent birds. I like to think they're friendly to humans because they know how much we've suffered at the hands of the sandroids."

The lohapa started to flap its wings harder. Slowly rising, it flew to a nearby tree. With its beak, the bird wrestled free a sprig of pale-green leaves. It descended and approached Kalani. With the bird inches away from her face, she nervously said, "What's going on here?"

"He's offering the sprig to you as a welcoming gesture," explained the Sand Monk. "He senses you're a newcomer and wants to welcome you to Sandtopia. Like I said, these birds are quite intelligent!"

"That's so sweet!" Kalani reached out to the lohapa and pulled the sprig from his beak. "Thank you, Mr. Lohapa!"

The lohapa let out a soft caw, picked up the pace of its flapping wings, and flew off.

"So, where are we headed?" asked Zach.

"I have a secret temple nearby," replied the Sand Monk. "It's similar to the one I have on Hawaii. But on Sandtopia, in addition to its religious functions, my temple is a meeting place for the Resistance. In fact, you'll likely meet some members when we get there."

"Cool!" exclaimed Kalani.

"Shall we get started?" The Sand Monk pointed ahead. "There's a path nearby. It leads to my temple."

They hiked toward the Sand Monk's secret temple. As they made their way up a particularly steep incline, Zach, out of the corner of his eye, noticed some movement. He brushed it off as being just a figment of his imagination. However, about

49

five minutes later, in his peripheral vision, he noticed movement again. He turned his head quickly and saw a very odd looking creature. Although it looked much like a human being, it was very short and had a large head, a big bushy beard, and thick eyebrows. It was wearing a plain brown frock, and it was carrying a bow. A full set of quivers—placed in a holder—was slung over its back.

The creature realized it had been spotted. It rapidly darted to and fro, hiding behind trees, until it vanished completely from sight.

"Did you see that?" Zach asked the Sand Monk.

"Yes, I did."

"See what?" asked Kalani.

"I just saw a strange little man darting between the trees over there. He was carrying a bow and arrow!" explained Zach.

Kalani gasped. "Are we in danger?"

The Sand Monk replied, "Oh, heavens no. You saw a menehune. They're native to Sandtopia. They were here even before the first humans arrived through the portal. They're—"

"Wait a minute," interrupted Kalani. "*Menehune?* As in Hawaiian leprechauns?"

"Yes. But we don't know if the menehune came to Sandtopia from Hawaii, or if they came to Hawaii from Sandtopia."

"What are they like?" asked Zach.

The Sand Monk answered, "They're very good builders and craftsmen. But they're quite mischievous and can be cranky at times. It's wise to stay on their good side. They hate the sandroids and often try to stir up as much trouble as possible for them. So, in a way, they're our allies."

"Are they also persecuted by the sandroids?" asked Kalani.

The Sand Monk paused. "Well, the sandroids stopped trying to subjugate the menehune many, many years ago. They discovered it just wasn't possible. The menehune were too cunning and difficult to control. They always seemed to be able to melt away into the forest."

"Well, he sure disappeared quickly," remarked Zach.

◆ II ◆

After investigating the sand underneath the Victorian door for signs of disturbance, and clearly not seeing any, Glen and Amanda returned to the temple's interior. They sat down in front of the sandstone Buddha. The candles still flickered, like they were each performing their own wild, unrestrained dance. Earlier, the effect of the candles seemed playful, but Amanda now thought their dance was macabre and menacing.

"I guess Kevin was right," concluded Glen. "I hate to admit it, after all my outbursts, but it looks like he actually saw the Sand Monk disappear—just like we did. This blows my mind!"

"Yeah, pretty amazing stuff," said Amanda.

"So, do you think you'll go through the portal next time?"

"Umm . . . I don't know." Amanda glanced at the Victorian door. "I guess that all depends on what Zach and Kalani say when they get back."

♦ III ♦

Zach, Kalani, and the Sand Monk continued their hike, crossing over to the next valley. They advanced deeper into its recesses.

"Mr. Sand Monk?" asked Kalani.

"Yes?"

"How much further until we reach your temple? Amanda and Glen are expecting us to return at five-thirty. We'll be late!"

"Don't fret. The passage of time on Sandtopia doesn't correlate exactly to Earth. For every hour that passes here, a fraction passes on Earth."

"Whew! That's a relief. I don't want Glen and Amanda to worry about us."

"No need for worries," said the Sand Monk evenly. "We're almost there."

The Sand Monk's mood grew increasingly buoyant as they drew closer to his temple. Perhaps he was looking forward to seeing his friends again, Kalani thought. Zach also noticed the Sand Monk's eagerness to reach his temple. He figured the old man was looking forward to sticking it to the Sand Queen; perhaps some dashing and daring plan was in the offing.

The Sand Monk started to hum and whistle a tune. Then he sang the following verses in a rich, deep, baritone voice:

Beedle, beedle, bo, it's time to get up and go,
Didn't you see them coming?
Can't you hear them marching?
Beedle, beedle, bo, you'd better get up and go!

He whistled briefly, then continued:

Beedle, beedle, boor, they're almost at your door,
Can't you hear them growling?
Can't you hear them stomping?

Beedle, beedle, bore, you'd better not open your door!

More whistling. Then:

Beedle, beedle, boor, they're banging on your door,
Can't you hear them hissing?
Don't you hear them clawing?
Beedle, beedle, boor, they've just bashed down your door!

Kalani blurted, "What's with the song, Mr. Sand Monk? Kinda scary!"

Zach asked, "Who bashed down the door? Sandroids?"

"No, not sandroids," answered the Sand Monk. "Sandroids don't growl. Lion men."

"Lion Men?" asked Kalani.

"Yes, they're the Sand Queen's henchmen," explained the Sand Monk. "They're quite vicious. The sandroids imported lion men to Sandtopia many years ago, before the portal to their home planet closed. They're employed as a kind of internal security police force to make sure we—humans—remain subservient and don't get out of line. Lion men are very well paid, and they're extremely loyal to the Sand Queen."

"What do they look like?" asked Zach.

The Sand Monk stretched his arm as high as possible above his head. "They're very big—over seven feet tall—and incredibly strong. They have bodies that look like ours, but their heads closely resemble lions. They also have tails and hands with long, incredibly sharp claws. They can't talk—they growl or roar—but they can understand language. Lion men make excellent henchmen, I suppose, because they follow orders but can't question them. In that respect, they resemble the Sand Queen's Praetorian Guard."

"Huh?"

The Sand Monk explained, "The Praetorian Guard protects the Sand Queen, her court, and her palace. The Sand Palace."

"Is the Praetorian Guard also made up of lion men?" asked Kalani.

"No," replied the Sand Monk. "Dacturions."

"What are they?"

"Huge birds, also imported from the sandroids' home planet. They have dark purple feathers, gigantic wingspans, and elongated yellow beaks. Dacturions walk upright—much like humans—and stand around ten feet tall. They're fearsome creatures with blood-red eyes, huge talons, and a penchant for ripping their prey to pieces before eating them."

"Oh my gosh!" exclaimed Kalani.

Zach asked, "Can they fly?"

The Sand Monk nodded. "That's what makes them so valuable as Praetorian Guardsmen. They're highly mobile. They also have an unpleasant, eerie, blood-curdling caw. You can often hear them when you're near the Sand Palace."

"Oooh, they sound spooky!" exclaimed Kalani. "Mr. Sand Monk?"

"Yes?"

"Are there any more verses to that song? I want to hear you sing some more!"

"Indeed there are." The Sand Monk licked his lips, whistled a little bit, and then sang:

Beedle, beedle, bace, they've just entered your place,
Look—don't you see their paws?
Oh my—they've just extended their claws!
Beedle, beedle, bace, you'd better get the mace!

♦ IV ♦

Zach, Kalani, and the Sand Monk rounded a sharp curve along the path and came upon a small temple, nestled between two large plumeria trees. It was fronted by a Japanese Zen-style garden of combed gravel. A Mexican stone fountain, over which water gently cascaded, abutted the entrance.

The breeze shifted. Zach immediately recognized the sweet, distinctive fragrance emanating from clusters of yellow and white plumeria flowers. Feeling impetuous, he bent down and picked up a stray plumeria flower. He placed it above Kalani's ear.

She smiled and blushed. "I see you have plumeria trees here on Sandtopia."

"They aren't native," explained the Sand Monk. "I'm quite fond of the trees, so I brought these two over from Hawaii many years ago. Along with that Mexican fountain. I wasn't sure my plumerias would survive in this realm. Thankfully, however, they're thriving. As far as I know, they're the only ones of their kind on Sandtopia." He chuckled. "Occasionally, I've even spied some menehune inspecting my trees. At first, they were very curious about these two newcomers to their forest. Now, I think they enjoy the trees as much as I do!"

"What makes you say that?" asked Zach.

"The menehune seem to like the flowers," explained the Sand Monk. "They gather the ones that have fallen to the ground."

"Why?" inquired Kalani.

The Sand Monk stroked his chin whiskers. "I haven't the slightest idea."

They approached the temple, which resembled the one in Hawaii, and walked up a flight of stone stairs to the entrance. The Sand Monk paused and cocked his head, as if he were listening for something. He gently slid the door open. Before entering, he turned to Zach and Kalani and placed his index finger over his lips, indicating that he wanted them to remain silent. He stepped inside, followed closely by the two kids.

♦V♦

The temple's interior was also quite similar in design to the one located in Hawaii. Soft sunlight and scores of flickering candles—along with the strong scent of sandalwood incense—created a gentle, welcoming ambiance. Zach spotted five individuals—three men and two women—sitting on cushions on the wood floor. They were meditating, with eyes closed, in front of a large sandstone Buddha.

The Sand Monk winked at Kalani and Zach. He clapped his hands together sharply, four times. The sound was crisp. It reverberated around the temple. The five meditators—much to Kalani's surprise— did not even flinch. However, after the passage of about ten seconds or so, they started to open their eyes.

"Hello, my friends!" The Sand Monk was beaming. "I'm sorry to interrupt your meditations, but I have some very special visitors I'd like you to meet."

The meditators slowly rose to their feet and walked toward the kids. The first one to reach them was an older man with thinning gray hair, a thick beard, and twinkling brown eyes. Standing at about six-foot-five inches tall, he had a very commanding presence.

The Sand Monk said, "Kids, I'd like to introduce you to Logarno. We've known each other for many, many years."

Logarno leaned down and embraced Kalani, then Zach. "Welcome to Sandtopia, my children. I trust your trip here was an eye-opening experience?"

"You bet," answered Kalani. "We sure saw some strange things—like the lohapa and the menehune!"

Logarno chuckled. "Yes, those would seem quite strange to you, wouldn't they?" He walked over to the Sand Monk and embraced him. "It's wonderful to see you again, my friend. You're looking well."

"Thank you," replied the Sand Monk. "As are you." He turned to Kalani and Zach. "I've known Logarno since childhood. He's a master strategist for the Resistance. In fact, the Sand Queen hates him almost as much as me. It incenses her that she hasn't been able to capture him over the years."

Kalani grinned. "I guess he's also a master at eluding capture!"

The Sand Monk chuckled. "Yes, I suppose you could say that."

"Hey, I like the way that sounds," declared Logarno. "Master of eluding capture. I think I'll add that to my résumé!"

Everybody laughed.

The Sand Monk said, "It hasn't hurt Logarno that the menehune love him. They've certainly saved his skin on several occasions. Isn't that right, Logarno?"

"Indeed they have," replied Logarno. He frowned. "But they certainly can be mischievous. Sometimes they play tricks on me!"

"What kinds of tricks?" asked Kalani.

"Here's one," said Logarno. "The showering facilities are detached from my house, so I have to walk clear across my lawn to reach my bathroom. Well, the other week, when I was showering, several menehune—I could hear them cackling with glee—somehow got into the bathroom and stole all my clothes. Can you believe it? They stole everything, including the towels. I had to run across my lawn—in full view of my neighbors, mind you— buck naked and dripping wet!"

"Did anybody see you?" asked Kalani.

"Yes!"

Everyone laughed uproariously. Logarno rubbed his hands together in front of his face and grinned mischievously. "Well, believe you me, I'm plotting a way to get back at them!"

A slight woman with gray hair and green eyes came forward to be introduced to the kids. The Sand Monk said, "Zach, Kalani—please meet Eraklena. She too has been a member of the Resistance for many years."

Eraklena embraced Zach and Kalani. In a soft voice she said, "It's a pleasure to meet you both. I'm glad to see our Sand Monk has been taking good care of you!"

The Sand Monk smiled. "Don't be fooled by Eraklena's small size and soft voice. She's a firecracker! Her tireless work and superior management skills have been indispensable to the Resistance. She's our master organizer!"

Eraklena smiled at the Sand Monk. "Thank you for your kind words. I try my best simply because our cause is so important." She turned to Logarno and pointed her finger at him. "You should take a page out of my book when it comes to dealing with menehune. Those pesky little guys certainly know better than to mess with me. They had better steer clear!"

"For goodness sakes, Eraklena, keep your voice down!" Logarno peered nervously over his shoulder. "You don't want them to hear you say such things!"

The Sand Monk chuckled.

A slightly bigger woman, also with gray hair, stepped out from behind Eraklena. "Allow me to introduce myself. I'm Mandalia."

The Sand Monk said, "Mandalia is a master musician. She and I often write songs together. She's skilled at playing many different types of instruments. Perhaps we'll sing a song for you later!"

"Cool!" exclaimed Kalani.

"And behind Mandalia," continued the Sand Monk, "is Pandalese. Other than you kids, of course, he's the youngest of the group here today."

"It's wonderful to meet the two of you," said Pandalese. He had sandy-brown hair and twinkling blue eyes. At about five-foot-eleven, with gentle facial features, he was less imposing than Logarno.

"What do you do?" asked Kalani.

"I'm a priest."

"Yes," said the Sand Monk. "Pandalese is the de-facto head of the religion when I'm gone. He makes sure everything runs smoothly."

Zach asked, "Why were you all meditating earlier?"

"Allow me to field that question," said Pandalese. "We meditate to clear our minds. To quiet all the mental clutter and chatter that seeps in during the course of daily living. With a clear and quiet mind, we can receive guidance."

"Guidance?"

"Yes Zach," confirmed Pandalese. "From the spiritual realm, from spirit guides. For example, suppose I'm wrestling with a thorny problem. I've studied it from all angles and just don't know how to proceed. Well, before I enter into meditation, I'll pray to my spirit guides and ask for their assistance. Often, when I'm in deep meditation, they'll send me a message. And this message, which is often a quick mental picture, shows me the best way to move forward. I trust my spirit guides completely. They've never led me astray, and they won't hesitate to deliver unpleasant news or warnings. For example, I received such a message today."

"Oh really? What was it?" asked Kalani.

"I saw a clear mental image of the Sand Queen. She was grinning."

The Sand Monk frowned. "Hmm . . . That's not good."

"What does it mean?" asked Zach.

Pandalese speculated, "It could mean that the Resistance will suffer some kind of setback in the not too distant future."

"Yes, that's possible," said the Sand Monk. "We must remain vigilant."

"Agreed," said a short man with salt and pepper hair. He was standing next to Pandalese. He had thick eyebrows and dark, furtive eyes. "Allow me to introduce myself—I'm Judlarthio. Now, if you'll excuse me, I have to step outside to attend to something. I'll be back momentarily."

"What does he do?" asked Kalani, after Judlarthio had left the room.

Mandalia answered, "Judlarthio handles the Resistance's finances. He's a very quiet man. He doesn't say much, and he's not very visible within the community. He likes to work behind the scenes."

"Shall we all sit down in front of the Buddha?" suggested the Sand Monk. "I'd like to have a brief meeting before I take the kids back to Hawaii."

The Sand Monk fetched some extra cushions and brought them to the center of the room. He arranged them in a large circle in front of the sandstone Buddha. They sat down, facing each other.

"Okay, what are the latest developments?" asked the Sand Monk.

Logarno said, "Several days ago, Bohanon was arrested for criticizing the Sand Queen in an underground newspaper article."

"How did she know it was Bohanon?" asked the Sand Monk. "After all, writers for the underground newspaper take great pains to hide their identity."

Logarno explained, "He slipped up. In the article, he mentioned the name of his street."

Kalani asked, "So? What's so bad about that?"

"Only a few people live on that street," answered Logarno. "It wasn't long before the lion men paid a visit to each house. Naturally, when they entered Bohanon's, they found all the evidence they needed to make an arrest."

"Wait a minute," said Zach. "They can just enter someone's house? Don't they need a search warrant, or something like that?"

"Haven't you been paying attention, silly?" Kalani said to Zach. "The Sand Queen can do pretty much whatever she wants here. Right, Logarno?"

"That's right, Kalani," he replied. "The lion men took that poor man to the Sand Palace and placed him in the dungeon. He was . . . interrogated intensely."

Kalani asked, "Don't you mean tortured?"

"I suppose so," replied Logarno. He was trying to be delicate. "Bohanon really angered the Sand Queen with that article."

"Is he still in the dungeon?" asked Zach.

"No," Pandalese answered solemnly. "He was executed this morning. In public."

Kalani gasped. "That poor man."

"Yes," agreed Mandalia. "The Sand Queen likes to make public spectacles of her executions. To her, they're pure entertainment."

"And a method of control," added Logarno.

Zach looked perplexed. "Huh? I don't understand."

Mandalia clarified, "The Sand Queen feels that if she shows the public what happens when you cross her, people will think twice about opposing her rule."

"Is it effective?" asked Zach.

"Highly," answered the Sand Monk. "Most people keep their mouths shut out of pure fear. But our non-violent tactics have been effective too."

"How so?" asked Kalani.

"Not too long ago the Sand Queen levied a new tax on bread, which most of us eat every day. And just how did she plan to use this tax money?" The Sand Monk paused for dramatic effect. "Salary increases for the lion men! Can you imagine? The Sand Queen was rubbing our noses in it, practically daring us to protest. Well, protest we did. We organized a huge march. It was attended by almost three-fourths of the island's population."

"How did she respond?" asked Kalani.

"The Sand Queen was livid," replied Logarno. "But she couldn't just go out and arrest everybody. Where would she put us? There wasn't enough room in her dungeon. So she stormed off, announcing she was going to raise the tax on bread even higher."

The Sand Monk said, "For us, it was a victory, even though she didn't repeal the bread tax."

"A victory? It sounds like you only made things worse," Zach remarked. "You pissed off the Sand Queen, and now you have an even higher bread tax!"

"It was a victory because, for once, she was powerless," explained Pandalese. "Our numbers were so large, there was nothing she could do. She couldn't simply kill us all, which is probably what she wanted to do. There wouldn't be anyone left to exploit!"

The Sand Monk grinned slyly at the kids. "You know, we're planning a protest march for next week. It'll be huge. They have to be huge, you know. Otherwise they would be ineffective. We're hoping to get eighty percent of the people to join us."

"Cool!" exclaimed Kalani.

The Sand Monk said, "Logarno's already busy at work, designing and supervising the creation of all the signs and banners."

"Indeed," said Logarno. He asked the kids, "Would you like to see an example?"

"Sure!"

"You bet!"

Logarno disappeared into an adjoining room. He emerged moments later, carrying a colored placard, on which the following message had been printed:

WIPE THE SLATE CLEAN:
GET RID OF THAT EVIL QUEEN!

Logarno held up his sign proudly. Suddenly, the temple's front door slid open violently, revealing a hissing and growling lion man. He roared in anger when he read the sign. Kalani could smell the lion man's breath. It stank. She saw a gob of drool roll off his bared fang. Even worse, she saw scores of other lion men behind him.

Acting swiftly, the Sand Monk leaned over to the kids and whispered urgently, "Run to the next room. There's a secret trap door under the incense table. It's your only escape. Go. Now. And lock the door behind you with the iron bar."

"But what about you?" asked Kalani.

"Don't worry about me. I'll follow you later. Go. Now!"

Kalani and Zach dashed into the next room. The lead lion man tried to follow them, but the Sand Monk stepped in front of him, blocking the way. Alertly, the Sand Monk picked up a staff, which was resting near the door. He swung it several times at the lion man, warding him off, buying time for the kids. By now, other lion men had streamed into the temple. In short order, they apprehended Pandalese, Mandalia, Eraklena, and Logarno. Using their sharp claws, they angrily set upon Logarno's sign and shredded it into hundreds of pieces.

The Sand Monk noticed that Judlarthio had not been apprehended; the lion men were not molesting him. The Sand Monk shouted, "Judlarthio! Is this your doing?"

Judlarthio was silent.

"How could you do this? How could you betray the cause like this?"

Judlarthio just stood there, stone-faced, showing no trace of emotion.

Zach and Kalani reached the trap door under the incense table. They opened it and descended a ladder.

"Where's the Sand Monk?" asked Kalani. "Isn't he coming?"

"I'll check," responded Zach. He climbed back up the ladder, opened the trap door, and peaked out.

"Well? Where is he?" asked Kalani.

Zach watched the Sand Monk swing his staff furiously at a lion man. The lion man reached out, snatched the staff away from the Sand Monk, and snapped it in half, like a twig. He threw it across the room, hitting Pandalese and Eraklena. Then, to Zach's horror, the snarling, slobbering lion man reached out and seized the Sand Monk.

♦ VI ♦

Zach closed the trap door and bolted it shut. He pulled down on a dangling white cord, turning on a light.

Kalani was shocked that Zach had just closed and locked the trap door without letting in the Sand Monk. "What are you doing?"

"The Sand Monk won't be joining us."

"What do you mean he won't be joining us?"

"Kalani, I'm sorry. A lion man just seized the Sand Monk. Probably the rest of them too."

Kalani started to scramble back up the ladder. "Zach, we have to help him!"

Zach shook his head and waved his hand, motioning for her to stop. "There's nothing we can do. There are just too many lion men. If we go back into the temple, we'll be apprehended. Or worse."

Kalani paused. "We have to do something, Zach. You know what the Sand Queen will do to them, don't you?"

"It won't be pretty."

"Then you agree we have to do something?"

"Yes."

"Good."

They heard scraping, clawing, stomping, and roaring in the room above.

"They must be looking for us!" exclaimed Zach.

"Okay, we'll figure out later how to help the Sand Monk. We better get out of here," said Kalani. "It's only a matter of time before they find the trap door. They're going to turn that room upside down!"

Hastily, the kids climbed down the ladder. After descending about thirty feet, they reached the bottom and found themselves at the beginning of a nondescript, narrow dirt tunnel. It was about five feet wide and six feet high. Lighting was provided on both sides by a series of light bulbs, which cast a soft, bluish, eerie glow. Kalani started to walk down the path. Zach quickly grabbed the back of her shirt and pulled her toward him.

"No, Kalani, please—let me go first," he said, trying to sound brave. "We don't know who—or what—we might run into."

She allowed Zach to step in front of her. "Be my guest."

Cautiously, they walked down the path. After approximately ten minutes, they started to hear banging and clanging from behind.

"Oh no!" exclaimed Kalani. A chill ran up and down her spine. "They found the trap door. They'll tear it open in no time!"

"That bolt will buy us some time, but not much," said Zach. "We better pick up our pace."

The kids started to run. They soon came to a fork in the path and had to decide which branch to take. Mindful that they did not have much time to make a decision, Zach chose the path on the right. Kalani followed closely behind, neither questioning nor protesting his snap decision.

In the distance, behind them, they heard wood groaning, creaking, and splitting. The sound echoed throughout the tunnel.

"Is that what I think it is?" exclaimed Kalani.

"I think so," said Zach, struggling to sound composed and in control of the situation. "I think they just tore open the trap door."

Soon, they reached another fork in the path. This time, however, there were three paths from which to choose. Zach stopped abruptly, causing Kalani to bump into him.

"What are you doing?" asked Kalani. "Pick a path!"

Zach was exasperated. "What's with all the forks? What idiot designed this escape route?"

"Actually, Zach, it's ingenious."

"What are you talking about?"

"Well, as we take more forks, fewer lion men will be able to pursue us. If we're lucky, we'll be able to give them the slip completely!"

"Let's hope so." Zach heard growling and stomping noises, close behind. A blood-curdling roar reverberated through the tunnel. "I suggest we make a decision."

"Let's take the center path," decided Kalani.

"Fine by me."

The kids ran down the center path. After five minutes or so, they rounded a sharp curve and came upon an entryway that led to a small room. The door was open. Cautiously, Zach peered inside. A round table—on which rested a bow, several arrows, and a cup—was in the center of the room. Several chairs ringed the table; a mandolin had been placed on one of them.

"Is anybody in there?" asked Kalani.

"No."

Kalani brushed by Zach and entered the room. "Kalani, wait—"

Brashly, she walked up to the table and touched the cup. It was filled with liquid. "Zach—it's still warm. Someone must've been here recently."

"Psst . . . psst . . . "

Kalani jumped and turned her head toward an opening at the far end of the room. She saw a small, strange looking man. His head was large, and he had big bushy eyebrows.

"Zach," she whispered, "is that a menehune?"

"Yeah. I think he wants us to follow him."

"Should we?"

"He can't be any worse than those lion men."

They approached the menehune. He dashed away from them, into the tunnel. He was very quick. Zach and Kalani had trouble keeping up with him.

Soon, they came upon yet another fork in the path. This one also had three prongs. Without missing a beat, the menehune took the one on the left. The kids followed him. After walking for about five minutes, Zach noticed they were starting to trek up a gentle incline. He saw the path end abruptly about ten yards in front of them. Momentarily, he panicked, thinking they had reached a dead-end and would be forced to double back—and possibly run into a lion man. He was greatly relieved, however, to see that the menehune, who had reached the tunnel's end, was quickly and deftly climbing a camouflaged ladder. The kids, after reaching its base, followed him up. The menehune opened a trap door above them and exited the underground labyrinth. The flash of daylight blinded Zach momentarily.

Soon, Zach reached the trap door and opened it slowly. He peered out, waiting a few moments for his eyes to adjust to the bright sunlight. The door was located by the edge of a small clearing in the middle of a lush fern forest. Zach hoisted himself out of the tunnel. He leaned over and helped Kalani out by grabbing her arm. Then he sank to his knees and flopped onto his stomach.

"What are you doing, Zach?" asked Kalani.

"Resting."

"Where did that menehune go? Did you see him?"

"No, he was long gone by the time my eyes adjusted to the sunlight. I guess he didn't want to chat."

"Apparently not."

"Kalani?"

"Yes, Zach?"

"Please close that trap door."

◆VII◆

Glen paced back and forth. Amanda sat on a cushion in front of the sandstone Buddha. She noticed it was getting darker outside.

"Glen, what time is it?" she asked.

Glen looked at his watch. "Six-forty-five."

"They should've been back over an hour ago. I'm worried."

"Well, maybe they're having a good time and just want to see as much as possible before returning."

Amanda shook her head. "I don't think so." She paused. "I have a really bad feeling."

"You're overreacting," said Glen. "They're only a little over an hour late!"

"Glen, I don't think the Sand Monk would be so late unless something went wrong."

"Amanda, I think—"

She interrupted him. "I think we should cross over. I don't know why, but I strongly feel that something's wrong. Seriously wrong."

Glen was about to continue arguing. But he remembered the brilliant flash of light and started to get excited about the prospect of crossing through the door to see what was on the other side (from a scientific point-of-view, of course).

Glen said, "If you really think they're in trouble . . ."

"I do," said Amanda. "Big trouble. Does that mean you'll go through the door with me?"

"Okay," said Glen. "But we need to wear sunglasses. Remember how bright that light was earlier?"

They each donned a pair of sunglasses and walked tentatively toward the looming Victorian door.

Glen stopped. "Wait a minute. Don't we need crystals?"

"Oh, that's right," replied Amanda. "The Sand Monk said their energy somehow helps during the trip through the doorway." She pointed to the Sand Monk's leather satchel. "I think he took some purple crystals out of that bag."

Glen walked over to the bag, leaned over, and thrust his hand inside. Amanda heard the distinctive sound of rocks banging and clinking together. Glen fished out two crystals.

"Are they purple?" asked Amanda.

"Yup," replied Glen. He held them out for her to see.

"Maybe we should each take two. We need all the help we can get!"

Glen handed Amanda two purple crystals. "Agreed."

They approached the Victorian door. Glen placed his hand on the brass handle. He turned to Amanda. "Ready?"

She nodded. "I think so."

Glen turned the handle and opened the door. A blinding light engulfed them and filled the interior of the temple. Squeezing their purple crystals, the kids walked through the portal.

CHAPTER 4

◆I◆

"What do we do now?" asked Kalani.

Zach shrugged his shoulders. "I don't know."

"We have to find the Sand Monk. He needs our help."

"How? We don't even know where *we* are right now!"

"There's no need to get snippy, Zach."

"I'm sorry, Kalani. I'm just trying to be realistic. I mean let's face it. Even if we *did* know how to find the Sand Monk and his friends, what could we do? You saw how awful those lion men are. The dacturions are probably even worse. We're just two kids. We're no match for them. How can we possibly help the Sand Monk?"

"Zach—" started Kalani.

"And what about Glen and Amanda?" interrupted Zach. "They're waiting for us back in Hawaii. I say we leave this weird island as soon as possible. Instead of trying to find the Sand Monk, we should try to find our way home!"

Kalani stared at Zach coldly. "You mean save our own skins? I thought you were better than that."

She stomped off toward the edge of the clearing.

"Wait. Kalani! Where are you going?"

"Where do you think? To help my friend, the Sand Monk. Go back to Glen and Amanda in Hawaii. Tell them you left us here high and dry."

Zach regretted his words. "Hold on." He ran up to Kalani. "You're right. I'm sorry. I was being selfish. Of course we have to rescue the Sand Monk. Somehow."

"Thanks Zach," said Kalani. She grabbed his hand and squeezed it. "We'll figure something out."

"Wait a minute!" exclaimed Zach.

"What is it?" asked Kalani. She was worried Zach might lose his nerve.

He pointed over Kalani's shoulder. "I think I see a path over there."

Kalani turned around and peered through the underbrush. "I don't see it. Are you sure?"

"Absolutely!" exclaimed Zach. "Right near that bush with the orange and black blossoms."

"I see it!" blurted Kalani. "Okay. That's our starting point. We'll follow that path."

"To where?" inquired Zach. "We can't just follow a strange new path without having some sort of destination."

"But we do."

"Huh?"

"Zach, it's obvious. We have to find the Sand Palace. I'm sure that's where the lion men took the Sand Monk and his friends."

◆ II ◆

Zach and Kalani were ascending a hill. The path was peppered with large, black lava rocks. After about ten minutes of walking (both kids were huffing and puffing), the trail became so steep that exposed tree roots provided the only possible sure footing.

"Don't slip and fall," cautioned Zach, who was behind Kalani. "You'll take me out."

"Don't worry." Kalani scrambled over the top of a precipice and disappeared from Zach's view. "Check it out!"

"You see something? What is it?"

"Just come up here and have a look."

Zach climbed the last few rungs of tree roots and hoisted himself onto a small plateau. He saw a whitewashed cottage with royal blue window-frames (and shutters), a red door, and a thatched roof.

"There's a wooden sign with white lettering on the door, hanging from that giant knocker," stated Kalani. "Go see what it says."

"Okay."

"And try not to make any noise!"

Zach tiptoed up to the red door and peered at the sign. He returned to Kalani.

"Well?" she inquired.

"It said: *Do not disturb under any circumstances. Unless you are an agent of the Sand Queen.*"

"Hmm . . ."

"What should we do?" asked Zach.

Kalani replied, "Whoever lives there might be able to tell us where the Sand Palace is located."

"True, but it doesn't sound like the owner wants to be bothered."

"I say we take our chances. Let's knock on the door."

"Maybe we should look through the window first," suggested Zach.

"Good idea."

They crept up to the window as quietly as possible (to Zach's consternation he stepped on and broke a few twigs en-route, creating several rather sharp crackling sounds). Zach peered inside.

"Do you see anyone?" asked Kalani.

"No," whispered Zach. "There's just a bunch of normal stuff: a bed, some drawers, a large mirror, a small cooking area."

"Let me take a look." Kalani nudged Zach to the side and looked in the window. "You're right. Nobody's inside. I guess—"

An old man suddenly appeared in front of Kalani at the window (just inches from her nose). He was chewing on a corncob pipe and looked very cross.

Kalani screamed.

"Let's get out of here!" Zach yelled.

Abruptly, the old man disappeared. Seconds later, the front door flew open. A small, thin, angry, bent old man stepped out. He was holding a rattle in his right hand. "Aye there! Can't you blasted kids read? The sign says 'Do Not Disturb.' Peeping in on me is a disturbance! Now get the hell out of here!"

For emphasis, he spat on the ground and shook his rattle, defiantly, at the two kids.

"But sir—" stammered Kalani.

"Get out of here!"

Kalani placed her hands on her hips and planted her foot firmly on the ground. "We're just two lost kids trying to find the Sand Palace. There's really no reason to be so rude!"

The old man cocked his head and looked at the kids quizzically. In a softer voice, he asked, "The Sand Palace? Why would you want to go to such an awful place?"

Zach explained, "We're trying to save the Sand Monk."

"How's that? Wait a minute, sonny. My pipe." The old man disappeared inside the cottage, retrieved his pipe, quickly re-emerged, and started to puff heartily. After blowing a few smoke rings in the air (and admiring his handiwork as they slowly rose to the sky), he continued, "Now, then. It sounded like you said 'save the Sand Monk.'"

"That's right," confirmed Kalani.

"Why? What happened to him?" asked the old man.

Zach answered, "He and some of his friends were captured by a whole gang of lion men. At his temple."

"Oh no!" shrieked the old man. He placed both hands on his head and gnashed his teeth. He ran inside the cottage and slammed the door. A few moments later he re-emerged, calmer. "How do you know that? Are you sure?"

"We're sure," answered Zach. "We saw it happen."

"How could such a dreadful, dreadful thing have come to pass?" asked the old man.

"He was betrayed by one of his own," replied Kalani.

"Oh?"

"By Judlarthio."

"Hmm . . ." said the old man. He shook his rattle several times, turned toward his door, and beckoned for the kids to follow him. "Please, won't you step inside my humble cottage? I'll brew some tea for you. It'll fortify your spirits."

They entered the sparsely furnished cottage and sat on several floor cushions. The old man immediately went to his stove. "Don't mind me," he said, "I'm just heating up some water for the tea. I do love my tea!"

"Me too," said Kalani. "Mister, what's your name?"

"I'm Jasper. Jasper the Hermit."

"You're a hermit?" asked Zach.

"Yes. I've lived in this cottage for a long, long time. I don't get many visitors."

"Why did you become a hermit?" asked Kalani.

Jasper answered, "I grew sick and tired of sandroids and their underlings."

"Lion men?" asked Zach.

"Yes. They're truly hideous, aren't they? After some bad experiences, I decided to remove myself from society. Entirely."

Kalani asked, "Do the sandroids know you live up here?"

"I don't know. They've never bothered me." Jasper stood up. "Excuse me." He walked to the whistling kettle, picked it up, and poured hot water into three cups. He placed a teabag into each one and brought the steaming beverages to the kids. "Be sure to wait a few minutes before drinking. That way, the tea will be stronger and more flavorful."

"Thanks Jasper," said Kalani.

"Yeah. Thanks," added Zach.

Jasper sat down.

"Do you know where the Sand Palace is located?" asked Kalani.

Jasper examined the kids carefully. "I can point you in the right direction. If you follow the path on the other side of this small plateau, you'll come to a fork. Take the path to the right. Follow that path for a while until you come to a three-pronged fork. Take the center prong. That will take you to the Hooded Blacksmith."

"The Hooded Blacksmith?" inquired Kalani.

Jasper nodded.

"He can help us?"

"Yes."

"So you don't know how to get to the Sand Palace directly from here?" asked Zach.

Kalani added, "Yeah, we're kind of in a hurry."

Jasper replied, "Trust me. Visit the Hooded Blacksmith."

Zach stood up. "Okay, well, we should probably be on our way. We don't have much time to lose."

"I understand," said Jasper.

The kids thanked him for his help and headed for the door.

"Wait!" Jasper shuffled over to a drawer, reached in, and pulled out a small leather necklace. It held a single amulet. "This is for the girl."

He approached Kalani and hung it around her neck.

"Thanks, Jasper." Kalani admired its rich turquoise coloring. "What is it?"

"It's a healing stone," explained Jasper. "It was given to me many years ago and has served me well. But it may be more useful to you, considering the task you face."

"A healing stone?" asked Zach.

Jasper answered, "Yes. Although she doesn't yet realize it, the girl is a natural healer. When the time comes, she'll know how to use the stone."

Jasper showed the kids out the door and wished them luck. As Zach and Kalani started walking toward the edge of the plateau, he shook his rattle several times and said, "Be sure to keep a low profile. If the lion men know you escaped—and it sounds like they do—they'll search for you relentlessly. The Sand Queen will see to it!"

◆ III ◆

The blinding light dissipated. Amanda saw that she and Glen had entered a tropical forest landscape, some distance away from the ocean. Excitement began to replace apprehension as she realized they had made it through the portal safely. She flexed her fingers (counting them to make sure they were all still there) and looked down at the rest of her body. Everything seemed to be okay. She turned to Glen and gushed, "Isn't this amazing? We made it through. Everything the Sand Monk said was true! Glen?"

"Yeah?"

"Do I look okay? I mean, I don't have three eyes or two noses, do I?"

"No, you look fine," reassured Glen. "What about me?"

"You look okay," said Amanda. "So, what do you think now, Mr. Skeptic?"

"I don't know what to say. This is absolutely incredible."

Amanda ran over to the nearby stream. "Glen, check this out. The fish are leaping in and out of the water. I wonder what other neat creatures we're going to encounter here. It's like entering a dream world!"

Glen walked over to the stream to take a look. "Wow, you're right! Those fish are really amazing. I wonder—"

In his peripheral vision, Glen saw something move. He turned his head quickly.

"What is it?" asked Amanda.

"Oh, probably nothing. I thought I saw something."

"Well, anyway, take a look at the neat coloring on those fish. They seem to be gulping air when they leave the water! I wonder if they can breathe air. What do you think?"

"There it is again!" cried Glen. "Movement. Over there!"

The kids saw a menehune dart away from them, taking cover behind a series of trees. Glen started to give chase.

"Glen, what are you doing?" yelled Amanda.

"It's okay," he shouted back, over his shoulder. "I just want to get a closer look. I've never seen anything like it!"

Amanda decided to stay put. A few moments later, Glen returned. He was sweating profusely.

"Well?" she asked.

"He gave me the slip. He was just too fast."

A blood-curdling caw reverberated around the forest.

Amanda shivered. "What in God's name was that?"

"Oh, probably just a vulture or something like that," replied Glen. "Nothing to get excited about."

Amanda looked up and saw a gigantic dark bird circling in the distance. She grabbed Glen's shoulder and pointed at the sky. "There it is!"

The bird let out another piercing caw. A flock of small birds from a nearby tree scattered away.

Glen said, "Come on, let's follow this path. Maybe we'll meet someone who saw Zach, Kalani, and the Sand Monk."

"Okay." Amanda glanced nervously at the bird circling above. "I think we had better find our friends as soon as possible."

◆ IV ◆

Amanda and Glen rounded a sharp curve along the path they were following and came upon a small temple.

"Check it out!" exclaimed Glen. "A temple."

"Yeah. It looks a lot like the Sand Monk's temple in Hawaii. Are those plumeria trees?" asked Amanda. "They sure look like plumeria trees."

"I don't know." Glen walked up to one of the trees, reached up, and plucked a flower. "It smells like one."

"That's a nice garden," commented Amanda. "It looks Japanese."

"That fountain doesn't look Japanese, though," remarked Glen. "It looks Spanish or something."

"Yeah. Well, let's take a look inside," suggested Amanda. "Maybe someone's in there."

They approached the temple and ascended a stone staircase to the main entrance. Glen pulled open the sliding door and stepped inside. Amanda followed close behind.

"Holy smokes!" exclaimed Glen.

The temple's interior had been completely ransacked. Numerous shoji screens on the far side of the temple had been ripped, and several meditation cushions had been shredded. Scores of candles, violently jolted loose from their holders, were strewn about the floor (beads of dried wax and black burn marks were everywhere). Hundreds of claw marks defaced and defiled the sandstone Buddha in the temple's altar, on which was written, in dark red, the following message:

BEHOLD THE FATE OF THOSE
WHO CROSS THE SAND QUEEN!

"Look at this," said Amanda. She ran her fingers across several scratch marks on the sandstone Buddha. "Who—or what—would do such a thing?"

"I don't know," remarked Glen. "They look like claw marks. And that message—"

"Yeah. I hope it wasn't written with blood."

Glen walked toward the adjoining room. He stepped on something, causing a loud snapping sound. He looked down and picked up a mangled pair of sunglasses. "Hmm . . ."

"Sunglasses," commented Amanda.

"Yeah. They look just like the Sand Monk's." Glen scanned the rest of the floor. "Oh no! Look—on the floor over there."

"Purple crystals," said Amanda. "Glen, what's going on here?"

"I think our friends were captured. Or worse."

"I feel sick." Amanda sat down on the floor and placed her head in her hands. She felt like vomiting.

Glen said, "Hey, wait a minute—is that what I think it is?"

Amanda looked at him. "What are you talking about?"

"Over there." Glen pointed toward an adjacent room. "It looks like a trap door."

They rushed into the next room and stood over a hole in the floor. "It's a secret passageway and the lights are still on!" Glen said excitedly.

Amanda bent over and picked up the badly damaged trap door, which had been torn from its hinges. "Claw marks."

Glen turned. "Huh?"

"Look—claw marks. All over this door. They look just like the marks on the Buddha."

"You're right," observed Glen. "Maybe this means Zach, Kalani and the Sand Monk escaped. It looks like they were at least able to close and lock the trap door behind them. Otherwise, it wouldn't be so badly scratched and damaged."

"Do you think?"

"Of course, that doesn't mean they weren't eventually caught. There's no way of knowing for sure."

Amanda kicked a wood splinter away from the opening. "Well, I know one way to find out."

"And that would be . . . "

"Go down into that passageway!"

◆V◆

Glen descended the ladder first. Amanda followed him closely. After reaching the bottom, they started to walk through a nondescript, narrow dirt tunnel.

"Wow, this tunnel isn't very wide," commented Amanda.

Glen hoped it might widen as they progressed. "Thankfully there's lighting."

"Glen, check it out!" Amanda pointed to the wall by her side. "More claw marks."

"Wonderful."

Soon, the kids came to a fork in the path. After flipping a coin (since they could not think of any other way to make the choice), they decided to follow the path on the left. After fifteen minutes of walking, they heard malevolent cackling.

The color drained from Amanda's face. "What was that?"

Glen tried to remain calm. "I don't know. But it definitely came from behind us."

"Do you think it was one of those claw creatures?"

"I don't know. But I sure don't want to stick around to find out. Let's get out of here!"

They sprinted down the passageway. After arriving at another fork, they took the path to the right. After another five minutes of hard running, they slowed down to catch their breath.

"We haven't heard that thing for a while now—maybe it went away," remarked Amanda.

"Perhaps," said Glen. "Look at the wall. More claw marks!"

"Why do those awful things feel the need to scratch things everywhere they go?"

They heard the shrill cackling again. It was noticeably closer. The kids turned around and saw a skeleton loping toward them. It wore a black eye-patch, and its bony hand was clutching a rusty dagger. The skeleton started cackling again. Its lower jaw was flapping repeatedly, wildly.

"Oh God!" moaned Amanda.

The skeleton shrieked, "Get out of my tunnel! Now!"

Amanda stammered, "Umm . . . umm . . . umm . . ."

"I said get out of my tunnel!" The skeleton, tossing its dagger from bony hand to bony hand, advanced menacingly toward the kids.

Glen and Amanda looked at each other. In unison, they shouted: "Run!"

They bolted away from the skeleton. They rounded a curve and were blocked by a closed door.

"Please be open, please be open, please be open," repeated Amanda as she reached toward the doorknob.

The moaning skeleton rapidly drew closer.

The knob turned, but the door would not open.

"Oh no!" cried out Amanda.

"Let me try," said Glen.

He turned the knob and pushed on the door. It would not budge.

Amanda started to panic. "What are we gonna do? What are we gonna do? God knows what that skeleton will do to us!"

"This door looks pretty old," observed Glen. "Maybe if I crash into it, we can break through. Quick, turn the knob."

Glen took a few steps back and rammed his body, leading with his right shoulder, into the door. Although it did not open, Glen heard the sound of splintering wood.

"Do it again," urged Amanda. "Hurry!"

Glen heard the moaning again, just around the corner. The skeleton would be upon them any second now. He took a few steps back and rushed the door again, throwing all his weight behind his right shoulder. This time, the door crashed open, shattering the wood around the dead bolt. Glen, losing his balance, fell through the opening and onto the floor of a large room. Amanda followed him and quickly slammed the door shut behind her. With her back toward Glen, she pushed against the door with all her strength. Glen lay on the ground, groaning softly, nursing his sore shoulder.

Amanda turned toward Glen, still pushing against the door. "I hope that skeleton doesn't try to—"

She stopped cold. They were not alone.

◆VI◆

Three very startled menehune, each wearing a different colored tunic (forest green, navy blue, and brown), sat around a small table on the other side of the room. They had been playing cards. Now they just sat there, silently, staring uncomprehendingly at the kids. One placed his cards on the table, picked up a silver goblet, and took a long drought.

"And just what do you think you're doing?" asked the menehune in forest green, in a heavily accented, singsong voice. "Barging in on us like that!"

"I'm terribly sorry, sir, but we were being chased by something horrible out there," explained Amanda. "We had no choice but to break down your door."

"And what were you running from? One of them lion men was it?"

"Lion man? What's that?" asked Amanda.

"Half-man, half-lion."

It dawned on Glen that they must be responsible for all those claw marks. "No, it wasn't one of those."

"Consider yourself lucky, then," said the menehune in forest green. "Now then. I'll ask you again. Why did you barge in on us like that?"

Amanda answered, "We were running from a horrible skeleton! It had a black eye-patch, a rusty dagger, and—"

"A black eye-patch? It was wearing a black eye-patch? Its jaw—did it flap up and down?"

"Yes," confirmed Glen. "You've described it exactly."

The three menehune exchanged knowing glances and cried out in unison, "Bones!"

"Excuse me?" said Amanda.

"Bones—he's a harmless one that he is!" said the menehune in navy blue. "He was just playing with you!"

Amanda scowled. "I'm not amused."

"Yeah, that was just Bones having his fun," said the menehune in brown. "He was murdered by them sandroids a couple years ago, don't you know. He don't know what to do with himself nowadays!"

"You knew him before he died?" asked Glen.

"Aye, we did," the menehune in brown said somberly. He flashed a wicked grin. "Obviously, that guy isn't resting in peace!"

The menehune in navy blue chuckled; the one in forest green guffawed. Amanda shot a horrified glance at Glen. The menehune in forest green saw it. After regaining his composure, he said to Amanda, "Don't take things so serious like. We're just having some fun, don't you know."

"Speaking of fun, would you like to join our party next door?" asked the menehune in navy blue.

"Party?" asked Amanda.

"Aye! Where do you think I got me beverage here?" He clinked goblets with the menehune in brown. "And don't you worry about a thing. Bones won't be joining us."

"That's a relief," said Amanda.

Glen and Amanda followed the menehune through a small passageway that led to a closed door. The menehune in forest green turned to them and said, "The party—it be waiting for us through this door!"

He opened the door.

A burst of music and laughter washed over the kids as they peered into a room filled with partying menehune, both male and female. There was a large vat in the middle of the room, inside of which bubbled and gurgled a viscous red liquid. A raging fire underneath it provided heat. Around the vat, a circle of menehune—their arms were interlocked—danced as a small band on the side of the room played instruments resembling mandolins and guitars. Several tables, on which a wide assortment of food had been placed, were on the other side of the room. A menehune was sprawled out on one of them. He lay on his back, unconscious. The contents of a silver goblet, which he clutched in his right hand, had spilled onto his chest. His tongue lolled. Drool was dribbling down the side of his mouth.

A menehune broke from the circle, moved in front of the band, and started to dance a little jig. She sang the following diddy, in a rich and melodious voice:

Gather all the berries,
We just picked off the vine.
We're a group of fairies,
About to make some wine!

Press all those berries,

Don't they look just fine!
We're a group of fairies,
About to drink some wine!

After the last line, a group of menehune raised their goblets and roared their approval.

"Not bad, eh?" said the menehune in brown to Amanda and Glen. He was grinning wildly.

"Do you want to try some?" asked the menehune in forest green.

"Try what?" asked Glen.

"Some of our brew," he answered. "You *must* try some of our brew!"

Without waiting for a response, he darted off toward the vat. Along the way, he grabbed a couple of goblets. He climbed a ladder that had been propped up against the vat. To his friends' hearty cheers, he dipped the goblets into the cauldron and filled them with the thick red liquid. He quickly returned to the kids and offered them each a drink. Glen gladly accepted and took a small sip. Amanda waited to see Glen's reaction.

"Well, how is it?" she asked Glen.

"It's pretty sweet," he replied. "But it's not bad. It tastes like thick cranberry juice."

"Okay, I guess I'll try it." Amanda took a small sip. Revolted, she spat the red liquid onto the ground. "Ugh . . . it tastes like cough syrup!"

The menehune cackled. The one in navy blue said, "Don't you worry about it none. Not many humans can stomach our brew!"

The menehune in brown said, "Come join our party. Have some fun!"

Amanda whispered to Glen, "We should get going. I want to find out what happened to Zach, Kalani, and the Sand Monk. I'm really not in a partying mood."

"Agreed," Glen whispered back.

"Hey, mister," said Amanda to the menehune in navy blue. She poked his shoulder to get his attention. "Did lion men make those claw marks in the tunnel?"

"Aye," he replied. "Not long ago, a bunch of them lion men came through here. Chasing a couple kids. Not too different from yourselves, come to think of it."

"You saw lion men chasing two kids earlier?" asked Amanda.

"That's what I said, didn't I?"

"Did they catch the kids?" asked Glen.

"No, them kids gave the lion men the slip," explained the menehune in forest green. "We made sure of that."

"Okay. Okay," said Amanda. "That's good. What about an old man. Did you see an old man with them?"

"No, that we didn't see. No old man. Just them two kids."

Amanda's heart sank. "Glen, that means they probably captured the Sand Monk!"

"How's that?" asked the menehune in brown, suddenly looking serious. "What was it you were saying? About the Sand Monk?"

Amanda explained, "Our friends—the kids you saw earlier were with the Sand Monk. He must've brought them to his temple, only to be captured by the lion men. He must've been captured; otherwise you'd have seen him with our friends!"

The menehune in forest green grew glum. "Oh, dear. That's not good."

"No, not at all," said Glen.

"Tell you what we can do," said the menehune in navy blue. "We can point you in the right direction, yeah?"

"Pardon?" said Glen.

"We can show you where them kids went," clarified the menehune in brown.

"That would be really helpful," said Amanda.

"While you go hunting for your friends," he continued, "we're going do some investigating ourselves."

"How are you going to do that?" asked Glen.

The menehune in forest green flashed a sly grin. "We have our ways, don't you know!"

"Well, if you learn something, can you let us know somehow?" inquired Amanda.

"Aye, that can be arranged." The menehune in forest green grabbed a nearby chair, stood on it, and shouted, "Oy! Oy! Oy!"

The music and dancing stopped abruptly. The room grew silent. Everybody turned around to look at the menehune in forest green, standing on the chair. "It seems the Sand Monk maybe was captured by them lion men we saw earlier," he shouted. Several menehune gasped; one fainted. "We need to find out what happened—maybe he's in serious trouble!"

With that, the party abruptly ended. The menehune packed up their instruments, extinguished the fire beneath the vat, and gathered up the food. One of them announced that there would be a meeting (in half an hour) to discuss the incident. Everybody quickly scattered. (Except, of course, for the menehune passed out on the table. Efforts to revive him were futile.) The menehune in brown escorted Amanda and Glen through the tunnels to the place where Zach and Kalani had made their escape earlier. He showed them which path to take, wished them luck, and quickly disappeared.

CHAPTER 5

◆ I ◆

Zach and Kalani paid close attention to Jasper's instructions after leaving his cottage. After walking briskly for a while, they began to hear a clanging sound in the near distance.

"We must be getting close to the Hooded Blacksmith's place," observed Zach. "That sounds like someone banging metal."

"Yeah, I think you're right," said Kalani. "And just in time too. Haven't you noticed the sun's about to set? It's also getting cooler."

Zach replied, "Yeah, but I didn't want to say anything."

The kids rounded a corner and saw a small cottage, with whitewashed walls and a thatched roof. The front door and window-frames (and shutters) were black. The cottage had a large annex, from which the metallic clanging emanated.

In unison, Zach and Kalani turned to each other and exclaimed, "The Hooded Blacksmith!"

The kids decided to peek inside the annex. They tiptoed up to a window and looked inside. They saw a tall man—his back was turned to them—pound repeatedly on a glowing piece of metal with a hammer. Scores of sparks flew through the air. He was wearing a black tunic. It had a hood, which was pulled over his head.

"What should we do?" asked Kalani.

"Jasper told us to go see him, so I can't imagine he won't talk to us," answered Zach.

"Yeah—let's make sure he knows Jasper sent us," said Kalani. Teasingly, she poked Zach in the ribs. "Don't be shy, go knock on his door!"

Zach, wanting to appear brave in front of Kalani, readily agreed. He walked over to the front of the annex, waited for a pause between hammer strikes, and knocked hard on the door. Inside, the Hooded Blacksmith cocked his head. Thinking he was imagining things, he grunted and resumed his pounding.

"Maybe he didn't hear you." Kalani was now standing beside Zach at the door. "Try again."

Zach rapped his knuckles against the door as hard as he could. After a few moments, the door flew open, revealing a middle-aged man with a goatee. The black hood still covered his head.

Looking mildly annoyed, he barked, "Yes? What can I do for the two of you?"

"Sir, we were sent here by Jasper the Hermit," explained Kalani.

The Hooded Blacksmith was surprised. "Jasper sent you?"

"Yes."

"Why?"

"Something terrible has happened," answered Kalani. "The Sand Monk's been captured by those horrible lion men."

The color drained from the Hooded Blacksmith's face. "Are you sure?"

"We're sure," said Zach. "We saw it happen with our own eyes. In fact, if it weren't for the Sand Monk's bravery, we'd have been captured too!"

The Hooded Blacksmith looked off into the distance, behind the kids, his eyes searching. He asked them to enter his cottage. Once inside, he offered the kids some water, which they accepted eagerly. He pulled a tap at the base of a wooden cask and filled a mug with a dark amber liquid.

"Whatchya drinking?" asked Kalani.

"Beer," replied the Hooded Blacksmith.

"Can I have some?" asked Zach.

"No. You're too young." The Hooded Blacksmith took a hearty swig and smacked his lips. "Now, tell me what happened to the Sand Monk."

Zach and Kalani explained everything. The Hooded Blacksmith listened intently. After the kids finished relating the events of the day, he leaned back in his chair and said, "The sun is about to set. Soon it'll be pitch black outside."

"Go on," said Kalani.

"The lion men will likely wait until dawn before resuming their pursuit of you," explained the Hooded Blacksmith. "That will give you time to rest; you both look very tired. You can sleep here."

"Thanks," said Kalani. "You think they'll still be searching for us tomorrow?"

"Count on it."

"There's one thing I don't understand," interjected Zach.

"Yes?"

"Why did Jasper send us to you?"

The Hooded Blacksmith leaned back in his chair and stared at the kids thoughtfully for a few moments. "Have you ever heard of the Black Knights?"

Zach and Kalani shook their heads.

"The Black Knights used to be a paramilitary group that often tried to assassinate sandroid leaders. Sometimes they were successful, sometimes they weren't. The Sand Queen cracked down on them brutally, wiping out a large portion of their membership. Afterwards, the Sand Monk persuaded the Black Knights to cease their violence, arguing that it wasn't really helping the cause. Instead of getting rid of the Sand Queen, the violence was strengthening her."

"Really? How?" asked Zach.

"The violence caused the sandroids to rally around the Sand Queen—even those who opposed some of her governing policies," explained the Hooded Blacksmith. "They essentially let the Sand Queen do anything necessary to stop the violence, which they called 'Black Knight terrorism.'"

Kalani asked, "Some sandroids oppose the Sand Queen?"

The Hooded Blacksmith stroked his goatee. "Yes. To explain why, I need to give you a brief history lesson. As the Sand King grew senile—he was the Sand Queen's father—there was talk among the sandroids of establishing a democratic ruling body with an elected prime minister. It was to be called the Sand Congress. In other words, they were planning to abolish the monarchy. They weren't idealists; they just wanted more power for themselves."

"A power grab," commented Kalani.

"Yes."

"The humans must've been happy, right?" said Zach.

"To a certain degree, because it meant they would no longer be at the mercy of one individual—the monarch," explained the Hooded Blacksmith. "Make no mistake, however. The sandroids weren't planning to allow humans to vote, or to be represented in the Sand Congress."

"I see," commented Zach.

The Hooded Blacksmith continued, "The senile Sand King died before the Sand Congress could be created. As you might guess, the Sand Queen would have none of this Sand Congress talk. She wanted to retain absolute power at all costs. The violence perpetrated by the Black Knights—they assassinated a prominent sandroid soon after she took power—played right into her hands. She exploited the situation by whipping up a frenzy of fear among the sandroids, especially among the more vulnerable older ones. She claimed that if they failed to support her, a strong leader, humans would gain power. In fact, the Sand Queen falsely claimed that humans were on the verge of taking over. She claimed the Sand Monk was behind all the violence and asked Sandroids to imagine life as slaves under his 'vengeful' rule. Therefore, when the Sand Queen declared an end to all talk of democracy, she was enthusiastically supported by each and every sandroid."

"Amazing. What did the Sand Monk do?" asked Kalani.

The Hooded Blacksmith gulped some beer. "Unlike many of us, the Sand Monk clearly saw that violence was strengthening the Sand Queen. We thought violence was the only answer, the only effective way to change things. But he argued that passive, non-violent resistance was the best way to weaken the Sand Queen, that over time it would strengthen and embolden her sandroid opponents. He was able to convince the Black Knights to renounce violence, which was no small feat."

"Were you a member of the Black Knights?" asked Kalani.

"Yes," replied the Hooded Blacksmith. "In fact, I still am. We are—or were, as the case may be—working very closely with the Sand Monk."

"If you're no longer a violent paramilitary group, what exactly do you do?" inquired Zach.

"The Black Knights gather intelligence. We focus our energies on keeping the Sand Monk apprised—as best we can—of what the Sand Queen is up to." The Hooded Blacksmith sighed deeply. "Unfortunately, we failed yesterday. The Sand Monk was captured."

"It's not your fault," said Kalani, trying to console him. "It was that jerk, Judlarthio. He betrayed the Sand Monk."

The Hooded Blacksmith responded, "Nonetheless, I can't help but feel responsible for not warning him in time."

"Can I ask you a random question?" said Kalani.

"By all means."

"Why do you always wear a hood?"

The Hooded Blacksmith chuckled. "To cover some damage I received long ago at the hands of some lion men."

Kalani was curious. "Can I see it?"

The Hooded Blacksmith stared at her. "It's not pretty." He slowly removed his hood, revealing two badly mangled ears. "During a fight, one of those lion men grabbed hold of both my ears and shook me around a bit. You can see the results."

Kalani felt sick to her stomach.

The Hooded Blacksmith placed the hood back over his head. "Now then, let me show you where to bunk down for the night."

◆ II ◆

Amanda and Glen were following the route recently taken by Zach and Kalani. As they climbed a steep incline, Amanda said, "Glen, it'll be dark soon. Do you think we should turn back?"

"We can probably spend the night in the tunnels with those menehune." Glen pointed to the top of the hill. "But first, let's see what's up there."

"Okay," agreed Amanda, "but if nothing's there, we should definitely turn back. I don't want to spend the night in this forest."

Grabbing onto exposed tree roots to keep from tumbling to the bottom of the hill, the kids climbed the rest of the steep incline. Glen was the first to reach the top. He scrambled over the precipice and disappeared from view.

"Do you see anything?" Amanda called out.

"A cottage."

"Really?" Amanda hoisted herself over the precipice and joined Glen. "You're right!" she exclaimed, pointing at Jasper's small, whitewashed cottage. Gingerly, they approached it.

Glen said, "There's a sign on that door. Let's see what it says."

They walked up to the front door. Amanda read the sign out loud: "Do not disturb under any circumstances. Unless you are an agent of the Sand Queen." She traced the white lettering with her finger. "Do you think we should knock on the door? I say we knock on the door."

"The person—or thing—who lives there might be a friend of the Sand Queen," warned Glen.

"It's possible," said Amanda.

Glen looked up at the darkening sky. "What the heck. We came this far, we might as well knock."

"Okay." Amanda smiled wryly. "Go for it."

Nervous—but trying to appear calm and collected—Glen rapped on the door. It opened slightly. "Hmm . . ." He pushed it open further.

Amanda gasped.

The interior of the cottage had been ransacked. Pots, pans, dishes, and shards of broken glass were strewn across the floor; the occupant's bedding material had been ripped to shreds (especially the pillows); and there were deep scratches—claw marks—all over the walls.

Amanda pointed at the wall. "Look!"

A message, written in crimson, said:

DEATH TO THOSE WHO HARBOR FUGITIVES!

She walked up to the message and touched the letters.

Glen picked a corncob pipe up off the floor. "Amanda, the intruders—probably lion men— must've been here recently."

"How do you know?"

"This pipe's still warm."

"I hope that message wasn't written with Zach and Kalani's blood."

"Yeah." Glen went to the window and looked outside. "I think we should stay here for the night."

"Good idea," observed Amanda. "Let's hope the lion men don't have the same idea."

◆ III ◆

The Hooded Blacksmith walked to his kitchen window and opened the curtains. He observed an orange glow on the horizon. Realizing the sun would soon rise, he muttered a curse and frowned. He poured some water into a kettle and fired up the stove. Several sharp pangs of hunger prompted him to place a few biscuits in the oven (and several more in a pouch to be eaten later). While the food and water was heating up, the Hooded Blacksmith slipped out to his workshop to retrieve his best sword and a couple of sharp daggers.

The Hooded Blacksmith re-entered the cottage and slammed the door shut. "Wake up, kids!" The kettle on the stove started to scream. "We have a busy day ahead of us. Gather your things and eat a biscuit or two. In the meantime, I'll pour us each a cup of tea."

Kalani pointed at the sword and daggers the Hooded Blacksmith was clutching. "Whatchya got there?"

"We may need these," he replied. "The sword is for me; the daggers are for you and the boy."

Zach was disappointed. "Why don't we get swords?"

"Because you don't know how to use one," replied the Hooded Blacksmith. "Now eat your biscuits."

Zach and Kalani sat down at a small table and started eating the warm food. The Hooded Blacksmith poured them some tea.

"Hey, this tea's pretty sweet and strong," observed Zach.

"Yes. It'll fortify your spirit," said the Hooded Blacksmith. He paused and cocked his head, as if straining to hear something. Sternly, he said, "We need to go. Now!"

Alarmed, Kalani asked, "What is it?" She heard a snarl in the distance. "Oh my God. They're here, aren't they!"

The Hooded Blacksmith barked, "Follow me!"

They scrambled out of the cottage and dashed down a path leading into the forest. A lion man, who had been waiting in ambush, dropped from a tree branch. He did a tuck-and-roll, to absorb the shock of the impact, and stood at his full height in front of the Hooded Blacksmith. He snarled and shook his head, splattering the Hooded Blacksmith with slobber—an insult. The Hooded Blacksmith promptly drew his sword and declared, "Get out of my way, you mangy half-breed, or I'm going to cut off your head!"

The lion man roared and leapt toward the Hooded Blacksmith. The Hooded Blacksmith deftly sidestepped him, managing to carve a line onto the lion man's upper arm with the tip of his sword. Blood started to ooze and spurt. Enraged, the lion man snarled, bared his teeth, and pounced directly onto the Hooded Blacksmith, pinning him to the ground. The kids were horrified.

"Oh God," shouted Kalani, "he's going to rip the Hooded Blacksmith to pieces!"

The lion man let out a terrible cry, rose up, and started to shake violently.

Zach said, "Look, the sword! The Hooded Blacksmith speared the lion man right through the belly with his sword!"

The lion man whimpered, twitched a few more times, and fell to ground, motionless. The Hooded Blacksmith stood up.

Kalani gaped at five deep scratch marks on each of his arms. "You're hurt!"

"I'll be fine. Just a few more ugly scars, that's all." The Hooded Blacksmith looked behind the kids. His eyes widened.

Kalani turned around to take a look. "Oh no!"

Five lion men were running toward them.

The Hooded Blacksmith commanded, "Kids— run! I'll ward them off."

He drew his sword. Fully expecting to die, he faced the rapidly approaching lion men. He hoped he could at least buy enough time for the kids to get a good head start. The Hooded Blacksmith glanced over his shoulder at Zach and Kalani. They stood there, frozen, watching him. He shouted, "For the love of God, run! Go save the Sand Monk! You can't do anything here—the lion men will rip you to pieces if you try to help me. I'll catch up with you later."

Kalani heard a *cloppety-clop* sound in the near distance.

The Hooded Blacksmith turned to her and exclaimed, "Could it be?"

Three large men, wearing black tunics and brandishing glistening swords, appeared from around the bend. They were riding creatures that resembled winged horses. The wings vastly increased the horses' speed (especially in rough terrain) by enabling them to glide several yards above the ground for brief intervals of time.

The Hooded Blacksmith, grinning wildly, cried, "They've come! By God, they've come!"

"Who?" asked Zach.

"The Black Knights!"

The lion men stopped in their tracks and turned around to confront the newcomers. The men in black tunics, however, were much too swift for them. They swooped down on the lion men, slashing and stabbing mercilessly with their swords. It was all over in a matter of seconds.

A Black Knight dismounted. The Hooded Blacksmith embraced him and said, "Thank God you showed up when you did, Palomar! I wasn't sure if I could take on five lion men at once."

"Well, as soon as we got your message, we raced to your cottage."

Kalani said, "Wow, you guys showed up in the nick of time. The cavalry, riding to the rescue!"

The Hooded Blacksmith said, "I sent them a message last night after you guys went to sleep. They got here quicker than I expected."

Palomar declared, "We drop everything to help a brother in need!"

◆IV◆

Amanda and Glen, happy they had survived the night without being visited by any lion men, left

Jasper's cottage. They followed a path into the lush forest. After about twenty minutes of walking, Amanda tugged Glen's shirt and said, "Look—over there!"

A gaggle of lohapa birds slowly flapped their way towards them.

"What the heck are those?" asked Glen.

"They're certainly different," stated Amanda. "Well, they don't look too dangerous."

"Are you sure about that? Look at those talons!"

"I'd rather not."

Trying to reassure Amanda (and himself), Glen reasoned, "They probably would've attacked by now if they meant us harm."

Amanda pointed at the lumbering birds. "Look—the one in the middle's carrying a brown sack, or something."

The lohapas drew closer. The one in the center broke from the pack and came within a few feet of the kids; the breeze generated by its flapping wings gently washed across their faces.

The bird fixed its gaze on Amanda, who was certain she could detect a high degree of intelligence and compassion in its eyes. It deposited the brown bag at her feet, emitted a soft caw, and flew away. Amanda bent over and picked up the bag.

"What's in it?" asked Glen.

"Hold on, hold on. Let me see." Amanda peered inside. "It's food!" She pulled out several large biscuits and two medium-sized pieces of pink fruit.

Glen was excited. "That'll certainly help us! I was worrying about our next meal."

"Me too." Amanda looked inside the bag again and fished out several small glass bottles. They were filled with a clear liquid and sealed with cork. "These will help if we get thirsty."

They continued walking through the forest. Soon, they came upon a sign that had been nailed to a tree, next to a path that branched away from the one they were following. The sign read:

This Way to Hollow Lookout

Glen suggested, "Let's follow the path to the lookout."

"This is no time for exploring, Glen," said Amanda.

"You don't understand; I'm not interested in exploring."

"What are you getting at?"

"We can probably get a much better view from the lookout. Maybe we'll spot the others."

Amanda grew excited. "Do you think?"

Glen answered, "It's worth a try."

Amanda brushed by Glen and strode purposefully toward Hollow Lookout. She glanced back at him. "Well, what are you waiting for? Follow me!"

◆V◆

They reached the top of the ridge, which was covered with rocks, boulders, and small shrubs. The drop to the valley below was precipitous. Glen scanned the horizon, searching for his friends.

"I don't see them," said Amanda. "Do you?"

"No." Glen pointed at a nearby tree. "Look—something's been posted on it." He approached the tree. A sign read:

Climb Tree for a Better View!

"I'm going to climb it," announced Glen.

"Are you sure that's a good idea?" asked Amanda.

"What do you mean?"

"It's right by the edge of the cliff!"

Glen tried to sound brave. "I'll be fine." He walked up to the tree. "Come on, give me a boost."

Reluctantly, Amanda approached Glen. "Be careful up there." She bent over and cupped her hands. "It's a good thing you're not that big."

Glen frowned. "Just give me a boost."

Amanda heard a rattling sound. "Did you hear that?"

"Hear what?"

"Never mind. It was probably just my imagination."

With some effort, Glen managed to scale the tree. "Wow, what a view!"

"Do you see them?" asked Amanda.

"No."

Amanda heard the rattling sound again. This time it was louder. "Did you hear that?"

Glen looked down at her. "Hear what?"

"A rattling sound. Like a rattlesnake."

"No."

Amanda was concerned that a snake might be hiding nearby, ready to sink its fangs into her. "I'm coming up there with you."

"Can you make it up on your own?" asked Glen.

"I'll manage."

Amanda deftly scrambled up the tree and joined Glen. "Quite a view, huh?" he commented.

"Sure is." Amanda scanned the horizon. "I don't see them either."

The tree started to vibrate gently.

Amanda was alarmed. "Do you feel that?"

"It's probably just the wind," answered Glen.

The vibrating grew in intensity.

"Hey, what's going on here, Glen? That's not wind."

"I don't know. Maybe—"

The tree began to shake violently. Its branches suddenly closed tightly around the kids, ensnaring them. The tree sank swiftly into the ground, pulling Amanda and Glen into a long, subterranean shaft.

Eventually, the tree slowed its descent and landed gently in front of a door. The branches relaxed their grip on the kids, allowing them to wriggle free and slide down to the dirt floor.

Glen pointed at an array of human skulls that had been placed on the door's lintel. They were bathed in soft, blue-gray light. "That doesn't look promising."

"Should we open the door?" asked Amanda.

"What other choice do we have?"

"We could climb back into the tree and wait."

The tree started to shake violently. It swiftly shot back up through the shaft, disappearing from sight.

"So much for that idea," Glen said dryly.

Amanda sneezed. "It's really musty down here."

THE HAILONA PROPHECY

Glen approached the door. "Are you ready?"

"As ready as I'll ever be."

He pushed it open. They stepped over the threshold into a thick, murky fog.

◆ VI ◆

The haze dissipated quickly. Amanda and Glen found themselves standing on a nondescript street corner in a city. The buildings were dull and drab; the weather was cold and grey. Although the streets were presently clear, dirty remnants of a recent snowfall could be detected in the gutters. Several pedestrians, wearing long pants and heavy coats, ambled down the sidewalks. An automobile sped by. It was not modern; the style reminded Amanda of cars she had seen in old movies, filmed in the 1930s or 1940s. The atmosphere was thick and heavy. Walking and talking seemed to take more effort than usual.

"Where are we?" asked Amanda. The words came out slowly, as if she had cotton in her mouth. She could see her breath. "It's awfully cold here."

"I have no idea." Glen was also speaking sluggishly. "I wonder if we went back in time."

"It's a little hard to talk."

"Yeah."

Amanda placed her hand on her forehead. "My forehead aches. Do you feel it too?"

"It's like a sinus headache," said Glen.

A group of people walked by and glanced at the kids. Their skin was unusually pallid. More shocking, however, were their eyeballs. They were completely black. The hair on the back of Amanda's neck stiffened. She tugged Glen's arm. "Did you see their eyes?"

"Yeah. Pretty creepy."

"Glen, where are we?"

A young man, standing on the sidewalk on the other side of the street, noticed the kids. He started to walk briskly toward them.

"Amanda, someone's coming!"

"Where?"

Glen pointed at the man. "Over there."

"Glen, don't point!"

"What should we do?"

As the man drew close, he smiled. "Please, don't be frightened. I just want to talk to you for a moment." Amanda noticed that his eyeballs were grey, not black. Moreover, remnants of his pupils and irises were still visible. "Allow me to introduce myself," he said. "I'm Jonus."

"I'm Amanda."

"Glen. Pleased to meet you."

"The pleasure is mine," said Jonus. "You've noticed my eyes."

"Some people with black eyeballs walked by earlier," said Amanda. "It was very unsettling. Why aren't yours completely black?"

"They will be," replied Jonus. He hesitated. "And so will yours."

"What!" blurted Glen.

"That's not funny," said Amanda.

"Unless you can somehow find a way out of here, your eyes will soon fade to black," explained Jonus. "Just like mine."

"Yours were once normal?"

"Yes. I was born on Sandtopia. I climbed that tree at Hollow Lookout to get a better view." Jonus shook his head ruefully. "I should have ignored that sign. Big mistake. Anyhow, next thing I knew, I was in front of that door with the skulls. I opened it, and here I am."

"How long ago was that?" asked Glen.

"I don't know. Several months?"

"And you haven't figured out how to get back to Sandtopia?"

"No."

Amanda shot Glen a concerned glance.

"Jonus, where *are* we?" asked Glen.

"You're in *Bad Land*. It's some version of hell, I think. At least it sure seems that way to me." Jonus' eyes darted about, scanning the street. "Let's get out of plain view. It's not safe for groups to gather in public. I'll take you to my apartment. It's not far from here."

♦VII♦

They entered a nearby building and climbed a flight of stairs to a small, dusty, one-bedroom apartment. It was sparsely furnished and in need of extensive renovations. However, to the kids' relief, it was well heated. Glen and Amanda sat down on an old couch in the living room. Jonus pulled up a chair next to them.

"How did you find this apartment?" asked Amanda.

"After I crossed over, I needed to find a place as soon as possible," explained Jonus. "I wasn't in any mood to spend my first night here homeless, out in the cold. Especially since I was wearing shorts and a t-shirt. So I picked a random building. The door to this apartment was open. I've been here ever since. Amazingly, nobody has bothered me."

"You mean the owner could come back at any moment?"

Jonus shrugged his shoulders. "I suppose so."

"That's a comforting thought."

"Jonus, can you see normally, what with your eyes darkening?" asked Glen.

"Yes, as far as I can tell. Actually, the longer I stay here, the better I seem to be able to see. And my head hurts less."

Amanda rubbed her temples. "You must be getting used to the heaviness."

"Yes, but my mind is slowing down," said Jonus. "I'll probably end up a zombie, just like the others."

"Excuse me?"

Jonus explained, "Those people with the black eyeballs you saw earlier—they're essentially zombies. I call them *vacants*. As far as I can tell, they can't think for themselves. They just seem to shuffle along, pretty much oblivious to everything."

"Where did they come from?" asked Glen.

"Beats me. Sometimes I think they're people who died and instead of going to heaven, came here."

"What makes you say that?" asked Amanda.

"Just a feeling. Nobody here seems to be truly alive. Except for the stormtroopers."

"Stormtroopers?" repeated Glen.

"They're the only ones who seem to function reasonably well here," explained Jonus. "They oppress the vacants." He paused. "But as far as I can tell, it's not so great for them here either."

129

"Really? Why not?" asked Amanda.

"The stormtroopers are incredibly paranoid. They're constantly plotting and fighting against each other. Their lives aren't peaceful."

"Don't they have a leader? You know, someone to crack the whip and keep them in line?" asked Glen.

"Yes, they have a supreme leader, but he lost his mind for some reason. He blathers incoherently all day long. Nevertheless, the stormtroopers venerate him. It's peculiar." Jonus changed the subject. "Where on Sandtopia are you two from?"

"We're not from Sandtopia," answered Glen. "We're from a place called Hawaii. We stepped through a portal that brought us to Sandtopia."

Jonus was intrigued. "Hmm. Another portal. Is Hawaii a nice place?"

"Hawaii no ka oi," Amanda said proudly. "Hawaii's the best!"

"Why did you come to Sandtopia?"

"To make a long story short, we met an old man called the Sand Monk in Hawaii," explained Amanda. "He offered to show us around Sandtopia. Glen and I said no, but two of our friends decided to go. They didn't come back when they were supposed to, so we became worried. We decided to step through the portal to see what happened. After we got to Sandtopia, we found trouble. The

Sand Queen's goons were chasing our friends. In fact, we were trying to help them when we got sucked down to this weird place by that tree."

"And what happened to the Sand Monk?" asked Jonus.

"We think he was captured."

Jonus sighed deeply. "That's terrible news. The Sand Monk is a good man. If he was captured, I hate to think what the Sand Queen is doing to him right now." He ran his hands through his hair several times. "Guys, I have a confession to make."

"Yes, what is it?" asked Glen.

"I lied to you earlier. I do know how to get back to Sandtopia."

"What!" exclaimed Amanda. "You know how to get back to Sandtopia?"

"Yes."

"Thank God!" exclaimed Glen.

Amanda squinted at Jonus. "Why did you lie to us?"

"Do you have any idea how lonely my life is here? Do you know how bad vacants are at conversation? I wanted some company."

"That was a terrible thing to do." Amanda thought for a moment. "Wait. Why are you coming clean now?"

"It's better that you go back to help your friends and the Sand Monk," answered Jonus. He smiled wryly. "See, I haven't completely lost my humanity. At least not yet."

"Jonus, I don't understand something. If you know the way back to Sandtopia, why are you still here?" asked Glen.

Jonus pointed at his eyes. "By the time I found my way back to Sandtopia, these had already started to fade. In fact, the last time I went there, I could hardly see anything. My eyes ached so badly, I could barely function. In fact, I passed out from the pain."

"But if you go back to Sandtopia, won't your eyes eventually return to normal?" asked Amanda.

"It doesn't seem to work that way."

"But if you stay here, you'll turn into a vacant!"

"Quite a dilemma, no?"

Amanda furrowed her brow and said tartly, "And you were going to let the same thing happen to us."

"I'm sorry." Jonus looked down at the floor. "It's just that I'm so lonely here."

Someone shouted and pounded heavily on Jonus' front door.

"Oh no!" shrieked Jonus. "Stormtroopers! Somebody must have tipped them off!"

Glen jumped to his feet. "I hope you know a way out of here."

Jonus pointed toward his bedroom. "There's a fire-escape ladder in there, off my balcony. It leads to the alley below."

A stormtrooper thudded loudly against the front door.

Jonus looked terrified. "Let's go! That door won't hold them much longer!"

They dashed into the bedroom. The front door broke open. Several stormtroopers, wearing black commando uniforms, plunged into the living room. They were yelling loudly in a foreign language. Jonus, followed closely by Glen and Amanda, opened the balcony door and scrambled down the escape ladder. The rattling and clanking caused by their descent quickly drew the stormtroopers' attention. They rushed to the balcony in time to see Amanda, then Glen, drop to the ground below. One of the stormtroopers drew a pistol and fired at Jonus. The bullet missed and ricocheted loudly around the alley. He took another shot. Jonus groaned deeply and fell to the ground.

"No!" screamed Amanda. She kneeled next to Jonus and held his hand. "Are you hurt? How bad is it?"

"I think the bullet just grazed me." His shirtsleeve was starting to turn crimson. "It hurts, but I'll be okay."

Two stormtroopers started to scramble down the ladder. A third ran back to the living room and exited through the apartment's front door.

Glen looked up at the descending stormtroopers. "Oh crap!" He pulled Jonus to his feet. "Let's get out of here!"

Jonus and the kids ran to the alley's entrance, which emptied into the main street. The two stormtroopers pursued them doggedly. Their heavy boots crunched and pounded against the pavement, sending shudders up and down Amanda's spine.

Jonus was the first to reach the street. He turned left and shouted, "This way!"

Amanda pivoted to make the turn, but slipped on a patch of ice and tumbled to the ground.

"Amanda!" exclaimed Glen. "Are you okay?"

"Help!" she offered meekly.

Glen pulled her to her feet. "Can you still run?"

"I think so."

In the alley, twenty feet away, the stormtroopers halted. One of them raised his pistol, pointed it at Glen, and shouted harshly in his language. The other one pulled out two pairs of handcuffs and held them aloft for the kids to see.

"I know what *that* means," said Glen.

The stormtroopers started walking toward the kids.

Jonus, around the corner and out of the stormtroopers' sight, shouted, "Glen, Amanda, what are you doing? Run!"

"Jonus, they're waving a pistol at us," said Glen. "There's nothing we can do."

The stormtrooper brandishing the gun barked at them again.

Jonus pleaded, "Get out of there! Don't let them capture you. It's better to be shot and killed. Trust me."

Glen looked at Amanda. "Jonus is probably right."

The stormtrooper ran out of patience. He pulled the trigger. The gun jammed. He cursed loudly.

"It jammed!" Amanda announced with delight.

"Get the hell out of there!" shouted Jonus.

The kids ran to Jonus while the stormtrooper attempted to un-jam his pistol.

Amanda said, "I sure hope that portal to Sandtopia's nearby!"

"It is." Jonus pointed at a building across the street. "It's in there."

Glen was perplexed. "In there? How on earth did you manage to find it?"

Jonus heard the stormtroopers' heavy boots again. "Follow me!"

They sprinted across the street, dodging several rushing cars along the way, and soon reached the building with the portal. Jonus tried to open a glass door, but it was locked. He pounded his fist against the glass. "Arghhh!"

He looked over his shoulder.

The stormtroopers were on the other side of the street, about to cross.

Jonus saw a rock nearby, picked it up, and hurled it against the door. The glass shattered into hundreds of pieces. Gingerly, he stepped through a jagged hole, into the building's entry hall. Amanda and Glen followed him inside, taking care not to slice themselves on the remaining shards of glass.

"Where's the portal?" asked Glen.

Jonus approached an elevator. "Right here."

"The elevator?" asked Amanda. "Are you sure?"

"Yes, it'll take you back to Sandtopia."

"How?"

"How should I know?" snapped Jonus. "It just does." He pressed the "up" button and glanced nervously outside at the approaching stormtroopers. His voice was taut. "Listen carefully. When the door opens, step inside and press the 'close-door' button immediately. Then press the button for the top floor."

Amanda was perplexed. "You're not coming with us?"

"No."

"Please, Jonus, you *have* to come with us. It's not safe for you here."

"I'll manage. Like I said, I can't really function on Sandtopia anymore."

The door opened. Glen entered the elevator car.

Amanda pleaded, "But Jonus, we know the Sand Monk. Maybe he can help you."

"Go. Please."

The stormtroopers reached the building's front door. They kicked away some of the remaining glass shards. Amanda stepped into the elevator. She turned around to take one last look at Jonus. Looking glum, he waved goodbye to her.

Abruptly, Jonus turned and dashed toward a nearby stairwell. Amanda heard loud shouting by the stormtroopers, followed by a gunshot. Glen pushed a couple buttons. The elevator doors closed. The carriage began to ascend.

CHAPTER 6

◆|◆

The Sand Monk opened his eyes and watched a plump rat scurry across the floor. Instinctively, he recoiled backwards, away from the rodent. Startled and confused by the sudden movement, the rat dashed off, splashing through several fetid puddles of water. A sharp stab of pain shot up the right side of the Sand Monk's body, causing him to grimace, moan, and clutch at his ribs.

The Sand Monk was lying on a damp stone floor in a dungeon. His ankles were chained to a nearby wall. The thick, rusting, metal bindings were very tight and had already started to chafe his skin. The Sand Monk worried he would soon start to bleed and become infected. Trying to ignore the pain in his ribs, he propped himself up slightly to survey the room; several flickering torches provided meager lighting. A stone staircase, at the top of which stood an imposing wooden door, hugged the wall. As far as the Sand Monk could tell, it was the room's only exit or entrance. There were no windows, and the air was stale. He noticed some words had been etched carefully into the stone wall next to him:

I am the one
Who will give you succor;

I am the one
Who will resurrect your shredded dignity;

I am the one
Who will lovingly tend to your skin and soul,
As it blisters and bleeds on the cold dungeon floor.

—Justinian

Anger engulfed the Sand Monk as he read the words carved by his close friend. The Sand Queen had executed Justinian recently. She thought his increasingly popular poems—many of which exhorted people to open their minds and take control of their lives—were subversive to her regime. She had him arrested and tortured. Then she let him languish in her dungeon for ten excruciating months before sending him to the gallows.

The Sand Monk whispered, "Yes, my dear friend, I'll remember your beautiful verses and draw strength from them."

The Sand Monk sighed deeply and looked over his shoulder. Logarno, Mandalia, Pandalese, and Eraklena were also lying on the dank floor, behind him, sleeping. Their ankles were chained to the wall. Assorted cuts and bruises were evident all over their bodies, some of which looked quite nasty. Logarno started to fidget.

"Psst . . . Logarno," said the Sand Monk, under his breath. He was trying not to wake the others.

Logarno opened his eyes. He rubbed them, trying to focus. "Who's there?"

"It's me, the Sand Monk."

Logarno peered at him and cried out, "Is it really you? Oh, thank God you're alright!" He grinned and slapped his knee in joy. "And there's Mandalia, Pandalese, and Eraklena. We're all here!"

"Yes, we're all here," confirmed the Sand Monk. "For now."

Logarno tried to walk over to the Sand Monk and embrace him. The chain around his ankle quickly grew taut, however, bringing him to the floor with a loud, unceremonious thud. He groaned.

"Be careful, my friend. Our bindings are rusty and will likely give us infections if we bleed." The Sand Monk rattled his chain. "I think these are the least of our worries, though."

"Agreed," Logarno said glumly.

The others started to wake up, one by one.

"Where the devil are we?" asked Pandalese. He strained against his chains and looked at his friends. "Oh no, we're in the Sand Dungeon, aren't we!"

"It would appear so," confirmed the Sand Monk. "Eraklena, Mandalia? Are you okay?"

Eraklena rattled her chains. "I'm okay, but these bindings are biting into my flesh a bit. I wouldn't mind having them loosened." She smiled wryly. "To whom should I lodge my complaint?"

Mandalia chuckled. "I'll schedule an appointment with the Sand Queen—at my earliest convenience, of course—and let her know."

"I'm glad to see the two of you haven't lost your sense of humor," said the Sand Monk.

Pandalese asked, "Any idea how we're going to get out of this jam?"

The Sand Monk responded, "I haven't had much time to think about it. But I did have a dream, while I was sleeping, that might be instructive. I was in a rather small room, not unlike this one. It was cold, damp, and—"

The door at the top of the stairs swung open, revealing the angular body of a tall, young, male sandroid. Holding a steel poker, he descended the staircase (his long robes made it appear as if he were gliding). Four sahus followed him closely. Sahus were the sandroids' slaves. When humans died, sandroids did not permit the dead bodies to be buried properly by their families. Instead, they were mummified, placed in storage, and later brought back to life through the use of black magic. The purpose was to humiliate living humans (particularly the family members of the deceased), and to provide a source of cheap, compliant labor for menial tasks. Sahus could not talk; they could only grunt or moan. Essentially mindless, they obeyed their sandroid masters without question.

The young sandroid, after reaching the bottom of the stone stairs, quickly approached the Sand Monk. The Sand Monk stared at the wall, ignoring him.

"You will look at me when you are in my presence!" the sandroid shouted in a tinny, otherworldly voice.

The Sand Monk ignored him.

"Look at me!"

The Sand Monk still refused to obey.

"Very well," the sandroid said harshly. "You were warned."

The sandroid barked a command at one of the sahus. The sahu approached the Sand Monk and savagely kicked him in the ribs. The Sand Monk groaned.

"Stop! You'll kill him!" cried Pandalese. "He's an old man!"

"Shut up!" spat the sandroid. He fixed his icy gaze on Pandalese. "You're next. Sahu!"

A different sahu shuffled over to Pandalese and punched him in the face. Blood started to trickle down the side of his mouth.

The sandroid chuckled. "That should shut you up for a while."

Pandalese glared at him. His lip started to swell.

"Now, back to you, Sand Monk," the sandroid said contemptuously. He snapped his fingers. "Sahus!"

Three sahus roughly picked up the Sand Monk and propped him against the wall. The Sand Monk, not wanting to give the sandroid any satisfaction, held his breath as pain shot up and down his body. The sandroid walked over to one of the torches and placed the tip of his steel poker into the flame. After a couple of minutes, he removed it to reveal a glowing red instrument of torture. He approached the Sand Monk. "I expect you to tell me everything you know."

The Sand Monk ignored him. The sandroid reached out and clasped the Sand Monk's face with his gelatinous hands. The Sand Monk cringed because they felt cold and clammy. The sandroid held the hot poker inches away from the Sand Monk's right eye.

"You will tell me everything."

◆ II ◆

"Kids, I'd like to introduce you to some of my closest friends," said the Hooded Blacksmith. He made a dramatic, sweeping gesture toward the three Black Knights. "I've known them a long time. We've fought many battles and skirmishes together."

"Pleased to meet you," said the largest one. He approached the kids. His face was fierce, and he wore a thick, black, bushy beard. "My name is Jaagdar."

"Jaagdar's specialty is the bow and arrow. He's an excellent marksman." The Hooded Blacksmith looked at the dead lion men. "Thankfully, he's also pretty good with the sword!"

"I try," Jaagdar said modestly.

"And, of course, you already know Palomar," observed the Hooded Blacksmith.

Palomar grunted.

"Hey, don't forget about me!" said the Black Knight standing next to Palomar. His hair was fair, and an ugly scar ran down the side of his left cheek.

"Right. Please allow me to introduce Scar Face!" joked the Hooded Blacksmith.

"Hey now!" responded the Black Knight with the scar. "My name is actually Duvar."

"Nice to meet you, Duvar," said Kalani. "Say, how did you get that ugly scar?"

"Kalani!" admonished Zach.

Duvar chuckled. "It's okay. I'm proud of this scar. It's from the Sand Queen herself!"

"Really?" blurted Kalani. "How did *that* happen?"

"It's quite a story, really," said the Hooded Blacksmith. "It happened during one of our most successful operations."

"Indeed," said Duvar. "Some time ago, before we renounced violence, we conducted an operation on Ascension Day."

"What's that?" asked Kalani.

"Ascension Day is the anniversary of the day the Sand Queen assumed power," explained Palomar.

"I see." Kalani looked at Duvar. "Go on. What kind of operation was it?"

"An assassination attempt," he replied.

"You were trying to kill the Sand Queen?" asked Kalani.

"We wish!" interjected Jaagdar.

Duvar continued, "Yes, we'd love to have killed her. But, as you may know, sandroids who aren't old are very, very difficult to eliminate."

"Yeah, we know," said Zach.

"Therefore," said Duvar, "we decided to target Maleus."

"Maleus?" asked Kalani.

"He was the Sand Queen's most trusted advisor," explained the Hooded Blacksmith. "He was very old."

"And therefore an easier target," said Zach.

"Right," said Jaagdar. "Like the Sand Queen, Maleus hated the prospect of democracy. He saw it as a threat to his own power, since he had so much influence on the Sand Queen. At the Sand Queen's behest, Maleus helped whip up hysteria and paranoia among the sandroids, claiming that humans—led by the Sand Monk—were plotting to take over Sandtopia."

Zach asked, "Did you kill Maleus?"

"At noon on that particular Ascension Day, a grand procession passed through the streets of the capital, Sand City," explained Duvar. "The Sand Queen and some of her advisors—including

Maleus—rode in open chariots. As you can imagine, security was very tight."

"Were a lot of people there?" asked Kalani.

"Yes," answered Duvar. "But the crowd wasn't enthusiastic; they were there because the Sand Queen had issued a decree requiring everybody in the capital to attend."

The Hooded Blacksmith smiled wryly. "The fact that she ordered so many humans to be present allowed us to melt into the crowd. It made our attack and escape that much easier."

"Indeed," said Duvar. "Anyhow, our plan was to shoot Maleus—and the Sand Queen—with arrows when the procession reached Jilomar Square. Jaagdar and I perched inside a couple of buildings along the side of the road, holding weapons we had hid underneath floorboards earlier. Jaagdar, being the better shot, aimed at Maleus. I targeted the Sand Queen."

"Wait a minute," interjected Zach. "Why did you even target the Sand Queen? Isn't she too young to be killed by arrows?"

"Yes," replied Duvar. "We wanted to humiliate her."

Zach chuckled. "I see."

Duvar continued, "As the procession went by, we shot our arrows. Jaagdar's arrow hit Maleus' head, shattering his hardened shell. Sand spilled out all over the place. He died right away."

"What about the Sand Queen?" inquired Kalani.

"My arrow punctured her soft shell and went deep into her head," replied Duvar. "Shrieking with rage, she plucked it out, snapped it in two, and threw it onto the ground. To my horror, she looked around and gazed directly at me. I was still holding the crossbow."

Kalani was riveted. "I'm listening."

"The Sand Queen pulled out a razor disk and hurled it at me." Duvar pointed at the scar on his cheek. "That's how I got this."

"Naturally, the Sand Queen's henchmen tried to apprehend us," said Jaagdar. "But they were blocked by the thick crowd. We were able to slip away."

"What a story!" exclaimed Kalani.

"Indeed." The Hooded Blacksmith looked off into the distance. "Guys, I think we had better get moving now."

◆ III ◆

Zach, Kalani, and the Black Knights headed toward the Sand Palace, in Sand City. After several hours riding through the forest (two to a winged horse), they came upon a gated entrance to a small village. Beside the entrance were two trees. At the bottom of each tree was a pile of human bones (skulls included). Two empty nooses swung gently from the branches above. Someone had nailed a large wooden sign with white lettering to one of the trees, just above the bones. The sign read:

Behold: Two Subversives
Eliminated, Courtesy of the Sand Queen

"Lion men," muttered the Hooded Blacksmith.

"Huh?" said Kalani.

The Hooded Blacksmith spat on the ground in disgust. "Lion men."

"How can you tell?" asked Zach.

Palomar said, "Look at the scratches on the trees, kid. Claw marks."

"And lion men love to leave messages, if you haven't already noticed," added Jaagdar. "As warnings."

"I see," said Zach.

"Come on, let's enter the village," Palomar said gruffly.

After passing through the gate, they walked down a gravel path. It led to the village's central square, where a large feast was taking place. The attendees were not celebrating; on the contrary, their collective mood was somber and sour. As the kids and the Black Knights approached the gathering, an old man with a long, white, flowing beard glimpsed them. He grabbed a walking stick and hobbled toward them with a sense of purpose.

"Allow me to introduce myself," said the old man. "I'm Keoluha, the village chief."

The Hooded Blacksmith introduced himself and the others to Keoluha. Then he asked, "What's the purpose of your gathering?"

Keoluha eyed him suspiciously.

The Hooded Blacksmith laughed, removed his hood to reveal his badly mangled ears, and said, "Don't worry, brother, we're no agents of the Sand Queen!"

Keoluha relaxed visibly. He pointed at the Hooded Blacksmith's ears. "Lion men, I presume?"

The Hooded Blacksmith nodded.

Keoluha glanced toward the gate and said, "I'm sure you saw the bones and nooses."

"We sure did," interjected Kalani. "Why did the lion men do that to them? Why would they do such a thing?"

Keoluha shook his head. "Those poor men were simply at the wrong place at the wrong time."

"What do you mean?" asked Zach.

"They failed to bow down when a group of lion men passed through here last year. The lion men reported it to the Sand Queen. She ordered their immediate execution."

"That's pretty harsh," commented Kalani.

"My child, the Sand Queen simply enjoys killing people." Keoluha frowned. "She's a black-hearted monster. By the way, I suggest you learn how to address lion men properly in case you run into one."

"With the edge of a sword," Palomar declared in an icy tone.

Zach pointed toward the feast. "Why's everyone so glum?"

Keoluha answered, "We just held a remembrance service for those men."

"The ones who were hanged?" asked Zach.

Keoluha nodded.

"How sad," commented Kalani.

Keoluha continued, "It's bad enough the black-hearted one ordered her goons to hang our men. But to rub salt into our wounds, she won't let us bury their bodies. She threatened to kill the entire village if those bones are removed from underneath the trees."

"That's awful," commented Zach.

"Yes, it is." Keoluha glanced toward the swaying nooses. "It was quite humiliating, you know, especially for the families of those dead men."

Kalani said, "I'm sure it was."

"Now then, would you like to join me in my cottage for a short rest?" inquired Keoluha. "If I may say, you all look a bit worse for the wear."

♦ IV ♦

They sat around a large, rectangular table. Keoluha poured them each a glass of fruit juice. "Now, what exactly brought you to my village?" He pointed at the Hooded Blacksmith's arms. "By the looks of those scratch marks, I gather you've had a recent run-in with those mangy lion beasts."

"Indeed," said the Hooded Blacksmith. His voice was grave. "Let me tell you exactly what has transpired."

After hearing about the recent events, Keoluha was stunned into speechlessness (which was unusual for him). Eventually, he muttered, "You know, I never thought I'd see the day. The Sand Monk has been captured. He always seemed to be one step ahead of the Sand Queen."

"We were all shocked to hear the news," stated the Hooded Blacksmith.

"Tell you what," said Keoluha. "I'm willing to provide some men to help you on your journey. I feel I must do something."

The Hooded Blacksmith replied, "Thanks for your kind offer, but we must decline." Kalani and Zach exchanged puzzled glances. "The smaller we keep our party, the easier it'll be for us to avoid detection."

Jaagdar added, "Besides, we only have three winged horses. They're already carrying two apiece. If anyone joins our group, they'll have to walk."

"Which will slow us down," added Palomar.

"I see. Well, at least let me offer you some extra provisions for your journey," offered Keoluha.

"Thank you," said the Hooded Blacksmith. "Extra food and water would be much appreciated."

"Furthermore, if anyone comes asking for you, I'll be sure to point them in the wrong direction," added Keoluha, smiling slightly.

"Much obliged," said Palomar.

The kids and the Black Knights galloped and glided out of the village on the backs of the three winged horses. Keoluha watched them depart. "God help them," he muttered under his breath. "God help us all." He heard a horrible caw. It was shrill and tinny. He looked up at the sky and saw a circling dacturion.

♦V♦

The sandroid held the hot poker inches from the Sand Monk's eye and hissed, "Tell me who shot Maleus."

The Sand Monk ignored him.

The sandroid grew shrill. "Who!"

The Sand Monk spat in the sandroid's face. "Go to hell, you beast!"

The sandroid howled with rage. He was about to jam the hot poker into the Sand Monk when the door at the top of the steps flew open. The sandroid turned to see what the disturbance was about. He immediately dropped the poker onto the stone floor—a loud clang echoed around the room—and dropped to his knees, bowing obsequiously. "At your service, my lady."

The Sand Queen descended the stone stairs and approached the Sand Monk. She was wearing a long, black, flowing gown, which was fastened by a white belt. A jewel-encrusted scabbard was attached to it. She wore white gloves and a wig (customary for sandroid females). Her hair was long, wavy, and black. It was set in place by a crown, adorned with exquisite pearls and seashells. At the center of the crown sat a giant red pixar (an extremely rare gemstone that had been imported from the sandroid home planet, before the portal closed). The pixar was a symbol of authority.

The Sand Queen drew close to the Sand Monk. He noticed the sand shifting and churning under her clear, gelatinous, humanoid face. "Well, well, well, if it isn't the infamous Sand Monk," she said in a tinny, mocking, otherworldly voice. She looked smug. "It appears your powers to elude me have finally failed. What do you have to say for yourself now, you wretch?"

The Sand Monk remained silent. Transfixed, Eraklena, Pandalese, Mandalia and Logarno looked on. Pandalese clasped his hands together and offered a silent prayer.

"I see," said the Sand Queen. She looked at the sandroid who was still on his knees in front of her and barked, "Get up and leave this dungeon immediately. And take those miserable sahus with you."

The sandroid rose to his feet and bowed deeply to the Sand Queen. He glided up the stairs, followed closely by the sahus, and left the dungeon. She peered at the Sand Monk. "I'll repeat myself. What do you have to say for yourself, monk?"

Once again, the Sand Monk ignored her. The Sand Queen removed a white glove and whipped it across his face, slapping him sharply. A red welt quickly appeared.

155

Mandalia gasped. The Sand Queen looked at her and snapped, "Shut up!" She returned her gaze to the Sand Monk and hissed, "Monk, you *will* answer my questions. Those kids you were with at the temple earlier. I want to know where they're from. Are they from Sandtopia? Tell me. Now!"

The Sand Monk said nothing. The Sand Queen whipped her glove back and forth across his face, slapping him twice.

"How many children are there?" she shrieked. "I demand to know!"

The Sand Monk remained silent.

The Sand Queen glowered at him. She was not used to being challenged in such a manner. Usually, her prisoners talked right away because they were so terrified. In a fit of pique, she slapped the Sand Monk once again with her white glove. "Fine." The Sand Queen picked up the iron poker, walked over to a torch, and placed its end into the fire. After a short while, she approached the Sand Monk and held the glowing red tip of the poker inches from his face.

The Sand Queen shook her head. "No, monk, I'm not going to use this on you." She squinted at Mandalia, sprawled on the floor. "I'm going to use it on your pathetic little friend over there. Let's see if you can remain silent while I torture her."

The Sand Queen walked over to Mandalia, grabbed a fistful of hair, and jerked her up to her feet. Mandalia groaned; the Sand Queen chuckled. The Sand Queen held the glowing poker inches from Mandalia's face and glanced back at the Sand Monk. "Tell me about those children, or else I'll disfigure your little friend here." She laughed derisively. "By the time I'm through with this wench, she'll need an iron lung!"

The Sand Monk sighed. "I know why you're so interested in the children."

"Do you now? Please, by all means, tell me. Tell us all! Why do I have such an interest in the children?"

"You know all about the Hailona Prophecy. You're worried those children are here to fulfill it."

The Sand Queen tightened her grip on Mandalia's hair. "Keep talking, monk."

"According to the Prophecy, an incredibly *evil* queen will be undone by four young newcomers to Sandtopia."

The Sand Monk smirked slightly because he had emphasized the word "evil." The Sand Queen was not amused. She threw Mandalia onto the stone floor and approached the Sand Monk. Mandalia moaned.

Inches away from the Sand Monk's face, the Sand Queen said, "I demand to know exactly where those kids came from. Now, I'll ask you one last time. Are they, or are they not from Sandtopia?"

"Those kids are not from Sandtopia."

The Sand Queen tapped the stone floor several times with her iron poker. "I see." She was silent for a few moments. "Monk, you've been able to elude capture for a long time. In fact, you disappeared every time I was about to get you. How?"

"I have many talents."

The Sand Queen frowned. "No. You're not talented at all. You're a hack. A malingerer. I think you merely stumbled upon a portal, one that allows you to slip in-and-out of Sandtopia at will." Her voice grew tense, as if she were about to unleash another spasm of violence. "And that's not the only thing, monk. I think that's also how you brought these children to Sandtopia. You criminal, you brought these children to Sandtopia! You *want* them to fulfill the Hailona Prophecy. How dare you!"

"Why do you find a group of children to be so threatening?" asked the Sand Monk. "What could they possibly do to you?"

"I don't know . . . I don't know." The Sand Queen glowered at the Sand Monk. "Where are the others?"

"What are you talking about?"

"Don't be stupid. Where are the other children? I know of two; there should be four."

"Well, you can rest easy. Only two children were with me at the temple when I was apprehended."

The Sand Queen scowled at the Sand Monk for a few moments. "Are you telling me that you only brought over two children?"

"That's what I'm telling you."

"You better be telling the truth, monk," said the Sand Queen. She sneered, turned abruptly, strode toward the stone stairs, and ascended them. At the top of the staircase, she looked back down at the Sand Monk. "May God have mercy on your worthless soul if I find out you've been lying to me. Because I sure won't."

The Sand Queen slammed the massive wooden door shut, leaving the dungeon. The echo reverberated around the dungeon. It was a cold, impersonal sound that cut to the bone. The Sand Monk, feeling helpless, shuddered.

CHAPTER 7

♦ I ♦

After reaching the top floor, the elevator door opened. Glen and Amanda saw nothing but blackness outside.

"Should we get off?" asked Amanda.

"You don't want to go back down there, do you?" inquired Glen.

"Good point."

Cautiously, Glen stepped out of the elevator and into the darkness. Amanda followed him. The elevator door closed.

Amanda pointed toward a small shaft of light in the distance. "Glen, look—over there!"

"Yeah. Maybe it's an exit." Glen sniffed the air. "It's dank in here."

They walked slowly and carefully over uneven ground toward the light. As they drew closer to it, they realized they were in a cave.

Glen pointed at the light. "That must lead to the forest, outside. See the trees?"

"Yeah. Well, as far as I'm concerned, the sooner we get out of here the better," said Amanda. She rushed toward the exit.

◆ II ◆

Glen and Amanda walked down a narrow path in the forest. They were completely lost. Eventually, the trail led to a huge clearing, in the middle of which stood two structures. The building on the left resembled Jasper's cottage; the one on the right looked much like a Hawaiian heiau (temple). The kids entered the clearing. To their amazement, a large, strange creature loped across the field and disappeared into the heiau. Although its face was human-like, it dragged its knuckles on the ground, grunted, and was covered in thick black hair.

Amanda worried she might have been hallucinating. "Did you see that?"

"I sure did," responded Glen. "It looked like an ape-man!"

"Do you think we're in Sandtopia?"

"I don't know. I hope so. The pressure on my head has lessened."

"Your speech sounds normal again."

Glen pointed at the cottage. "Should we take a look?"

"I don't know," answered Amanda, sounding nervous. "That thing might be dangerous!"

A youthful-looking man, wearing a flowing white gown emerged from the cottage. He was tall, thin, and bearded. Appearing relaxed and in no hurry to do anything in particular, he stretched and yawned. He noticed the kids staring at him. Amanda froze. She wanted to turn and run, but she could not get her muscles to obey. Glen grabbed Amanda's arm and started to pull her off the meadow, back into the forest.

"Wait!" said Amanda, planting her leg to resist Glen's tugs. She pointed at the man. "He's smiling at us. He's friendly—he doesn't want to harm us."

Glen turned around. The man was waving his arm, beckoning the kids to come join him. "Are you sure it's safe?"

"Come on!" urged Amanda, tugging Glen back toward her. "Maybe he can tell us where we are."

The kids approached the man, who smiled and greeted them with outstretched arms. "Isn't it a glorious day? It's sunny, the air is fresh—" He tilted his head back, placed his hands on his hips, and closed his eyes. "And I can smell the flowers blooming in my garden." He opened his eyes and looked at the kids earnestly. "Can you smell them?"

"Yes," said Glen.

Amanda nodded.

"Excellent! Now, allow me to introduce myself. I'm Gavendo the Mystic. Feel free to simply call me Gavendo. What are your names?"

"Amanda."

"I'm Glen."

"Gavendo, are we in Sandtopia?" asked Amanda.

"Yes, of course," he answered.

"That's a relief. You wouldn't believe where we just came from."

"Oh?"

Amanda explained, "Yeah, we climbed a tree at Hollow Lookout. The tree plunged into the ground and left us in a strange, cold place that was filled with vacants and stormtroopers."

Gavendo looked puzzled. "Vacants and stormtroopers? What are those?"

"You don't want to know," said Glen.

"It sounds like quite an unpleasant place," said Gavendo. "Perhaps you should tell me the entire story."

They entered Gavendo's cottage and sat down at a dining table. Amanda and Glen told him everything that had transpired since they first materialized in Sandtopia.

After listening to their story, Gavendo sat silently for a while, stroking his beard. Finally, he said, "So, you don't know the fate of your friends, and you suspect the Sand Monk has been captured."

"That's right," said Glen.

"That is bad news indeed."

"Can you help us?" inquired Amanda.

Gavendo looked at the kids thoughtfully. "Perhaps. Let's retire to the heiau next door."

Amanda sat up stiffly. "I'm not going over there."

Gavendo was perplexed. "Why wouldn't you want to enter the heiau? It's a very peaceful place, and it has a wonderful energy." He smiled wryly. "You're not an atheist, are you? You don't look like an atheist."

"No, it isn't that," answered Amanda. "I don't want to have anything to do with that strange ape-man creature."

"You saw him?" asked Gavendo.

Amanda nodded vigorously. "He entered your heiau."

"Hmm . . . he must be gaining strength."

"I don't understand," said Glen.

Gavendo stood up. "Come, join me in the heiau and I'll explain everything. Don't worry. The creature won't harm you."

◆ III ◆

Amanda and Glen sat on cushions in the middle of Gavendo's meditation room (inside the heiau). The room did not look like the Sand Monk's meditation hall; there was no sandstone Buddha and it was teeming with crystals of varying sizes and colors. Moreover, numerous painted wooden masks adorned one of the walls. Some of the faces were angry, others were sad. A few were jolly.

Gavendo lit some incense and placed the smoking sticks into four stone holders. The sweet smoke quickly started to fill the interior of the heiau. Amanda asked, "What happened to that awful creature we saw earlier?"

Gavendo, with a twinkle in his eye, turned to her and said, "Oh, he must have run off somewhere."

"What was it?" asked Amanda.

"A tulpa."

"Huh?"

"A tulpa. You don't know what that is?"

"No."

Gavendo pondered the best way to explain. "Are you familiar with meditation?"

Glen said, "I've seen people meditate, but I'm not really sure what they're doing. It looks boring."

Gavendo frowned. "Meditation is a way of focusing and disciplining the mind."

"I don't understand," said Glen.

"During the course of the day, how many thoughts do you suppose you have?" asked Gavendo.

"Too many to count!" exclaimed Amanda.

"Exactly!" said Gavendo. "Your mind is constantly racing. You know, wondering what to wear, what people think about you, worrying about tomorrow's mathematics test. I could go on and on."

"So what does that have to do with meditation?" asked Glen.

"Meditation quiets all that mental chatter," replied Gavendo. "It's quite relaxing and therapeutic in that sense. When you're meditating, you're essentially taking a break from worrying about all life's stresses and problems."

"How exactly do you do that? I mean, how do you quiet all the mental chatter?" asked Amanda.

"Well, one way to do it is through concentration," replied Gavendo.

"Concentration?"

"Yes." Gavendo stood up, walked over to the corner of the room and picked up a small piece of black cardboard. A solid white circle had been painted in the center. He returned to his cushion and displayed it to the kids. "Do you see this white disk?"

They nodded.

"I want you to concentrate on it. It's pretty easy to do when it's right in front of your eyes, right?"

"Right," said Glen.

"Now, close your eyes and try to visualize the white disk."

Amanda closed her eyes and furrowed her brows. "It's easy to do at first, but I lose the image pretty quickly."

Glen agreed. "Yeah, me too."

Gavendo said, "Okay, when you lose the image, open your eyes and take another look at the piece of cardboard. Keep doing that until you're able to increase the amount of time you can hold the image with your eyes closed."

They followed his instructions. After several minutes, Amanda declared, "This is hard."

"Precisely," said Gavendo. "You see, with practice, you'll be able to hold the image for increasingly longer periods of time."

"How long can you hold it, Gavendo?" asked Amanda.

"A long time. I've been meditating for many, many years."

"You probably don't even need the picture!"

"No, I don't. But let me ask you this. While you were concentrating on the picture of the white disk, and as you were trying to visualize it with your eyes closed, were you thinking about anything else?"

"Not really," said Amanda.

"Exactly!" exclaimed Gavendo. "You see, concentrating on the disk quieted your mind. You weren't worrying about the hundreds of things you normally worry about. When you do such meditation for extended periods of time, it's quite healthy, actually. I find that after meditation, I'm able to think more clearly. In fact, answers to problems that may have been vexing me for some time often pop suddenly into my mind. It's quite magical. You see, life is much like walking through thick fog. You don't know where you're going, because you can't see more than a few feet in front of your face. You might be walking toward a wonderful garden, or you might be headed toward a terrible trap. Meditation clears the fog somewhat. If you're adept enough, it helps you avoid the terrible trap and leads you to the wonderful garden."

"That's all very interesting," said Amanda, "but you haven't told us what a tulpa is."

Gavendo stroked the bristles of hair on his chin. "Right. Tulpas have to do with concentration during meditation. As I told you, I've been meditating for a long time. When I visualize, I don't picture simple discs. I visualize creatures."

Amanda's eyes bulged. "Creatures?"

"Yes. If you're advanced enough, and you spend a lot of time visualizing a certain object or thing, you can actually make it materialize."

Glen laughed uneasily. "You're joking."

Gavendo looked at Glen intently. "What do you think you saw earlier? I've been visualizing that ape-man for quite some time now."

Glen said, "Are you saying that that strange ape creature is a product of your imagination? That we saw something you've been visualizing in your meditations?"

"That's what I'm saying," answered Gavendo. "You see, here's the thing about tulpas. When other people start seeing your visualizations, you know you've been successful at creating one. Fortunately, not many people can create tulpas."

"Why do you say that?" asked Amanda.

"Most tulpas are controlled by their creators. Although they look and feel real enough, their minds are rather empty. They'll do the bidding of their creator, without question. The tulpa you saw earlier protects me. That's why I created him. As you know, Sandtopia can be a dangerous place with all those lion men and sandroids running around."

Amanda was concerned. "You said most tulpas are controlled by their creators."

"Yes, that's right."

"What about the ones that aren't?"

"Creating tulpas can be dangerous. That's why it's a secret art known by very few people. You see, sometimes tulpas are able to slip away from their creator's control."

"What do you do if that happens?" asked Amanda.

"If I feel that the tulpa is sinister and may cause harm," replied Gavendo, "I go through an arduous process of deconstructing it."

"And that gets rid of the tulpa?"

"Yes, but it's not easy, and it's quite exhausting. Tulpas don't like to be destroyed once they've achieved a certain degree of independence."

"No, I imagine they wouldn't," Glen said with a twinge of sarcasm.

"You know, Glen, even if you don't believe in tulpas, the concept has interesting implications for daily life," remarked Gavendo.

"How so?"

"Some of us on Sandtopia—myself included— believe strongly that nothing in our life happens by accident. In other words, we believe that an unseen force—Daijar—works behind the scenes to guide our life by bringing us the people we need to meet and the events we need to experience at just the right time. It's as if Daijar is writing a play. In response to our choices, He's constantly bringing in new characters and new scenes for us to experience. Some are pleasant; others are not. Some characters exist for minutes; others are with us for years. Daijar is the unseen playwright. The hidden hand."

"He has complete control?" asked Amanda.

"Not exactly. Remember, we do have free will. That means we can make our own decisions; we're able to think critically and independently." Gavendo looked at Glen. "We can even reject Daijar, if we so choose."

Glen shifted uncomfortably on his cushion.

Gavendo continued, "Think of it this way— we're Daijar's tulpas and we've slipped away from His conscious control. We're able to make our own independent choices. However, it's quite easy for Daijar to de-visualize us if He so chooses."

"How?" asked Amanda.

"Death," answered Gavendo.

"This is really too much—" started Glen.

Amanda interrupted. "Glen, how is it that you can step through a portal, materialize in a completely new realm, be chased by a skeleton, not to mention gun-toting stormtroopers, and still be so closed-minded? I mean, come on!"

"I just find it hard to believe someone can sit down, close their eyes for a while, and conjure up creatures out of thin air," said Glen. "I have my limits, you know."

Gavendo chuckled. He was not bothered by Glen's skepticism. "Well there's another concept I want to talk to you about."

Amanda was intrigued. "What's that?"

"As I mentioned earlier, we have free will and can make our own choices. However, some decisions obviously carry more weight than others. For example, deciding what shirt you intend to wear for the day isn't particularly significant. In most cases, it won't change the course of your life. Other decisions, of course, are much more important."

"Like deciding whether or not to marry a particular person," said Amanda.

"Yes. Fortunately, such weighty decisions don't occur everyday," stated Gavendo.

"I'd go crazy!"

"But here's the interesting thing. Unbeknownst to us, some of the decisions we make *are* extremely significant."

"Can you give an example?"

Gavendo paused. "Remember the shirt example I just mentioned? Let's say you decide, on a whim, to purchase a bright orange shirt—you're tired of your usual dark ones. You put it on after leaving the store. Because the shirt is so bright and unusual, it catches the attention of a handsome young man who's standing behind you in line while you're waiting to purchase a cold beverage—it's hot outside. Intrigued, he strikes up a conversation with you. The two of you hit it off immediately and start dating. In time, you get married, have children, and spend the rest of your lives together."

"I see. It's all because I decided, on a whim, to purchase an orange shirt."

"That's right, Amanda." Gavendo grinned. "That's the hidden hand at work. After all, who do think made sure the handsome guy was there to notice you in your smashing new shirt?"

"Daijar!" she exclaimed.

Glen pursed his lips. "Hmm . . . "

Gavendo suddenly closed his eyes and said nothing for a while. The kids looked at each other nervously. He began to breathe very deeply. As Amanda was about to say something, Gavendo opened his eyes. He handed Glen a crystal and said, gravely, "My boy, hold onto that crystal. I'm not exactly sure how, but in the coming hours you'll be tested."

"Well, we'll see about that," responded Glen. He stood up brusquely. "Come on, Amanda, we'd better get going."

"Wait a minute. I want to ask Gavendo something," she said.

"Yes?"

"Would it be possible for you to go into meditation and find out where our friends are, and if they're safe?"

Gavendo glanced at several crystals to his left, picked them up, and placed them in front of him. "I'll see what I can do."

He began to meditate. Amanda watched keenly, anxious to get some information.

After several minutes, Gavendo opened his eyes. "Your friends, including the Sand Monk, are indeed still alive. But they're all in grave danger. The Sand Queen is convinced that your friends are part of an ancient prophecy describing her downfall. She'll stop at nothing to protect her throne."

"What should we do next?" asked Amanda.

"You must find your way to Sand City."

"But what do we do once we're there? Please, tell us what's going to happen!"

"That information is hidden."

CHAPTER 8

◆ | ◆

Soon after leaving Keoluha's village, Zach, Kalani, and the Black Knights reached the edge of a vast, rolling plain. It sloped downwards, gently, toward the ocean (which they could see in the distance). Small shrubs and lava rocks of varying sizes, shapes, and colors—mostly black, red and gray—peppered the grassy plain. The dusty path they were following snaked its way down to the distant shoreline. The group slowed to a halt and gazed at the spectacular view.

The Hooded Blacksmith said to Zach and Kalani, "As you can see, this path goes down to the coast." He pointed. "We have a hideout down there, where we can plan our next moves."

Zach was concerned they would lose valuable time. "You mean we're not going directly to Sand City?"

"Don't be stupid," replied the Hooded Blacksmith. "We can't just saunter into Sand City without a plan."

"Kid, Sand City is the Sand Queen's stronghold," explained Palomar.

"Okay, I get it," said Zach. "Shall we get going?"

"Good idea," said the Hooded Blacksmith, kicking the side of his winged horse, sending it into a quick gallop.

The others followed closely. Not long after leaving the protective canopy of the dense forest, they heard a series of chilling, frantic, high-pitched caws.

"Oh hell!" shouted the Hooded Blacksmith, peering up at the sky.

Kalani, perched behind him, also looked up at the sky. "What are they?"

"Dacturions!"

"The Sand Queen's Praetorian Guard?"

"Yes." The Hooded Blacksmith's voice was tense. "We must get to our secret hideout immediately." Wasting no time, he shouted "Hiyaaagh!" and kicked the sides of his winged horse forcefully, trying to coax as much speed out of the animal as possible.

The others quickly followed suit. After ten minutes or so of hard galloping and gliding, the winged horses were frothing at the mouth. They heard the chilling caws again. Zach looked up at the sky and saw about a dozen dacturions circling overhead. Each one was carrying a curious payload in its talons.

Zach, who was sitting behind Jaagdar, tugged at his tunic. "What are they carrying?"

"Huh?"

"Look up!"

Jaagdar's eyes widened. "Lion men!" he exclaimed. "They're carrying lion men!"

The dacturions buzzed over the group—their blood red eyes were blazing and flickering malevolently—and deposited their payloads about one hundred yards ahead of them. The birds swiftly returned to the group and pounced. With their long talons, they snatched the Black Knights and the kids from the backs of the winged horses and lifted them up to the sky (Palomar managed to slice off a dacturion's talon with his sword before being seized).

Kalani was dangling just several yards from Zach. She yelled, "Zach, I hope they don't drop us onto the ground from up here!"

"No, it's worse." He pointed directly ahead. "They're taking us to the lion men!"

The lion men had formed a large circle, and the dacturions deposited the kids and the Black Knights directly into its center. The circle of lion men suddenly parted at one end to let the leader—by far the largest of the bunch—make a dramatic entrance. Snarling and shaking his head back and forth, he was clearly very angry. He was also carrying the lifeless body of one of his comrades— killed earlier by the Black Knights near the Hooded Blacksmith's cottage. He threw his head back and roared loudly. With the dacturions hovering just overhead (their long yellow beaks glistened in the sun, and their huge, dark purple, flapping wings created an unpleasant breeze), the lion men started to close the circle around the group.

"This is not good," said Kalani. "What are we going to do?"

The Hooded Blacksmith looked at Palomar. "Got any ideas?"

Palomar grunted. "I'm not letting those mangy beasts capture me!" He drew his sword and charged the closest lion man.

"Palomar—no!" shouted the Hooded Blacksmith.

Feigning a slice attack, Palomar plunged his weapon deep into the lion man's belly. He roared in agony. Unfortunately, Palomar had trouble removing his sword. Exposed and defenseless, several lion men pounced, driving him hard to the ground.

Instinctively, Duvar drew his sword. Seeking to save his friend, he rushed Palomar's attackers. Screaming at the top of his lungs to stiffen his resolve, Duvar drove his sword into one of the lion men on top of Palomar. He withdrew it and was about to stab another adversary when six or seven lion men jumped him. It was over very quickly.

"I think we had better surrender," concluded Zach.

With disdain, several lion men flung the two lifeless Black Knights onto several adjacent lava rocks.

"This is not good," stated Kalani. "Beedle, beedle, boor, they've just bashed down our door."

With a heavy heart, the Hooded Blacksmith tossed his sword to the ground—a sign of surrender. Jaagdar did the same. The lion men quickly moved in and apprehended them.

◆ll◆

"So, what did you think about that meeting with Gavendo?" asked Glen. He and Amanda were walking down a forest path toward Sand City.

"It was really interesting. I think—" Amanda stopped abruptly, stiffened her back, and cocked her head to the side. "What was that?"

"What was what?" asked Glen.

"Didn't you hear it?"

"No. I didn't hear anything. It was probably just—"

"Shut up and listen, Glen!"

Silence.

"Amanda, I don't hear anything unusual."

She shook her head. "No. No. I swear I heard something."

"You're just spooked, that's all," said Glen.

"Huh?"

"Gavendo's crazy talk. It's got you spooked."

"I don't know . . . At any rate, let's get moving."

They pressed on, deeper into the forest.

Several guttural grunts emanated from somewhere behind them.

Glen froze. "*That*—I heard."

"It's getting closer," Amanda said tensely.

"What do you think it is?"

"I don't want to know. Run!"

Amanda shot up the path ahead of Glen. Straining, he raced to catch up to her. Meanwhile, the grunts increased in frequency, like a dog panting.

The kids rounded a gentle turn. A large gray net, weighted with small stones, fell from the trees on top of them. Arms flailing, they fell to the ground, toppling over one another. Trapped, they flopped around like two fish out of water.

"Get this thing off of me!" shouted Amanda.

The grunting stopped, only to be replaced by an earthy, sinister growl and a pungent smell. Amanda stopped punching her arms against the net and looked up.

"Uh-oh."

"What is it?" inquired Glen. He could not see anything because his head was pinned to the ground.

"You don't want to know."

A hairy creature, clutching a long spear, yanked the net off the kids. He motioned for them to stand up.

Glen spat a wet gob of dirt and a couple of small pebbles out of his mouth. He turned his head to size up his captor. "It's a tulpa!" he exclaimed.

◆ III ◆

The tulpa forced the kids to march into a nearby cave. Several torches provided meager lighting. Glen stumbled over a boulder and tumbled to the ground. He picked himself up and dusted off his trousers. Impatient, the tulpa jabbed Glen under his shoulder blades with the blunt end of his spear.

"Okay, okay!" snapped Glen. "Hold your horses. I just wanted to rub the dirt off my pants."

"Glen, don't antagonize him!" exclaimed Amanda. "After all, he might be able to understand you."

The tulpa grunted.

"What do you think he's planning to do with us?" asked Glen, whispering.

"I don't know," Amanda whispered back.

"Do you think he's going to kill us?"

"Wouldn't he have already done so by now?"

"Good point."

Amanda scrunched her face. "He really needs to take a bath."

The tulpa grunted and jabbed Glen's back again.

"Ouch! Take it easy!"

The tulpa forced the kids to enter a large side room with a black and white tile floor. It was lit by a row of flickering oil lamps. The tulpa motioned for Glen and Amanda to sit down at a long rectangular table.

Neither Amanda nor Glen moved.

Agitated, the tulpa grunted several times, pulled out several chairs, and motioned toward the table again.

"Okay, okay!" said Amanda. She and Glen approached the table and sat down uneasily in the chairs. "Are you happy now?"

The tulpa snapped his feet together and stood rigidly at attention (as best he could). He puffed out his chest conspicuously and gripped his spear tightly. A creature that looked completely human— save for a slightly more pronounced brow-ridge— entered the room from an adjoining passageway. Walking completely upright, he wore a flowing black gown. His head was shaved tightly, he had a black goatee, and he wore a pair of round spectacles. Eight more tulpas, each resembling the one standing at attention (ape body, human-like face) filed into the room. They grunted and dragged their knuckles on the ground. Each one sat down at the table.

The bald, human-looking creature sat at the head of the table. He raised his arm (the grunting ceased abruptly) and surveyed the kids closely for a while. Then he said, "Welcome to the Council Room. Allow me to introduce myself. I'm Plathor the Leader." He smiled tightly. "But you can simply call me Plathor."

"Okay. I'm Glen."

"Amanda."

Glen eyed the room's main exit. The tulpa who had captured the kids was now guarding it.

Plathor had a habit of oddly cocking his head to the side whenever he spoke. It made him appear slightly unhinged. "I wouldn't recommend trying to escape, young man," he said to Glen. "You won't get far."

Amanda changed the subject. "What exactly are you the leader of, Plathor?"

Plathor gestured at the ape-men sitting at the table. "I'm the leader of this group. We're all tulpas."

"You're a tulpa too? But you look different from the others," Amanda remarked.

"Indeed," said Plathor. "I was created to be a little bit more—how shall I say—advanced."

"Who created you?" asked Glen.

"Gavendo. He created all of us."

"Gavendo?" asked Amanda.

"Yes, the man you met earlier. He created us to protect him."

Glen smiled. "Well then, this has all been just one big mistake. We have no intention of harming Gavendo. We're his friends. We're no threat to him. So, you see, you can let us go."

Plathor frowned. Sternly, he said, "There has been no mistake."

"I'm confused," said Glen.

"As I explained, Gavendo created us to protect him. Being the most intelligent and advanced tulpa, my duty was to supervise the others. But you see, as time progressed, I became more and more independent-minded. I didn't like being Gavendo's stooge. And I really hated it that he could eliminate me whenever he pleased." Plathor slammed his fist against the table. "I'm not expendable!"

Amanda did not like where this was going. "Are you still taking orders from Gavendo? Are you still protecting him?"

Plathor smiled crookedly. "Let's just say that I broke away from that fool and his overbearing ways. I convinced the rest of the tulpas here to join me."

"How did you manage that?" asked Amanda.

"It was simple—I offered them their eternal freedom."

"So all of Gavendo's tulpas joined you?" asked Glen.

Plathor spat on the table contemptuously. "No."

"Why are we here?" asked Amanda. "This is all very interesting, but we do have urgent business elsewhere."

Plathor pounded the table again and shouted, "I'm not finished!"

"Sorry," Amanda said meekly.

"Gavendo is well aware of my rebellion," stated Plathor. "In fact, he already eliminated three of us. It's only a matter of time before we—"

"Why don't you just eliminate Gavendo?" suggested Glen.

"Glen!" blurted Amanda.

"I already thought of that," snapped Plathor. "Don't you think I would have thought of that right away?" He paused. "Do you think I'm stupid?"

"No, not at all," stammered Glen. "I just thought—"

"Gavendo has far too much protection. We can't get close enough to kill him. Too many tulpas are still on his side." Plathor grinned malevolently. "That's where the two of you come into play."

Amanda shuddered.

"I don't understand," said Glen.

"It's simple," said Plathor. "You're going to do it for us. Glen, you're going to kill Gavendo."

"What!" exclaimed Glen. "I'm not killing anyone."

"Yes you will," hissed Plathor. He looked at the tulpa guarding the exit. "Seize the girl!"

The guard dropped his spear, loped towards Amanda, and plucked her from her chair. He held her up in the air, legs dangling.

"Put her down!" demanded Glen. "She hasn't done anything to you!"

"Shut up!" barked Plathor. "You're going to listen to me, and you're going to listen well."

Plathor looked at one of the tulpas sitting at the table and made a motion with his arm. The tulpa loped into an adjoining room. He swiftly returned, wheeling a contraption made of tightly meshed iron bars. It closely resembled a coffin.

"Strap her in!" commanded Plathor.

The tulpa threw Amanda into the mesh-iron coffin and restrained her with metal manacles, which were locked tightly around her ankles and wrists. Next, he closed the lid and spun her upright, several feet above the ground. Amanda gazed plaintively through the iron bars.

Plathor laughed derisively. He said to Glen, "You, my boy, are going to eliminate Gavendo. If you refuse, or fail, we'll bury your little friend here alive. I assure you, her death will be slow and extremely unpleasant."

"What makes you think I'll be able to kill Gavendo?" asked Glen. "Even if I wanted to, which I don't, how could I possibly succeed? I'm not a cold-blooded killer."

Plathor glared at Glen. "Follow me."

They walked into an adjoining room. The guard wheeled in Amanda. In the center of the room was a large pit, next to which lay an enormous pile of dirt. Plathor snapped his fingers, prompting the guard to lower Amanda, on her back, into the hole. Plathor grabbed a shovel, scooped a large helping of dirt, and heaped it onto Amanda. She coughed and spat some of it out.

"Hey, what are you doing!" exclaimed Glen.

"Glen, each tulpa here will scoop a shovelful of dirt onto Amanda every thirty minutes. Until Gavendo dies. That's eighteen shovels of dirt per hour. More if I decide to join in. Which means you have one day, perhaps less. When you kill Gavendo, we'll release her. It's as simple as that."

"Glen, do something!" implored Amanda.

"How do you expect me to kill Gavendo? Strangle him with my bare hands?" Glen gestured toward himself. "Look at me!"

Plathor smiled deviously. "Gavendo trusts you. Dare I say, he even likes you? He'll let you into his cottage, and you'll be able to get very close to him. We'll provide you with a small knife. When the opportunity presents itself, you'll use it. And that will be that." Plathor's eyes were gleaming. "Gavendo will be dead and we'll finally have our freedom!"

"How do I explain myself to Gavendo?" asked Glen. "He won't be expecting me."

Plathor made a dismissive gesture. "That's not my problem." He kicked some dirt onto Amanda.

"Hey, stop that!" she exclaimed.

Plathor said, "I suggest you get moving. Your little friend here doesn't have much time."

◆ IV ◆

Glen knocked on Gavendo's front door.

188

Nobody answered.

As quietly as possible, Glen opened the door and stepped inside. His forehead glistened with sweat. The dining room and kitchen were empty. Glen unsheathed his knife and gripped it tightly. Steeling himself, he slowly peered into Gavendo's bedroom.

It was empty.

"Hmm . . . Where is he?" Glen muttered.

He looked out the window and saw the heiau (temple).

"Maybe he's in there."

Glen placed his knife back in its sheath and tiptoed to the heiau. Cautiously, he glanced inside. Gavendo was cleaning some of the masks on the wall, whistling quietly. His back was turned to Glen.

"Okay, you can do this."

"I can't do this."

"No, you must! Amanda's life depends on you!"

"What the hell am I doing?"

Glen wiped the sweat from his brow and entered the heiau.

Gavendo whirled around. "Glen, what a nice surprise! What brings you back here?" His expression grew serious. "Is something wrong?"

"Yes, something has happened," replied Glen.

"What?" asked Gavendo.

"Amanda and I were walking down the forest path, away from your cottage."

"Yes."

"She tripped over a boulder, fell, and cut her leg."

"I see."

"So I came back here to see if you had any medicine and bandages we could use."

"Was there a lot of bleeding?"

"No, it's not that bad. There wasn't much bleeding. I was just hoping you had a bandage or two we could use to keep the cut from getting dirty. It's really not that serious."

Gavendo looked at Glen quizzically. "Well, I might have a few in my cottage."

◆V◆

Inside the cottage, Gavendo quickly disappeared into the bathroom. Glen unsheathed his knife again and gripped it firmly. He approached the bathroom entrance and peeked inside. Gavendo was rummaging through some drawers; his back was turned. Glen approached him from behind and raised the knife into the air. Glen took a deep breath.

Gavendo heard him. He whirled around and grimaced. Glen hesitated. Gavendo seized the opening. He reached out and clutched Glen's knife-wielding arm.

"Drop it!" commanded Gavendo. He was squeezing Glen's arm tightly, like a vice.

Glen froze. Pain shot up and down his arm.

"I said drop it!"

Glen released the knife and sank to his knees. He buried his face into his hands and began to sob.

"I failed," wailed Glen.

Gavendo quickly bent down and snatched the knife. "What in blazes has gotten into you, Glen? Why did you try to stab me?"

"Oh, it's awful! It's just awful!" cried Glen. "I've failed her."

"Okay, okay," said Gavendo calmly. "Try to relax and pull yourself together."

"You must hate me!"

"No, I don't hate you. But I am stunned." Gavendo took Glen's hand and helped him up. "Shall we go to the next room for a cup of tea?"

"Alright."

Gavendo guided Glen to a seat at the dining room table and entered the kitchen to prepare some tea. After a short while, he placed a steaming cup in front of Glen. "Now, why don't you tell me all about it."

"I'm so sorry, Gavendo."

"I know."

"They forced me to do it."

"Who?"

"Your tulpas."

"What? My tulpas?"

Glen sipped some tea. "Yes, they captured us soon after we left your place earlier. They took us to a cave. They put Amanda in an iron contraption. Plathor said if I don't kill you, he'll bury Amanda alive."

"Plathor's behind all of this?" asked Gavendo. He pursed his lips. "I should have known. He's getting desperate."

"For every thirty minutes that pass without me having killed you, they'll shovel more dirt onto Amanda. They're slowly killing her!"

"Then we don't have much time."

Glen looked hopeful. "You'll still help us? Even after what I just tried to do to you?"

"Of course," replied Gavendo. "Plathor must be stopped. I'll redouble my efforts to deconstruct him."

"How? I mean, why haven't you been able to deconstruct him so far?"

"Plathor is the most powerful, independent-minded tulpa I've ever created. As you've seen, he's slipped out of my control."

"And you're just letting him run amok?"

"Of course not. But as I explained to you earlier, it takes a lot of energy to deconstruct a wayward tulpa. Up until now, I've been focusing on deconstructing the less powerful ones that surround and protect Plathor. He feeds off their energy. So far, I've eliminated three of his lackeys. Once they're all gone, Plathor will be much, much easier to deconstruct. He knows this. That's why he's growing increasingly bold and desperate."

Glen looked at Gavendo earnestly. "I think he really means to kill Amanda."

"Indeed," Gavendo said gravely. "Therefore, I must change my strategy. Since time is of the essence, we must target Plathor directly."

Silence.

"We?" asked Glen.

"Yes," confirmed Gavendo. "I must confront Plathor face to face. That will enable me to deconstruct him—and the others—much more quickly. And Glen, you're the only one who knows where he's currently hiding. Therefore, you must take me to Plathor at once!"

♦VI♦

Glen waited outside the heiau while Gavendo prayed and chanted inside. After finishing, Gavendo stood up and approached Glen.

Glen remarked, "I was just thinking about something. Won't the tulpas be able to spot us on the way to the cave? They'll surely kill Amanda as soon as they see you're still alive, that I didn't kill you."

Before Gavendo could reply, several friendly tulpas walked up to Gavendo, grunting emphatically. They were very agitated. Gavendo calmed them down.

"What's wrong?" asked Glen.

"They don't want me to go on this mission," explained Gavendo. "They think it's too dangerous and are worried that I'll be killed. They want to come along, to protect me."

Glen brightened. "Yes! That's a fine idea. Surely we could use the extra bodies. In fact, why don't we bring a whole bunch of them? That way, we can simply overpower Plathor and the other rebels."

"No, that won't work. Tulpas can't kill other tulpas. Remember, only the person who constructed the tulpas can deconstruct them. That's how it works. Otherwise, I would have set my tulpas on Plathor long ago."

"So we're just going to saunter up to the cave alone? Won't the tulpas see us coming?"

"They'll be able to see *you*, Glen. But they won't be able to see me."

"Huh?"

"When I was praying and chanting a moment ago, I made it such that the rebellious tulpas won't be able to see me. I'll be invisible to them."

"But they'll see me?"

"Yes."

"And how exactly is that a good thing?"

"Don't worry, Glen. It's part of my plan."

Glen looked unconvinced.

"Here's the important thing," continued Gavendo. "When we approach the cave, it's imperative that you look confident. You must act as though you actually killed me."

"Oh, I get it." Glen gestured toward Gavendo's cottage. "Do you have any ketchup in there?"

"Pardon?"

"Ketchup."

"What's that?"

"I guess not. Do you have any red ink, or something like red ink?"

"Brilliant!" exclaimed Gavendo. "Part of the illusion. Spatter your clothes with red ink and it'll look like you're covered with my blood."

"Exactly."

♦VII♦

Wearing a shirt carefully stained with blotches and streams of dark red ink, Glen led Gavendo to the cave of the renegade tulpas. Upon seeing Glen, the tulpa guarding the entrance became exited and began to grunt repeatedly. He led Glen into the cave while Gavendo, standing unnoticed under a nearby tree, waited patiently.

Glen entered the Council Room. Plathor was sitting alone at the head of the table. "From the looks of your shirt, I trust the deed has been done?"

"Yes, I killed Gavendo," Glen said solemnly.

Plathor smiled broadly. He clapped his hands four times and grunted. Soon, the rest of the tulpas filed into the room.

"Everyone! I have a wonderful announcement to make," shouted Plathor. "The despicable Gavendo is dead! Gavendo, he is dead!"

Plathor leapt onto the table and danced a jig. "Long live Plathor! Long live Plathor!"

The tulpas broke into a macabre dance, circling the table while grunting wildly.

"Plathor!" shouted Glen.

"Yes?" he responded, still dancing his jig.

"What about Amanda? Aren't you going to free her?"

"Oh, we already killed her."

"What!"

"Just joking!"

"That's not funny. I want to see her."

"Oh, in good time, my dear boy. In good time. You must join our celebration. We're finally free! We're finally free!"

Glen stomped his foot on the ground. "No! This is all fine and dandy, but Amanda and I have pressing business. We were on our way somewhere when you captured us. I held up my end of the bargain. I killed Gavendo. Now it's time for you to let us go."

Plathor stopped dancing and glowered at Glen. "How dare you interrupt my celebration, my moment of glory." He shifted his gaze to the guard who had escorted Glen into the cave. "Seize the boy!"

The guard apprehended Glen roughly.

"I have a surprise for you," said Plathor.

"Huh? I don't understand," responded Glen.

"Take him to the pit!"

The guard shoved Glen into the same room as Amanda. To his horror, Glen saw another mesh-iron coffin next to a second freshly dug pit.

"Are you okay, Amanda?" asked Glen.

"Yeah."

"Shut up!" barked Plathor. "Strap him in!"

Several tulpas lifted Glen into the mesh-iron coffin. He struggled against them, but they were far too strong.

"I guess you didn't kill Gavendo after all," said Amanda.

Glen decided to maintain the illusion. "No, I did."

"Really?"

"That's right, I killed him."

"Oh my God, Glen, you actually did it?"

"Yeah, well look what good it did."

Anger started to well up inside of Glen as the tulpas lowered him into the pit. Plathor scooped a shovelful of dirt onto Glen and laughed derisively.

"You double-crossed me, Plathor!" shouted Glen. "After I gained your freedom, this is how you repay me? I should've known better."

"Oh, you poor dear," said Plathor. He suddenly grew stern. "Say your goodbyes."

Plathor snapped his fingers. In response, the tulpas grabbed shovels and feverishly started to bury the kids.

"You back-stabber!" shouted Glen, spitting out a mouthful of dirt.

Plathor rested on his shovel, surveyed the other tulpas, and faked a yawn. "Oh, don't be such a bore. Can't you come up with a more colorful insult?"

"Cease burying those kids at once!" boomed a voice at the room's entrance.

Plathor whirled around.

Gavendo smiled at him.

The color drained from Plathor's face. "But . . . but . . . you're supposed to be dead! Dead, I say!"

The other tulpas looked around the room in bewilderment.

Plathor regained his composure. "Tulpas—seize Gavendo!"

The tulpas did not respond.

Plathor was irate. "I said seize Gavendo! Why aren't you seizing him?"

"They can't see him, stupid," explained Glen, from the grave.

"Shut up!"

"What's going on?" asked Amanda. "Is that Gavendo?"

"That's right!" Gavendo answered triumphantly.

"But I thought you killed him, Glen!"

"He did no such thing," announced Gavendo.

"A trick!" spat Plathor. He ran to the pile of dirt. In a spasm of hatred, he kicked as much of it as he could onto Glen. "You tricked me!"

After a short while, Plathor stopped to wipe his sweaty brow and rest. He was breathing heavily. He squinted at Gavendo and pondered his next move. "Tulpas, seize Gavendo!" he shouted. "He's standing at the entrance to this room!"

The tulpas rushed to the doorway. With arms flailing, they tried to grab the invisible (to them) Gavendo. He deftly sidestepped them. The tulpas comically crashed into one another, causing a small pileup.

"Idiots!" shrieked Plathor. "To your left! To your left!"

The tulpa on top of the pile rose and lunged at Gavendo. He moved out of the way, but not before the tulpa managed to grab and hold onto his ankle, causing him to trip and fall.

"Gavendo has fallen!" Plathor yelled gleefully. He was jumping up and down. "Get him!"

Several tulpas piled onto Gavendo, pinning him to the floor.

"Ha ha!" celebrated Plathor. "I got him!"

Glen was alarmed. "What?"

Plathor leaned over the pit so Glen could see his face. "We just captured Gavendo, you little twit! Nothing can save you now!" Plathor turned to address Gavendo. "Well, well, well. It looks like I'm the one who will live, not you. I'm going to enjoy killing you. You and your little friends." He snapped his fingers. "Tulpas—dig a third pit. We'll have ourselves a mass burial. A mass burial!"

Gavendo smiled. "Not so fast, Plathor."

"Oh, you have something to say, do you?"

"No, something to show you."

Gavendo closed his eyes. The two tulpas holding his arms started to fade and shimmer. Gavendo opened his eyes. Plathor looked at him apprehensively. Gavendo winked and closed his eyes again. This time the two tulpas faded and disappeared entirely.

Plathor dropped his shovel and pointed at Gavendo. "Seize him!"

Two more tulpas grabbed onto Gavendo. They held his arms tightly. Gavendo closed his eyes. They also faded into non-existence.

Plathor panicked. He ordered the rest of the tulpas to swarm Gavendo at once, in an attempt to overwhelm him. "And don't bother bringing him to me," he yelled. "Kill him immediately. Kill him! Kill him!"

Plathor's tulpas did not move.

"Kill him!'"

No movement.

"What's the meaning of this?" yelled Plathor.

Gavendo was calm. "The tulpas aren't as dumb as you think."

Gavendo waved his arm and became visible to the tulpas. They approached his side and glared at Plathor.

201

Plathor held out his arms and pleaded, "Guys, guys. Siding with Gavendo is a dead end. Don't be rash, come back to me."

The tulpas stood fast.

"Game over, Plathor," said Gavendo. "Your time is up."

"But Gavendo, perhaps we can work something out. This has all been just a silly mistake. A minor misunderstanding."

"You're the mistake."

Plathor sank to his knees. He cupped his hands together in front of him, as if he were praying, and begged, "Please Gavendo. Please have mercy on me. Can't I have just one more chance?"

Gavendo looked at the tulpas standing by his side. "Bring Plathor to me."

Terrified, Plathor looked up at the approaching tulpas. "No!" he shrieked.

The tulpas dragged him, kicking and screaming, to Gavendo.

Gavendo placed his hand on Plathor's shoulder and closed his eyes.

Plathor cried, "It can't end like this! It just can't, I tell you!"

Gavendo whispered a prayer. Plathor began to fade.

"Noooo!"

"What the heck's going on?" asked Amanda, from her pit.

Plathor disappeared.

"Gavendo?"

"Plathor has just been deconstructed," Gavendo announced triumphantly.

CHAPTER 9

♦I♦

The Sand Monk took a deep breath and tried to muster his courage and resolve. "Mandalia, are you okay?" he asked. "You were treated rather roughly, I should think."

"I won't lie to you—I've seen better days," she replied. "But I'll survive. What about you?"

"I'll be okay. I just wish I could forget the feel of those clammy hands."

"The Sand Queen's?"

The Sand Monk nodded.

Mandalia shuddered. "I don't blame you."

"Are you okay, Pandalese?" asked the Sand Monk. "That sandroid certainly roughed you up a bit too."

"I'll be okay," said Pandalese, holding his jaw. "I don't think anything's broken, and I still have all my teeth."

Mandalia asked the Sand Monk, "Did you tell the Sand Queen the truth? Did you really come over with just two kids?"

"Indeed. There were four kids in my temple in Hawaii. Two of them decided to come to Sandtopia. But the other two were hesitant. In the end, they decided to stay in Hawaii. My intention was to bring all four of them over at some point. But Judlarthio—"

"That traitor!" blurted Logarno. "He's the reason we're in this awful mess."

"Agreed," said the Sand Monk.

"What do you suppose happened to the two kids you brought over?" asked Mandalia. "Do you think they were able to escape?"

"I don't know," admitted the Sand Monk. "I certainly hope so."

"Why don't you go into meditation to find out? Maybe your spirit guides will be able to give you some insight."

"Well, my nerves are a bit jangled, but I suppose it can't hurt to give it a try."

The Sand Monk took a few deep breaths to calm down. He sat up straight, his back rigid. He closed his eyes and started to breathe slowly and rhythmically.

Suddenly, the massive wooden door at the top of the stairs swung open again, revealing the Sand Queen. She was carrying a tall, white, pointed hat and a furled up scroll. The Sand Monk, his concentration broken, opened his eyes and looked at her.

"Meditating won't get you out of your predicament, you fool." The Sand Queen descended the staircase. "Stand up."

The Sand Monk rose to his feet slowly.

The Sand Queen approached him and grinned sadistically. "I've been dreaming of this day for a long time. You're finally going to get your comeuppance." She unceremoniously placed the pointed hat on the Sand Monk's head. "Since you're a moron, I've declared that from now on, you must wear this dunce cap at all times."

"So, your intent is to humiliate me."

"Naturally. Much like your partisans humiliated me by firing that arrow into my face. What goes around comes around, monk."

The Sand Monk was about to deny responsibility—they were not his "partisans" after all—but he knew the Sand Queen would not believe him. She would just become further agitated and possibly take out her anger on his friends. Therefore, he said nothing.

The Sand Queen drew back and became rigid, like a soldier standing at attention before a drill sergeant. She unfurled the scroll she was clutching and held it aloft. Trying to sound as official as possible, she declared, "Sand Monk, you have been formally charged with treason."

Silence.

She looked at the Sand Monk and continued, "Your trial will commence in one hour. Someone will come for you. Are you aware of the penalty for such a crime?"

"I can guess."

"Yes," the Sand Queen said smugly. "Death."

◆ II ◆

Kalani kicked a pebble and watched it tumble down the dirt path in front of her. To her horror, it entered a divot, popped out, went airborne, and struck the back right calf of one of the lion men. He peered back at Kalani and snarled. A gob of spit rolled off his left incisor.

"Sorry," she offered meekly.

He grunted and continued walking.

Kalani, Zach, the Hooded Blacksmith, and Jaagdar—escorted by the lion men and a lone dacturion, which circled above—entered Sand City through a massive stone archway. Along the top of the arch, the following words had been carved:

**Long Live the Sand Queen
and Her Merciful Rule!**

The Hooded Blacksmith laughed contemptuously. "Merciful."

"Yeah," said Jaagdar. "The sad thing is, she's probably told it to herself enough times to actually believe it."

They passed under the archway. Zach looked up and noticed the dacturion was no longer circling above.

"Where did it go?" he asked the Hooded Blacksmith.

"Where did what go?"

"The dacturion."

"I don't know. It probably returned to the Sand Palace."

Zach whispered to the Hooded Blacksmith, "Let's make a dash for it after we enter the city!"

"That wouldn't be wise," said the Hooded Blacksmith. "We're about to enter a well-guarded, walled city. Trust me, it wouldn't take long for them to capture us."

After passing under the archway, they proceeded down a large, cobblestone street.

"This road leads to the center of the city," remarked the Hooded Blacksmith.

Kalani noticed that many of the townhouses along the route—the colonial-style architecture reminded her of a trip she once took with her family to Washington D.C.—were flying black flags.

"What's with all the black flags?" she asked.

"They're a symbol of mourning," replied the Hooded Blacksmith. "They're flown when someone has died, or when a tragic event has occurred."

Kalani gasped. "Are we too late? Do you suppose the flags mean the Sand Monk's dead?"

"I don't know."

Three male sandroids, wearing black robes, appeared in front of the group. Stunned—and somewhat horrified—Zach and Kalani gaped at them. The sight of sand churning underneath their translucent skin transfixed Zach. Kalani stared at the sandroids' curious golden-brown hair; she thought it resembled *Pele's hair* (thin strands of volcanic glass).

"They really give me the creeps," Kalani whispered to Zach. "Bad energy."

"Yeah."

The Hooded Blacksmith looked at Kalani and put his finger to his lips. He wanted her to be quiet.

The sandroid in the center approached Kalani and stroked her face. Kalani cringed.

"This one is quite cute," said the sandroid. "For a human."

Kalani recoiled; the sandroid laughed. His breath smelled like slate.

"So, I suppose we're headed for the Sand Dungeon," said the Hooded Blacksmith, trying to get a fix on where they would be taken next.

"All in good time," replied the sandroid. "But first your presence is required at a trial. In Central Plaza."

The Hooded Blacksmith was surprised. "We're going to be tried? So soon? What are the charges?"

"Today's trial isn't for you," replied the sandroid. He pointed at Kalani and Zach. "Nor is it for these children."

"Who's it for, then?" asked Kalani.

The Hooded Blacksmith shot Kalani an irritated glance because he wanted her to remain silent.

"The trial is for the Sand Monk," announced the sandroid.

Kalani brightened. "So he's still alive?"

"Yes. Whether or not he will remain so—that's for the jury to decide."

Kalani whispered to Zach, "Well, at least he's still alive."

The sandroid continued, "The timing of your capture couldn't have been better. You see, the Sand Queen will probably call on you as witnesses. The fact that the Sand Monk brought you to Sandtopia will strengthen her case."

The Hooded Blacksmith retorted, "Strengthen her case? Give me a break. The Sand Queen will be the judge, jury, and prosecutor—all wrapped up in one. This trial will be a sham. We already know what the verdict will be."

"That's where you're wrong, human," said the sandroid. "The Sand Queen has assured the public that this trial will be fair. Plus, she won't even participate. Except, perhaps, as a witness."

The Hooded Blacksmith was suspicious. "She won't participate in the trial?"

"Naturally, she'll observe the proceedings. But she won't be the judge, she won't be the prosecutor, and she most certainly won't be a member of the jury."

Zach was hopeful. "Maybe it *will* be a fair trial."

"Don't be naïve," said the Hooded Blacksmith.

Jaagdar added, "Zach, what do you think will happen to members of the jury if they return an 'innocent' verdict?'"

Zach thought for a moment. "Nothing good."

"Precisely," said Jaagdar.

"Nonsense!" declared the sandroid, trying to sound optimistic and upbeat. He smiled. "The jury won't be tainted; I assure you, the trial will indeed be fair."

Jaagdar sneered. "I'm amazed you just said that without laughing."

The sandroid frowned.

♦ III ♦

The Sand Monk, still wearing the dunce cap, sat in a chair, alone, on an elevated platform in Sand City's Central Plaza. He looked unhappy. The judge—a sandroid wearing black robes and an ostentatious, powdery white wig—sat behind him at a large desk, on a platform, elevated even higher. The twelve members of the jury—six sandroid, six human—were off to the side, also sitting on an elevated platform. Pandalese, Eraklena, Mandalia, and Logarno were sitting in chairs reserved for witnesses—directly in front of the Sand Monk, in the front row. A second row had been reserved for members of the sandroid ruling class. Members of the public filled the numerous rows of chairs behind them (set back at a distance, for security reasons). The trial had generated so much public interest— and sympathy for the Sand Monk—that there were not enough chairs to accommodate everyone; throngs of people filled the plaza, hoping to catch a glimpse of the proceedings. The atmosphere was electric. People were amazed the Sand Queen had not simply executed the Sand Monk and his friends immediately after their capture. They were spellbound by the spectacle of a public trial (something which had never previously occurred).

The Sand Queen's advisors—sitting in the second row of seats—were strongly against the idea of a public trial. Of primary concern to them, because they were older and therefore more vulnerable, was security. They were worried about assassination attempts. They had implored the Sand Queen to execute the Sand Monk swiftly—without a trial of any sort—and be done with him once and for all, since it was well within her power to do so. And, if a trial *were* to occur, they had urged it be held behind closed doors. Also of concern to the advisers was letting humans be part of a jury, something the sandroids had hitherto never considered, let alone done. They held the deep conviction that humans were inferior and therefore had no right to render judgment in any court case. Only sandroids were qualified to do so.

To her advisors' great consternation, the Sand Queen ignored their advice. To justify her decision and alleviate their concerns, the Sand Queen delivered the following speech to them right before the trial: "A fair public trial will expose to the world exactly how awful the Sand Monk really is. He's just awful, isn't he? People will learn all about his devious machinations to install himself as the new ruler of Sandtopia. He'll be exposed for the fraud he truly is. And I'm certain the vast majority of the populace will support my case against him. After all, people love me. My rule has brought such a great amount of security and prosperity to Sandtopia. People are afraid of what might happen if I'm deposed. Yes, I assure you, the Sand Monk will be convicted and there will be rejoicing in the streets after his execution."

◆IV◆

Although the Sand Queen ignored her advisors by deciding to hold a public trial, she did promise to make security as tight as possible. Therefore, each entrance to Central Plaza was closely monitored and guarded by lion men; every public spectator had been thoroughly searched for weapons; a protective shield had been erected behind the seats for the high government officials; and scores of lion men patrolled the grounds (while dacturions hovered above).

To the sound of blaring bugles and crisp drum rolls, the Sand Queen made her grand entrance. Flanked closely by two large, ferocious-looking dacturions, she walked down the central causeway and ascended the platform on which the Sand Monk and his friends sat. Except for a cluster of ten young sandroid spectators, the crowd did not cheer; its response was tepid. This vexed the Sand Queen.

She addressed the crowd: "Ladies and gentlemen, I stand before you today to announce the commencement of perhaps the most important trial in the history of Sandtopia." She gestured dramatically. "Behold the Sand Monk. At long last, he will be required to answer for his crimes. The charge? Treason!"

The young sandroids applauded boisterously. The Sand Queen smiled approvingly and continued, "I assure you, the trial will be fair. As you can see, six members of the jury are human, and six members are sandroid. The decision by the jury need not be unanimous. A simple majority—at least seven votes—will do. If the jury is deadlocked, with six members voting to acquit and six members voting to convict, the deciding vote will be cast by the judge."

A large, burly man sitting in the tenth row stood up and shouted, "You don't seriously expect us to believe this trial will be fair, do you? We all know the sandroids will vote to convict and the humans will vote to acquit. It'll be up to the judge. And there's no way a sandroid judge will vote to acquit!"

The Sand Queen snapped her fingers and pointed at several lion men. "You. You. You." Then she pointed at the burly man. "Take him away."

The lion men seized the burly man. "Get these sloppy beasts off of me," he shouted, several times, as they dragged him out of Central Plaza, kicking and screaming.

Satisfied, the Sand Queen announced, "Now, does anyone else have something to say?"

Silence.

"I didn't think so," she said. "Now, where was I? Oh, yes. The Sand Monk has been provided with an attorney who will argue his defense. I assure you, his attorney is well qualified to do so. As for the prosecutor, I selected him myself. He's very skilled." She gave the prosecuting attorney a cold stare. "I'm confident he will do an excellent job."

He shifted uncomfortably in his front-row seat.

There was a commotion at one of the entrances to the plaza. Zach, Kalani, the Hooded Blacksmith, and Jaagdar were being led down the central causeway by a group of lion men. The Sand Queen smirked. After they had been seated in the front row, she announced, "Ah, I'm glad you're all able to attend today's proceedings."

Jaagdar muttered, "Like we had a choice."

The Sand Monk was relieved to see Zach and Kalani. Although he was deeply disappointed they had been captured, he was glad they were still alive and did not look as though they had been mistreated.

Logarno leaned over and asked the kids, "Are you guys okay?"

"We're fine," replied Zach. "The lion men treated us okay."

"They smell bad, though," remarked Kalani. "They need to take baths."

A lion man at the end of the row, patrolling, growled at her.

Logarno chuckled.

"Why's the Sand Monk wearing that silly hat?" asked Zach. "It looks like a dunce cap."

"Indeed, that's what it is," replied Logarno. "The Sand Queen wants to humiliate him."

The Sand Queen addressed the crowd again. "Here's how the trial will be conducted. First, the prosecuting attorney will make his case, calling witnesses to the stand, should he so choose. Then it will be the defense's turn. After that, we'll listen to closing arguments. Finally, the jury will vote to acquit or convict the Sand Monk."

A man in the crowd shouted, "Will the jury's vote be secret?"

The Sand Queen hesitated. "Yes."

The same man added, "Will you abide by the decision?"

She shot the man a nasty look. "Of course. If the jury votes to acquit, the Sand Monk will be a free man." The Sand Queen did not want to answer any more questions and announced, "Now, without further ado, let the trial begin!"

She sat down on her throne, next to the judge's bench. It had been elevated such that she perched slightly above him. Two dacturions stood at attention on either side of her, flapping their wings slowly. She peered down at the proceedings.

The Sand Queen's prosecutor—an older sandroid with a square jaw and chiseled facial features—stood up and mounted the elevated platform on which the Sand Monk sat.

With a flourish, he turned to the jury. "Ladies and gentlemen," he began, "we have assembled today in Central Plaza to decide the Sand Monk's fate. He sits before you, accused of high treason, of plotting to overthrow the regime." He paused for dramatic effect. "And I'm here to tell you today—to prove to you—that he's guilty of this serious crime. And why is treason such a serious offense? Well, let me tell you. Imagine what would happen if the Sand Queen's regime were to be toppled. How would people react?"

A man in the audience shouted, "We'd get down on our knees and thank the good Lord!"

The Sand Queen stood up and scowled. "Who said that? I demand to know who said that!"

The audience was silent.

"Identify yourself!"

Silence.

"I see." The Sand Queen's expression grew sinister. "From now on, I'll be watching you all closely. Should I catch anyone making another outburst like that, well, the consequences will be most unpleasant. Most unpleasant indeed."

In a huff, she sat down and crossed her arms in front of her.

The prosecutor looked at her. "May I continue?"

"Of course."

The prosecutor continued, "Now, as I was saying. How would people react if the Sand Queen were to be deposed? There would be chaos. Chaos and mayhem. People would rampage through the streets of our great city, looting and pillaging, pillaging and looting. Yes, they would. You see, the Sand Queen's rule has been so effective because she's a master at keeping order. That's why it's so important she remain in power. Let me give you an example. The crime rate in Sand City has plummeted since the Sand Queen ascended the throne. Children can roam around and play without worrying about being harmed."

A young sandroid shouted, "You said it, brother!"

"Here, here!" shouted another young sandroid.

The Hooded Blacksmith whispered to Kalani, "You've got to be kidding me."

The prosecutor continued, "Let us pray. For the continued safety of the children."

"Oh, come on," snapped Jaagdar.

The Sand Queen gave him a long, hard, cold stare.

"Let me give you another example of life under the Sand Queen's enlightened rule," continued the prosecutor. "Have you noticed that when you walk down the city's streets these days, you won't see a speck of graffiti or trash? Our streets are immaculate. Not like the old days, when trash pickup was erratic and offensive graffiti was rampant. Indeed, the Sand Queen has made sure the trash gets picked up on time in Sand City!"

Jaagdar whispered to Zach, "That's because the trash collectors know what'll happen to them if it isn't. And I'm not talking about pay cuts."

"Death?" asked Zach.

"Painful death."

"I guess they can't go on strike."

"No."

The prosecutor continued, "The Sand Queen has truly created a sand utopia! A sandtopia!" The young sandroids cheered and stomped their feet. "Now, as I mentioned earlier, the Sand Monk plotted to overthrow the Sand Queen. But it gets worse. He also planned to install himself as the new ruler of Sandtopia. Can you imagine it? A human ruler. Had he succeeded, everything would have fallen apart. All the Sand Queen's accomplishments would have been for naught, because the Sand Monk would have been a completely incompetent ruler, a total nincompoop. Tell me, what does he know about governing?"

"Nothing!" one of the young sandroids shouted.

The Sand Queen smiled.

"Nothing indeed," said the prosecutor. "Obviously, the Sand Monk's behavior is totally unacceptable. He's incorrigible. He's wildly dangerous." The prosecutor gestured dismissively at the Sand Monk. "Why just look at him."

"Kill him now!" shouted a young sandroid.

The prosecutor continued, "Because the Sand Monk is such a menace, such a devious plotter, he must be removed from society permanently. Therefore, the prosecution seeks the death penalty!"

The young sandroids whooped and hollered their approval. The prosecutor acknowledged them, walked off the platform, and sat down.

"Alright. Alright," said the judge, trying to temper the sandroids' exuberance. "The defense may now present its opening statement."

The public defender—a sandroid who had volunteered for the thankless and highly dangerous task of defending the Sand Monk—ascended the platform. Smiling, he faced the crowd. "The defense readily admits the Sand Monk isn't the Sand Queen's biggest fan."

Many members of the crowd laughed.

He continued, "However, the fact that the Sand Monk dislikes the Sand Queen's policies doesn't automatically mean he was plotting to overthrow her regime. Indeed, the Sand Monk is a religious man, a man of peace. He doesn't condone violence in any form and therefore would never be involved in some nefarious plot to assassinate the Sand Queen. In fact, he's been working assiduously to rein in various violent paramilitary groups, claiming their actions have hindered his ultimate goal, which is to reform the existing system."

The Sand Queen glowered at the public defender; one of the young sandroids pointed at him and shouted, "Hang him! Hang the human-lover!"

The judge banged his gavel. Tufts of powder flew from his wig as he growled, "Order! Order! We'll have order in this court!" He looked at the public defender. "Proceed."

"Thank you, your Honor." The public defender faced the jury. "Now, as I was saying, before being so rudely interrupted. The Sand Monk's goal has always been to reform the system, not overthrow it. For example, observe the case of the bread tax. As you may recall, the Sand Queen implemented this tax to pay for the lion men's most recent salary increase. Needless to say, this was hugely unpopular among humans. Had he so desired, the Sand Monk could easily have organized a massive, violent response. He probably could have recruited at least two-thirds of the humans on this island. Who knows what the repercussions might have been. Yet he didn't. In response, he organized a large, peaceful protest march. Was the goal of this march the overthrow of the Sand Queen? Hardly. The Sand Monk's goal was the repeal of the unpopular bread tax. That's it. This case—and there are many others just like it—proves the Sand Monk is a gentle soul. He seeks change by working within the system. He's not a revolutionary, and he's certainly not guilty of treason. Therefore, I implore you to acquit the Sand Monk of all charges that have been leveled against him. Thank you."

"Thank you, counselor," said the judge. "The prosecution may proceed."

The public defender sat down.

The prosecutor ascended the platform and took a deep breath. "Ladies and gentlemen of the jury, as my first witness, I call Zenoga to the stand."

A burly lion man approached the witness chair and sat down. A bailiff shuffled over and swore him in.

Kalani leaned over and whispered to the Hooded Blacksmith, "How's that lion man going to testify? I thought they can't talk."

"Watch—the prosecutor will ask him 'yes' or 'no' questions."

The prosecutor asked, "Zenoga, were you responsible for apprehending the Sand Monk in his temple?"

Zenoga nodded.

"Excellent," said the prosecutor. "Now, when you opened the temple's door, was one of the Sand Monk's men carrying a sign?"

Zenoga nodded.

"Uh-oh," said Logarno.

The prosecutor inquired, "Did the sign say: 'Wipe the slate clean, get rid of that evil queen?'"

Zenoga nodded.

"Wipe the slate clean, get rid of that evil queen," repeated the prosecutor. "Are those the words of a pacifist, someone who just wants to reform the system? I think not. Could it be any clearer that the Sand Monk wants to get rid of the Sand Queen?"

The Sand Queen glared at the Sand Monk. He did not return her gaze, choosing instead to ignore her. The sight of her face made his eyeballs ache.

"Zenoga, were there two children in the temple at the time you apprehended the Sand Monk?" asked the prosecutor.

Zenoga nodded.

"These children were not arrested at that time because they escaped, correct?"

Zenoga nodded.

"Did the Sand Monk help them escape?"

Zenoga nodded. He turned and growled at the Sand Monk because he was still cross with him.

"I have no further questions, your Honor," said the prosecutor.

"Very well," responded the judge. He looked at the public defender. "Your witness, counselor."

The public defender ascended the platform. "Zenoga, when you burst into temple, was the Sand Monk holding the sign that said: 'Wipe the slate clean, get rid of that evil queen?'"

Zenoga shook his head.

"Therefore, you can't say that it was actually his sign, can you? You can't say the sign conveyed his true sentiments about the Sand Queen, right?"

Zenoga looked confused.

The prosecutor jumped out of his seat. "Objection, your Honor! Those are two separate questions. As such, they should be asked separately."

"Objection sustained," announced the judge. He looked at the public defender. "Counselor, please ask those questions again—one at a time."

"Very well," said the public defender. "Zenoga, can you say the sign belonged to the Sand Monk?"

Zenoga shook his head.

The public defender continued, "Good. Now, for the second question. Are you certain the sign—which wasn't being held by the Sand Monk and which you just said you aren't sure was actually his—are you certain the sign conveyed the Sand Monk's sentiments about the Sand Queen, and not someone else's?"

Zenoga did not respond.

"Let me remind you that you are under oath, Zenoga. What's your answer?"

Zenoga looked at the Sand Queen searchingly, seeking guidance. She stared at him severely.

"Zenoga, please answer the counselor's question," said the judge. "Are you certain the sign conveyed the Sand Monk's sentiments about the Sand Queen?"

Zenoga nodded.

"Really?" asked the public defender.

Zenoga growled at him and then nodded again.

"No further questions, your Honor," stated the public defender.

Zenoga stood up and quickly bounded off the elevated platform. He did not want to answer any more questions.

"Would the prosecution please call its next witness," commanded the judge.

The prosecutor stared at Kalani. "The prosecution calls the young lady who escaped capture at the temple."

"Do I have to?" Kalani asked Hooded Blacksmith.

"You don't want to know what the Sand Queen does to those in contempt of her court," he replied.

Kalani sighed. "Alright."

She sat down on the witness stand and was sworn in by the bailiff. The prosecutor approached Kalani and smiled broadly, trying to put her at ease. She knew it was disingenuous. "Young lady," he said, "what's your name?"

"Kalani."

"Where are you from?"

"Hawaii. The Big Island."

"And where exactly is Hawaii?"

"Planet Earth."

"How many times have you come to Sandtopia?"

"This is my first time." Kalani glared at the prosecutor. "And hopefully my last."

Zach chuckled softly.

The prosecutor was not amused. "Young lady, you just said this is the first time you've been to Sandtopia. How did you come here?"

"Through a portal."

"Did you come here by yourself?"

"Of course not."

"Whom did you come with?"

"My friend Zach."

"And who is he?"

Kalani pointed. "That guy over there."

Zach waved at the prosecutor.

"So, only you and Zach came to Sandtopia through the portal? There weren't any others?" asked the prosecutor.

"That's what I just said. Weren't you listening?"

The prosecutor frowned. "Who brought you here? Why did you come?"

Kalani looked at the judge. "Sir, those are two separate questions. Could you please have him ask them one at a time?"

The judge smiled slightly. "Would the prosecution please ask those questions again, one at a time?"

The prosecutor squinted at Kalani. "Who brought you through the portal to Sandtopia?"

"That's fairly obvious, isn't it?"

"Don't be flippant with me, young lady. I'm going to ask you this question one last time: Who brought you to Sandtopia?"

Kalani sighed. "The Sand Monk."

"And why did he bring you here?"

"I don't know, I guess he wanted to show me around. Maybe he actually likes this place."

The prosecutor contemplated his next question carefully. "Young lady, have you ever heard of the Hailona Prophecy?"

"The Hailona Prophecy?" asked Kalani.

"Yes."

Kalani feigned ignorance. "I'm not sure I understand."

"The prophecy stating that the Sand Queen's rule would be ended by four children who aren't from Sandtopia."

"Oh, that one," said Kalani. "I may have heard of it."

"Have you heard of it? Yes or no?"

"Yes."

"Good. Who told it to you?"

"The Sand Monk."

"Why did he tell you about the Hailona Prophecy?"

"How should I know? I can't read his mind."

"Listen, young lady," snapped the prosecutor (while waving his finger at her), "you had better—"

"Objection!" interrupted the public defender. "The prosecution is berating the witness."

"Sustained," said the judge.

The Sand Monk smiled.

The prosecutor, sweating profusely, took a deep breath to regain his composure. "Okay, okay, I apologize for that. It won't happen again." He paused. "Perhaps I should approach this from a different angle. Did the Sand Monk tell you at any time that he thought you might be part of the Hailona Prophecy?"

Kalani replied, "He may have said something like that, yes."

"Okay. So, isn't it a fact, then, that the Sand Monk brought you here to topple the Sand Queen?"

"No, he never said that. The purpose of the trip was to show us around Sandtopia. To open our minds a bit. Our plan was to stay for a short while and then return to Earth." Kalani got snippy. "Which is where I'd be right now if it weren't for those smelly lion men. I couldn't care less about the Sand Queen and her precious rule. I just want to go home."

The Sand Queen was displeased. She stood up and said to the prosecutor, "May I have a word with you?"

"Of course, my lady," he replied obsequiously.

Petrified, the prosecutor approached the Sand Queen. She whispered into his ear, and he nodded several times. He returned to the witness stand.

The judge said, "You may proceed, counselor."

"Thank you, your Honor," said the prosecutor. He turned to Kalani. "How many kids did the Sand Monk want to bring to Sandtopia at the time you crossed over?"

"Like I said, just Zach and I crossed over."

"I know that. Were there any other kids on Earth intending to cross over to Sandtopia with the Sand Monk's help?"

Kalani paused. "No, there weren't any other children intending to cross through the portal at the same time we crossed."

"Liar!" shouted the Sand Queen, unable to restrain herself. "Remember, you'll suffer intensely if I discover you lied to this jury."

Kalani said, "I'm telling you the truth. Zach and I are the only ones the Sand Monk brought through the portal. Two children, not four. If anyone else came through, it's news to me."

"Okay, okay," said the prosecutor. "But the Sand Monk did say that you may be part of the Hailona Prophecy?"

"I already answered that question," snapped Kalani.

"So you did," said the prosecutor, smiling wanly. "So you did. Your Honor, I have no further questions for this witness."

The judge peered at the public defender. "The witness is yours, counselor."

"Thank you, your Honor." He approached Kalani. "Did the Sand Monk at any time give you instructions on how to actually carry out or fulfill this so-called Hailona Prophecy?"

"No."

"How many kids are supposed to be involved in the Hailona Prophecy?"

"Four."

"And how many kids did the Sand Monk bring to Sandtopia?"

"Two."

"How long were you planning to stay here?" asked the public defender.

"The Sand Monk planned to take us back to Hawaii after a couple of hours," replied Kalani.

The public defender addressed the jury, "Two hours? The prosecution seriously thinks the Sand Monk planned to depose the Sand Queen in two hours, aided by two children who had never before been to Sandtopia?"

"I guess that's their argument," interjected Kalani. "Pretty thin, huh?"

"Shut up, you little twit!" barked the Sand Queen.

The public defender gazed at the judge. "Your Honor, the prosecution's case is preposterous. They're grasping at straws. They've got no hard evidence against the Sand Monk. I mean, come on. A sign the Sand Monk wasn't even holding? Some flaky prophecy? Is this the best they can come up with? Your Honor, I move that this case be thrown out immediately. Let's stop wasting everyone's time!"

The judge looked at the Sand Queen. She raised her eyebrow at him.

"Motion denied," announced the judge. "There will be a two hour recess."

He banged his gavel.

The Sand Queen sprang from her chair and approached the prosecutor. She removed her white gloves.

CHAPTER 10

◆I◆

"Hey Amanda, look at that!" exclaimed Glen, pointing about thirty yards ahead. They had resumed their trek toward Sand City.

"I don't see anything."

"I swear I saw something scamper across the path. It looked like a menehune."

"Maybe he can help us," said Amanda. "Maybe he's got some news. Let's check it out."

They jogged to the area where Glen thought he saw the menehune. They did not see anything remarkable—no footprints, no paths.

"I guess I just imagined it," Glen said sheepishly.

Amanda heard some rustling noises nearby. "Did you hear that?"

"I sure did."

Glen jumped into the brush. Amanda followed closely. After pushing forward approximately ten yards—in the direction of the noise—they approached the beginning of a subtle, lightly traveled path. After about twenty yards or so, the path widened, became more gravelly, and began to slope gradually into the ground, deepening into a trench. The walls of the trench were reinforced with sandstone, on which numerous hieroglyphs had been carved. Soon, the kids' heads were below ground level. They saw a huge, polished, stained-wood door just ahead.

Amanda pointed at the door. "Where do you suppose it leads?"

Glen replied, "Probably to a bunch of underground tunnels—like the ones we were in earlier." He hesitated. "Should we investigate?"

"I'm not sure I want to step through any more doors."

"We could just take a quick look."

"I don't think that's a good idea."

"Maybe the menehune went in there."

Amanda paused. "You have a point. Hmm . . . Well, okay. A quick look."

They approached the door. It did not have any handles or knobs. "There's nothing to pull," Glen remarked.

"Maybe you push it," said Amanda. She lightly pushed on the door. It did not budge. To Glen's surprise, she tried again, throwing most of her weight into it. The door swung open. Amanda fell through the threshold, disappearing into a dazzling and blinding white light.

"Not again," muttered Glen. He gazed at the opening for a few moments. Concerned about Amanda's fate, he quickly pulled himself together and plunged in after her.

◆ II ◆

Amanda felt as if she were being suspended in mid-air. Suddenly, she crashed unceremoniously onto a stone floor. She could not see anything at first; it took a while for the fog and light to clear up. Glen crashed down beside her. It also took him a few moments to get his bearings. Quickly, an overwhelming feeling of calmness washed over the kids; like they had just returned to a place they knew intimately after a long, arduous journey.

Amanda stood up and surveyed the room. It appeared as if they were in some kind of ancient Egyptian tomb. Elaborate paintings and hieroglyphs on the walls depicted scenes of daily life. The colors were vibrant, like they had been painted yesterday. The floor was made of polished granite, arranged in a black and red checkerboard pattern. A large, dark red, granite sarcophagus was in the center of the room. Someone had placed a nondescript wooden box and a vase—filled with freshly cut flowers—on its lid (a hint of their aroma wafted throughout the chamber).

"Neat!" exclaimed Amanda. "It looks like we're in some kind of ancient Egyptian tomb." She looked at Glen. "Do you feel as relaxed as I do?"

"Yeah." He pointed at the sarcophagus. "It looks like someone's been here recently. Those flowers are fresh."

"That box looks interesting," said Amanda. She approached the sarcophagus carefully and opened the box.

"What's inside?"

Amanda fished out several black and white photographs and showed them to Glen. His jaw dropped.

"I know," said Amanda. "Pictures of us."

"But how can that be?"

Amanda started flipping through the photographs. "Look. Here you are walking into your house on the Big Island. You look a lot younger. Here I am walking down the hallway at school. This must've been taken several years ago as well. Here you are having dinner with your folks. Here I am walking my dog."

Glen started to say something but Amanda interrupted, "Whoa, look at this one! It's recent. Here we both are at the Sand Monk's temple."

"How did these pictures get here?" asked Glen. He grew indignant. "Amanda, someone's been spying on us!"

Amanda continued to flip through the photographs. "Here we are in the tunnels. Here we are having breakfast in the cottage. Here we are talking with Jonus in Bad Land. Here we are with Gavendo." Amanda came to the last picture and held it aloft. "Glen, look at this one."

"Holy smokes! That's a picture of us in the trench, opening the door that led to this room."

Suddenly, a secret door in the back of the room opened. A middle-aged woman wearing a long, flowing white gown entered. Her long black hair contrasted starkly with her milk-white skin. She had piercing blue eyes, the edges of which had been painted black. She exuded gentleness and compassion. With a quick gesture, she motioned for the kids to follow her as she stepped back through the door and exited the chamber.

"Should we follow her?" Amanda asked Glen.

"She seems nice enough. Why not? Let's see what she has to say."

The kids followed the woman into an adjoining parlor room. Music was being played.

"Would you look at that!" exclaimed Amanda, pointing toward an instrument closely resembling a piano. "Is that what I think it is?"

Sitting upright on the piano bench was a rust-colored cat. It was frantically banging the piano keys with its paws, creating a surprisingly complex and slightly haunting melody. The cat was puffing away on a cigarette, which dangled out the side of its mouth.

Glen rubbed his eyes in disbelief. "That looks like a cat! Not a cat-person, but an actual cat!"

"Indeed, a cat is playing my piano," confirmed the woman. Her voice was soft. "He's quite talented, no?"

"Yes, he is," remarked Glen.

Amanda nodded.

The woman sat down at a large table in the middle of the parlor. "Please, join me for a cup of tea. You both look thirsty. Would you like a cup of tea?"

"That would be nice," said Amanda.

"Sure," said Glen.

"Wonderful!" She craned her neck toward an adjoining room. In a raised voice, she said, "Mr. Tribbles, tea for five!"

Amanda and Glen sat down across from her.

"Allow me to introduce myself," said the woman. "My name is Valencia."

"Glen."

"I'm Amanda."

Valencia nodded. "Two of my friends will soon join us. They're interested in meeting you. We're all quite astonished here, you know. We haven't had human visitors for quite some time. Menehune cross over occasionally, but not humans."

"Why not?" Amanda inquired.

"From what I understand, the doorway through which you came is fairly well hidden," replied Valencia.

"That's true," confirmed Glen.

"Where are we?" Amanda asked Valencia.

"You're in *Pure Land*."

"Pure Land?"

"Yes, that's the name of this place. It's very, very different from Sandtopia and Earth."

"It sounds a lot better than Bad Land," commented Glen.

Valencia smiled knowingly. "Of course."

Mr. Tribbles entered the room. He was a burnt-orange cat with a slightly crooked left ear. He was quite thin and walked erect, on his hind legs, like a human. Mr. Tribbles was carrying a silver tray with five cups of steaming water, five teabags, a bowl of sugar cubes, and a small ceramic flask filled with fresh cream. He placed the tray on the table.

"Thank you, Mr. Tribbles," said Valencia. "Where are Miss Cassie and Miss Angel?"

Mr. Tribbles shook his head. "Thwaaaak-hiss-hiss!"

"Oh, you don't know," remarked Valencia. "Well, be a dear and please get them, okay? They're keen to meet Amanda and Glen."

Mr. Tribbles left the room.

"Now then, please have some tea," said Valencia.

Amanda and Glen each grabbed a tea bag and dunked it into their cups.

"Valencia, how's Pure Land different from Earth and Sandtopia?" asked Glen. "Besides the fact that cats here can play the piano and serve tea."

"Do you remember the inscriptions on the walls you saw earlier?"

"In the trench?"

"Yes. They warn people not to come here."

"That would've been good to know," Amanda said dryly.

"Why do the hieroglyphs warn people not to come here?" asked Glen.

Valencia continued, "People who come here often go insane after they return to Sandtopia. Sometimes the descent into insanity is rapid; sometimes it's slow."

"What!" exclaimed Glen. "Why?"

"The experience is too much for some people to handle."

"I don't get it."

Two cats entered the room. Valencia turned her head sharply. "Ah, Miss Cassie and Miss Angel. I'm so happy you could join us." She motioned toward two empty chairs at the table. "Please, have a seat."

Miss Cassie was a gray Calico. She was slightly overweight and had fluffy fur. It made her appear larger than she really was. She had a regal bearing, as if she were accustomed to giving orders. Miss Angel, on the other hand, was smaller, younger, and thinner. She was white, with black and tan patches on her back. Like Mr. Tribbles, Miss Cassie and Miss Angel walked erect, like humans.

Miss Angel sat at the table, wearing a mischievous grin on her face; Miss Cassie, on the other hand, had a serious expression, one that indicated she was not to be trifled with. Miss Angel reached into the bowl filled with sugar cubes, speared one with a claw, reached back, and launched it at Miss Cassie, hitting her square between the eyes.

Miss Angel laughed uproariously, a wild laughter that was interrupted by the occasional "Thwaaack!" and "Khhhhh!"

Miss Cassie glared at her and hissed.

"Girls, we'll have none of that tomfoolery in front of our guests," Valencia said sternly. She looked at the kids. "Now then, where were we?"

"Valencia, you were saying that people who come here often go insane," said Glen. He sounded concerned.

"Indeed. After they return to Sandtopia. Let me explain. You see, those of us who live in Pure Land vibrate at a higher rate than people on Earth and Sandtopia."

"Huh?" said Amanda.

"Inhabitants of Pure Land are like spirits. We can't be killed, we don't feel physical pain, and we don't need food in order to survive. Violence is unthinkable because it simply isn't possible. You can't force me do anything against my will. In other words, coercion—which, unfortunately, is such a big part of life on Sandtopia and Earth—is non-existent here." Valencia paused for a moment. "Just imagine what life would be like on Earth or Sandtopia if people couldn't hurt each other."

"Wow!" exclaimed Amanda. "What a place this is."

Glen was not convinced. "Come on, you can't be serious."

"Glen, if that's what you think, why don't you try to touch me?" challenged Valencia. "You might be surprised."

Glen stood up, walked over to Valencia, and tried to put his hand on her shoulder. To his amazement, it passed right through her. "What the—" he muttered.

"How did your hand feel when it was inside my shoulder?"

"Warm. As if the molecules in my hands were being energized."

Valencia smiled. "Like I said, we vibrate at a much higher rate here in Pure Land. Your hand would pass through Miss Cassie as well." Valencia chuckled. "I don't recommend trying, though!"

"Thwaaaak-hiss-hiss!"

Stunned, Glen walked back to his chair and sat down.

Valencia continued, "You asked why people often go insane after coming here. Well, I'll tell you. If the average human were to visit Pure Land, he or she would observe first-hand how we live. The visitor would see that we treat every living creature here with unconditional love. Moreover, he or she would not see the violence and negativity and fear that are endemic to Earth and Sandtopia. In fact, in most cases, the visitor wouldn't want to leave. But

244

leave they must. After returning to Sandtopia, well, that's when the problems would start."

"How so?" asked Amanda.

"When people come here, all their assumptions on how to live their life, how the universe is structured—all these assumptions are challenged in a fundamental way. Their values are turned upside down. For example, take a man who's used to getting his way through intimidation and bullying. If he were to come here, such crude methods would be completely ineffective. This sudden impotence would shock and trouble him profoundly. To make things even worse, the inhabitants of Pure Land would see his behavior as a personal defect, a moral failure. And they would let him know this. Upon returning to Sandtopia, the man would face a choice: apply the lessons learned in Pure Land, or ignore them and revert to boorish behavior. Let's say he decides to apply the lessons by making a sincere effort to treat people with more love and compassion. In such a case, he would likely be okay. His trip to Pure Land would have been a fruitful experience. However, if he denies the lessons learned in Pure Land and starts treating people poorly again—the easier route, taken by most people—well, that's the danger alluded to in the inscriptions. Mental breakdowns in the future are likely to occur because he hasn't reformed his behavior to be more like the people he met in Pure Land. Deep down, he's aware that he's not living a proper, ethical life."

"So, people who are excessively violent or negative would be in the most danger?" asked Amanda.

Valencia replied, "Yes. But there's more to it."

"I thought there might be," said Glen.

"Exposure to the peaceful and loving nature of our existence in Pure Land is a strong shock to someone used to violence and negativity. However, such people aren't the only ones in danger when crossing back over to Sandtopia."

"Who else is in danger?" asked Amanda.

"Most people aren't very open-minded. Simply coming through a portal and experiencing—however briefly—such an alternate reality is too much for them to handle." Valencia sipped some tea. For a few moments, she listened to the haunting melody being played by the cat at the piano. "Indeed, after returning to Sandtopia, most people have great difficulty determining what's real and what isn't. In other words, coming to Pure Land is dangerous for people who are very rigid in their thinking, people who have difficulty accepting the possibility of alternative ways of thinking or existing. It's very difficult to assimilate the experience."

Amanda glanced uneasily at Glen and said, "So, if you're closed-minded or prone to negativity and violence, then you really shouldn't come through the portal to Pure Land."

"Yes, that's right," confirmed Valencia. She smiled wryly. "And if you're both, then you're really in trouble."

Glen said, "But you don't know if that's still true, right? After all, humans haven't come here from Sandtopia for such a long time. Maybe things have changed."

"I assure you, things are the same," replied Valencia. "Human nature hasn't changed."

Glen continued, "Okay. For the sake of argument, let's say you're right. There's a chance Amanda and I could go insane after we return to Sandtopia. Maybe we should just stay here forever and not even risk it. From what you were saying earlier, Pure Land sounds like paradise!"

Valencia replied, "You and Amanda can't stay here long. You *must* leave at some point because your bodies won't survive. They're too dense. Think about it. What would you eat? There's no food here to give you energy. There's no water here to quench your thirst."

Amanda lifted her cup. "But what about the tea?"

"Although it looks and feels real to you, it isn't. It simply won't sustain you. It's just for effect. In addition to the fact that there's no food or water here for you, the high vibratory rate of Pure Land would, over a relatively short period of time, loosen the molecules of your body, causing it to fall apart. In other words, you would disintegrate."

"So, you find paradise, but the thing that makes it so special causes you to die," Glen said glumly.

"Ironic, isn't it?" commented Valencia.

"Valencia, I have a question," said Amanda.

"Yes?"

"Okay, so we know the inscriptions in the tunnel warn people about coming to Pure Land. Do people from Pure Land ever cross to Sandtopia?"

"Never."

"Why not?"

"Because the environment in Sandtopia—all the oppression, negativity, and violence—is much too dense and toxic for us to bear. We'd never want to go there. A place like Bad Land would be even more unthinkable."

Amanda grew wistful. "It sure must be nice to live here in Pure Land."

Glen decided to change the subject. "It sounds like you know what's going on in Sandtopia right now."

"Yes," replied Valencia. "It's an unfortunate situation."

"Then you know all about the Sand Queen?"

Miss Cassie and Miss Angel hissed, spat, and shook their heads in disgust.

Valencia looked at them and nodded. "My sentiments exactly."

Miss Cassie: "Thwaaack!"

Valencia turned to Glen. "Yes, I know all about the Sand Queen."

"Thwaaack!"

"Hissssssss!"

"And I also know about the capture of the Sand Monk," she continued.

"How do you know all this?" asked Amanda.

"We don't need to cross through the portal to know what's going on in Sandtopia and Earth."

"Valencia, you must've been the one who put those pictures in the box in the other room," remarked Glen.

"Indeed I was."

"How did you know we were coming?"

"Some of the elders told me you were going to pay a visit. They're very advanced, knowledgeable beings."

"Can they read the future?" asked Amanda.

"Yes. They have their ways of knowing what will happen on Earth and Sandtopia in the coming years."

Amanda decided to press for information. "Do you know what'll happen?"

"You want to know if you'll find your friends."

"Yes," admitted Amanda.

"I haven't been given that knowledge. But I can do this." Valencia turned toward the other room and said, "Mr. Tribbles, please bring me the two latest photographs. Mr. Tribbles?"

Moments later, Mr. Tribbles entered the room. He placed two photographs, each turned upside down, onto the table.

"Would you like some more tea?" asked Valencia.

"No, I'd really like to see those photographs," said Amanda.

"Of course."

Valencia flipped one over.

Amanda gasped.

The photograph, in black and white, showed several lion men apprehending Zach and Kalani.

"When did that happen?" asked Amanda.

"Recently," replied Valencia.

"Where were they taken?"

"Probably the Sand Palace. But that's just my guess."

"The Sand Palace?"

"That's where the Sand Queen lives."

"Makes sense."

Glen pointed to the picture that had not yet been flipped over. "What about that one?"

"I'm not sure I want to see the other picture," said Amanda.

Valencia said, "The next picture is in color."

"Does that have some special meaning?" asked Glen.

"Yes," Valencia replied. "All the pictures you've seen up to now have been in black and white, which means the scenes have already taken place. Color pictures represent future events."

Valencia turned over the color picture.

"Oh no!" exclaimed Amanda.

The photograph showed the Sand Monk standing on a platform, with a noose around his neck.

"How much time do we have?" inquired Amanda. "How far into the future is the hanging?"

Valencia shook her head. "I don't know."

◆ III ◆

"Valencia, can we take a quick look around Pure Land before returning to Sandtopia?" asked Amanda. "It's so peaceful here."

"Pure Land is a vast place. I certainly wouldn't be able to show you everything."

"Well, even if you could show us just a little bit . . ."

"I get the sense you don't really want to leave," remarked Valencia. "I don't blame you. I certainly wouldn't want to return to Sandtopia. But don't you remember what I explained earlier?"

"It isn't possible for us to stay here permanently. Yes, I know."

"And the longer you stay, the harder it'll be for you to readjust to Sandtopia."

"Amanda, I think we should leave now," Glen said firmly. "Personally, I don't want my molecules to dissolve."

Valencia smiled slightly. "Yes. Of the two of you, he's the one who needs to worry about his sanity the most."

Glen frowned.

"But why so soon?" asked Amanda. "We could take just a few minutes, really." She paused and looked at Glen. "Don't you just love it here?"

"Amanda," he said, "you're forgetting something important."

"Yes?"

"The Sand Monk. Zach. Kalani. They need our help. Remember?"

"Yeah, you're right. I know it."

Glen looked at Valencia. "How do we get back to Sandtopia?"

"To do that," said Valencia, "we must retire to the next room."

"The room with the sarcophagus?" asked Amanda.

"Yes."

"But there was only one door in that room, and it led to this one."

Valencia grinned. "My dear girl, you won't be leaving Pure Land through a door. The path back to Sandtopia leads through that sarcophagus."

"Huh?"

"You must lie down inside that sarcophagus— with the lid closed."

"What! Are you kidding me?" exclaimed Amanda. She was aghast. "There's no way I'm getting inside that thing. Oh God! There isn't a mummy in there right now, is there?"

"No, not anymore," said Valencia. "Just some dust and old bandages. That's all."

"Oh God! Oh God!" exclaimed Amanda. "So there *was* a mummy in there. And to get home I have to lie in its old bandages!"

"I'm afraid so," said Valencia.

Glen asked, "Valencia, aren't there any other portals we can use?"

"No."

Valencia led the kids into the room with the sarcophagus. She approached the stone coffin and raised her arms. The heavy lid began to shake before levitating several feet into the air. With her arms, Valencia gently guided the stone cover to the floor, off to the side. There was a soft thump when it touched the ground.

"Now get in," she said to Amanda.

"No."

"You don't have a choice. Get in."

Amanda crossed her arms defiantly. "Absolutely not. There's no way I'm getting into that used coffin."

Glen tried to ease the tension. "I'll go first."

"You don't mind?" asked Amanda.

"Well, I'm not thrilled. But it beats having my molecules dissolve. Or whatever happens if you stay here too long."

"Okay, get inside Glen," said Valencia.

Glen crawled inside the sarcophagus. Valencia stretched her arms out and gently guided the stone lid back on top of the coffin.

"It is done," she said dramatically.

"That's it?" asked Amanda. "You mean he's back in Sandtopia right now?"

"Yes," replied Valencia. She guided the sarcophagus lid back onto the floor. "Now get in."

Amanda peered at Valencia for a moment before stepping haltingly up to the coffin's edge. She looked inside, only half believing that Glen would actually be gone.

"He's not there!" exclaimed Amanda.

"Indeed," said Valencia.

Amanda observed a cluster of musty old mummy wrappings in the corner of the sarcophagus. She felt nauseous.

"What's all this dust on the bottom?" she asked suspiciously. "Where did it come from?"

"Please, just get in," said Valencia. "It's time for you to join your friend in Sandtopia. Don't worry, you'll be fine."

Mustering all her courage and fighting the urge to vomit, Amanda crawled into the stone sarcophagus. She lay on her back, rigid, on the layer of fine dust.

"Valencia, please hurry up!" she cried out.

There was a loud thud as Valencia sealed the sarcophagus with the lid. Darkness. A small backdraft inside the coffin caused a piece of mummy wrapping to float into the air. It fell directly onto Amanda's face, draping itself across her cheeks, caressing her upper lip. It smelled stale and musty. She screamed.

CHAPTER 11

◆1◆

Amanda opened her eyes. She lay on her back in a subterranean tunnel, much like the ones she and Glen had traveled through earlier. Relieved that she was no longer in the coffin, Amanda took a deep breath and exhaled slowly. She checked her cheek to make sure the repugnant mummy wrapping was gone. It was. Behind her, she heard moaning, followed by a shuffling sound.

"What was that?"

She stood up.

More shuffling and moaning. Amanda saw a mummy appear around a bend in the tunnel. She screamed. It was trailing dirty wrappings, and it emitted a putrid smell. She sprinted in the opposite direction. Amanda rounded a bend, looked behind her to see if she had given the mummy the slip and, to her horror, collided with another one. There were scores more behind it. The mummy groped at her, clutching her shirt. Amanda screamed and tried to break free. The mummy moaned—its breath smelled like moldy cheese—and held fast while the other ones approached, ready to seize her. Amanda redoubled her efforts and managed to break free, ripping her shirt in the process.

"Glen!" she screamed. "Where are you? Help!"

A nearby trap door opened.

Glen popped his head out. "Psst! Psst! Amanda, over here. Quick, get in!"

Amanda descended into the secret passageway and bolted the trap door shut. She scurried down the ladder. Above, she heard moaning, shuffling, and frantic clawing.

"Thank goodness you popped up when you did, Glen. I was a goner!" Amanda peered up at the trap door. "Do you think it'll hold them off?"

"It better."

After reaching the bottom of the ladder, Amanda paused to catch her breath.

Glen remarked, "It's good you screamed. That's how I knew to open the trap door."

"So you were chased by the mummies too?" asked Amanda. Glen showed her a big rip in his shirt. "I'll take that as a yes. Strange. You'd think that Valencia would've known better than to deposit us in such a place."

"Maybe she doesn't have any control over that," offered Glen.

"I guess not. Hey, how did you find out about the trap door? I never even saw it!"

"After I screamed, a menehune popped it open for me. When I got to the bottom, he was gone. I didn't go looking for him, because I figured you were on your way."

"Well, what do we do now?" asked Amanda.

"I don't know," admitted Glen. "I suppose we should look for that menehune. Maybe he—or some of his friends—can point us in the right direction."

◆ II ◆

Amanda and Glen followed a tunnel, praying the mummies would be unable to open the trap door and pursue them. Soon, they came to a fork.

"Yet another fork," commented Glen. "Which way should we go?"

"I don't know," replied Amanda. "Let's just flip a coin."

"We simply don't have time for this! Our friends need our help, and here we are, scurrying around underground tunnels, like lost rats!"

"Take it easy, Glen."

He pounded the wall with his fist. "It's just so frustrating!"

"I know, I know."

"What if we never make it out of here, Amanda? Oh, God! Why did I ever step through that stupid portal?"

"Glen, pull yourself together. Now's not the time to—"

"Pssst! Pssst!"

"Did you hear that?" asked Amanda.

"Hear what?" responded Glen.

Amanda pointed at the tunnel on the right. "Look—over there."

In the distance, a menehune beckoned for them to follow him. The kids entered the tunnel on the right and the menehune promptly disappeared. After walking for about ten minutes, they came upon yet another fork.

They waited.

Silence.

"Hello, Mr. Menehune?" shouted Amanda.

Silence.

"I said hello, Mr. Mene—"

"Pssst! Pssst!"

"There!" exclaimed Glen, pointing at the tunnel on the left.

Again, in the distance, a menehune—it looked like the same one they saw earlier—beckoned for them to follow him. They entered the tunnel to the left. As before, the menehune promptly disappeared.

After walking for about fifteen minutes, they came to a closed door. Glen reached out, turned the doorknob, and shoved it gently. The door creaked open.

Everyone in the large room was shocked to see the kids. Two male sandroids, two menehune, and two humans were sitting at a large conference table. The two humans quickly stood up and strode across the polished red-granite floor to greet the kids.

"Allow me to introduce myself," said the first one. He was a tall, lanky, middle-aged man with curly black hair and a scraggly beard. He had a casual, amiable air about him. "My name is Jephratus."

"I'm Amanda."

"Glen."

Jephratus turned to his friend. "Please allow me to introduce Zorjin."

Zorjin was of average height but very muscular. His sandy brown hair was straight, and he had piercing gray eyes. He was slightly younger than Jephratus and had a much fiercer air about him. He looked like a seasoned warrior.

Zorjin shook the kids' hands firmly. "Nice to meet you."

"How the heck did you find us here?" asked Jephratus.

Amanda explained, "We came here through a portal. It deposited us here in these tunnels."

"You're not from here?" asked Jephratus.

"No," answered Glen. "We're from a place called Hawaii."

"Who brought you to Sandtopia?" inquired Zorjin.

"The Sand Monk," responded Glen.

"So you're the other two," said Jephratus. "There *are* four outsider kids here on Sandtopia!"

Jephratus and Zorjin exchanged knowing glances.

Amanda pointed discreetly at the sandroids sitting at the conference table. "Are those sandroids?" she asked in a hushed voice.

Jephratus chuckled. "Yes, my child, those are sandroids. Don't worry, they won't harm you."

Curiosity got the better of Amanda. She walked over to the conference table to gaze at the sandroids. She was amazed to see the sand churning underneath their skin. Their yellowish, fibrous hair also looked very peculiar to her. They appeared to be relatively young.

One of the menehune, dressed in a green tunic, laughed. "This must be the first time you've seen a real live sandroid!"

"It is," said Amanda, still transfixed by the churning sand.

"What are you all doing here?" asked Glen. "I thought humans and sandroids don't like each other."

"Aye, they don't," said the menehune in green. "What you've stumbled on here is an emergency meeting. For the trial."

"Trial? What trial?" asked Amanda.

"You mean you don't know?" asked Jephratus.

"Know what?"

"The Sand Monk is currently on trial."

"Really? What's he being tried for?"

"Treason."

"What'll they do to him if he's found guilty?"

"Execute him."

Amanda grabbed Glen's shoulder. "The picture!"

Glen nodded.

"What picture?" asked Jephratus.

"To make a long story short," said Amanda, "we just returned from a place where future events are known. They showed us a picture of the Sand Monk with a noose around his neck."

"Were you in Pure Land?" asked the menehune in green.

"Yes," answered Glen.

The menehune in green said, "Jephratus, if them kids were in Pure Land, the picture they saw's real. If we don't act soon, don't you know, the Sand Monk will die."

Jephratus said, "But if the picture showed the Sand Monk hanging, I'm afraid there's nothing we *can* do. It is written."

Amanda corrected him. "No, the picture wasn't of a dead Sand Monk. In the photo, the noose was around his neck, but he wasn't hanging. He was still alive."

Zorjin announced, "Then perhaps we *can* do something about it!"

"Superb!" exclaimed Jephratus. "Okay. Okay. Let's hammer out a plan."

The menehune grabbed two extra chairs for Amanda and Glen.

After they were seated, Jephratus said, "Glen, Amanda, I know you're wondering why such a strange group has gathered in a secret chamber deep beneath the ground. Well, as you know, the Sand Monk has been captured, along with the top leaders of the Resistance."

"Our friends Zach and Kalani have also been captured, don't forget," added Amanda.

"Indeed," said Jephratus. "As I said earlier, the Sand Monk is currently on trial for high treason. Strangely, the Sand Queen has decided to make the trial public. Normally, she'd conduct it behind closed doors and simply have the Sand Monk executed. It's well within her power to do so."

Amanda asked, "So why did she decide to make it public?"

"Probably to humiliate and discredit the Sand Monk," replied Jephratus. "Obviously, she thinks her case is strong, and she likely expects the jury to decide in her favor, no matter what. You know, it's strange. She's actually letting the Sand Monk defend himself, in public. That's unprecedented for the Sand Queen. It's the first time she's ever conducted a trial this way."

"Yeah, I don't know why she's doing this," remarked Zorjin. "But we see it as an opportunity. In fact, as soon as we found out the trial would be held outside in Central Plaza, with all the sandroid ruling elite present, we called for this meeting."

Jephratus said, "You see, the two sandroids here—oh, I forgot to introduce you to them." He gestured at the one wearing a white robe, fastened with a black sash. "This is Pepros."

Pepros nodded.

Next, Jephratus pointed at the sandroid wearing a gray robe, fastened with a red sash. "This is Haljan."

Haljan nodded.

"Now, where was I?" said Jephratus. "Oh, yes. These sandroids are prominent members of a reform-minded group."

"A reform-minded group?" asked Glen.

"Right. A kind of sandroid resistance movement," explained Jephratus.

"What on Earth do they need to resist?" asked Amanda.

"They're unhappy the Sand Queen has made herself all powerful," explained Zorjin. "They want to strip away her power and transfer it to the Sand Congress. They want her to be a figurehead. A powerless monarch."

"Like the British system?" asked Glen.

"The what?"

"Oh, right. Never mind."

"In essence," said Jephratus, "the sandroid rebels are tired of the Sand Queen being able to do whatever she wants, whenever she wants. Also, they're sympathetic to humans and are open to the idea of human representation in the Sand Congress."

"I see," said Amanda. "So how do you and Zorjin fit into all this?"

"We're members of the Resistance," said Jephratus. "We've become the de-facto leaders since the Sand Monk and some of his associates were captured."

"And why are the menehune here?" asked Glen.

"They helped facilitate this meeting," answered Zorjin. "Without them, it would have been nearly impossible—because of the mistrust—to bring us all together. Plus, they offered whatever assistance they can to help us reach our goal."

"Your goal?" asked Amanda.

"Stripping the Sand Queen of her power."

"Yes, there are a lot of us menehune on Sandtopia, don't you know, and we've offered our services," said the menehune wearing a black tunic. "But, most important, we've agreed to import some taurgogs."

"What are they?" asked Amanda. "By the way, what's your name?"

"I'm Kabar," replied the menehune in black. He pointed to the menehune sitting next to him—a female wearing a turquoise tunic—and said, "This is Mindia."

"Nice to meet the both of you," Mindia said cheerfully.

"To answer your question," continued Kabar, "taurgogs are fierce creatures we met in a different dimension. Through a portal."

"You're going to bring them here?" Glen asked, sounding worried.

Mindia tried to reassure him. "Don't you worry none. Taurgogs love menehune. And we'll tell them to be nice to humans!"

Jephratus said, "The taurgogs will be indispensable. You see, they're an integral part of our plan, which we'll now have to revise."

"Revise? Why?" asked Glen.

Jephratus smiled. "You and Amanda showed up."

"Yes," Pepros said in a tinny voice. "I already have a great idea for incorporating the kids."

Amanda did not like the sound of that. Pepros' metallic voice sent a shiver up and down her spine.

Jephratus was intrigued. "What's your idea, Pepros?"

"As we discussed earlier, we'll initially use the taurgogs to help neutralize the dacturions and the lion men."

"Agreed," said Zorjin. He looked at Kabar. "How many taurgogs can you muster?"

"Right away? Maybe fifty or sixty."

"Will that be enough to do the job?" asked Pepros.

"It'll have to," replied Kabar. "If we had some more time . . ."

"Understood," said Pepros. "Okay, so we can muster fifty or sixty taurgogs. Haljan, how many sandroids sympathetic to our cause can we gather? Young ones, mind you."

"Ready for the task at hand? Perhaps twenty."

"Okay, so our sandroids will neutralize the Sand Queen's young sandroids," said Pepros, "while the taurgogs go to work on the dacturions and the lion men."

Haljan cautioned, "But there are scores of lion men patrolling the plaza. I don't think we'll have enough taurgogs to neutralize all of them."

"Don't you worry about that," said Kabar. "I can recruit hundreds of menehune at a moment's notice, don't you know."

Pepros responded, "Thanks, but menehune are no match for lion men."

"You're forgetting that we have many marksmen—with the bow and arrow!" Kabar stated proudly.

"That's right," said Haljan. "Menehune can sneak up and pick off lion men from a distance."

"Okay," said Jephratus, "this is a good start. What's the rest of your idea, Pepros?"

"This is where the kids figure into it," he explained. "You see, it'll be a ruse. Haljan and I will approach the trial with Amanda and Glen, pretending we just captured them. We'll have the twenty other young sandroids with us. The menehune and taurgogs will be nearby, hiding, ready to ambush when we give the signal. Since the Sand Queen is already suspicious of us—she knows Haljan and I support the Sand Congress idea—this will be a non-threatening way for us to get near her. In fact, if we have the two kids in tow, she'll welcome us with open arms!"

"Now wait just a minute," said Glen, sounding anxious. "This is your plan?" He looked at Jephratus and Zorjin. "Do you trust these sandroids? I mean, they could simply hand us over to the Sand Queen!"

"What choice do we have?" asked Jephratus. "This is the best chance we've ever had to overthrow the Sand Queen. Such a golden opportunity may never happen again. Besides, if we don't act quickly, the Sand Monk, the other Resistance leaders, and your friends will surely be executed."

Glen shook his head. "I don't like it."

Amanda looked at Glen. She noticed a nervous twitch in his left eye. "Well, it's a plan," she said to him. "And it just may work."

Glen crossed his arms defiantly. "No, it won't. We're just pawns. These hideous sandroids are surely going to serve us up to the Sand Queen on a silver platter. She's going to execute us all!"

Amanda stood up. "Glen, may I have a word with you in private?"

They walked to a corner of the room.

Amanda whispered to him, "Our friends need our help. I don't like being taken to the Sand Queen any more than you do. But if you have a better plan, I suggest you come up with it right now."

Amanda placed her hands on her hips and waited for Glen's response. He was silent.

"Remember, they were going to go through with some operation against the Sand Queen before we even showed up," continued Amanda. "Yes, there's a possibility of a double-cross, but I'm willing to take that risk for the sake of our friends."

Glen said nothing.

"Well, are you with me?"

"I guess so," Glen responded reluctantly.

"Okay. Good."

They walked back to the conference table and sat down.

"We're in," announced Amanda.

"Terrific!" exclaimed Jephratus. "Now, let's get down to the details of our operation."

♦ III ♦

The judge banged his gavel (a tuft of powder flew off his wig, into the air). "Order! I'll have order in this court!" He waited for the crowd to grow silent. "I now officially reconvene the trial of the State versus the Sand Monk. The defense may now call its first witness to the stand."

The Sand Queen stood up and stomped her foot on the ground. "No! The defense may not call witnesses. I hereby decree that that right solely belongs to the prosecution."

The judge did not know how to respond. He simply banged his gavel and announced, "Sustained."

"So much for fairness," the Hooded Blacksmith muttered to Zach and Kalani. "I knew this whole thing was a crock."

The prosecutor, who had several nasty red welts on his face, stood up. "The prosecution calls the child who goes by the name 'Zach.'"

"Here we go," said Zach.

Reluctantly, he took the witness stand.

The prosecutor approached him. "For the record, please state your name, son."

"Zach."

"And where are you from?"

"Hawaii."

"I see, I see. You're friends with Kalani, are you not?"

"Yes, we're friends." Zach pointed at the prosecutor's cheek. "Sir, it looks like you're bleeding a bit."

The prosecutor produced a handkerchief and dabbed at one of the bleeding welts on his face. Trying not to look flustered, he continued, "How did you arrive in Sandtopia?"

"The Sand Monk brought me to Sandtopia through a portal in his temple. Didn't Kalani already tell you all this?"

"Please bear with me. There's a reason I'm asking you these questions. Now, at the time you decided to come to Sandtopia, were there any other children in the Sand Monk's temple in Hawaii?"

Zach froze. "Um . . . there might have been."

The prosecutor continued, "Let me be specific. Do you have any other friends, still at the Sand Monk's temple in Hawaii, who are planning to cross over to Sandtopia at some point in the future?"

Zack was silent.

"Answer the question!" spat the Sand Queen. She strode over to Zach and peered down at him. Her eyes flamed with anger and self-righteousness. "Your reluctance to answer the question proves you're hiding something. May I remind you, if I discover you've been lying, I'll execute you."

Zach looked at the Sand Monk for guidance. The Sand Monk nodded, indicating that it was okay to tell the truth.

"Yes, there were other children in the Sand Monk's temple at the time Kalani and I crossed over," announced Zach.

Numerous people in the crowd gasped.

"I knew it!" the Sand Queen exclaimed triumphantly.

She returned to her throne.

"How many other children, Zach?" asked the prosecutor.

"Two."

"So, in total, how many children were in the Sand Monk's temple in Hawaii before you crossed to Sandtopia?"

"Four."

"There were four of you!" the prosecutor repeated gleefully. "And now, perhaps the most important question. Did the Sand Monk want to bring all four of you to Sandtopia?"

"Yes, he wanted to show us Sandtopia," replied Zach. "But only Kalani and I actually crossed over with the Sand Monk."

"Who cares?" blurted the Sand Queen. "It's obvious that in his twisted and sick way, the Sand

Monk was seeking to fulfill the Hailona Prophecy. What clearer indication of his intentions could there possibly be? He planned to bring four outsider children to Sandtopia to depose me. It doesn't matter that he planned to show you around just a little bit on this trip. He was merely preparing you for later operations."

"Here, here!" said the prosecutor, trying to ingratiate himself to the Sand Queen. "I couldn't have said it better myself."

The Sand Queen announced, "The defense will be allowed one question for cross-examination."

The Hooded Blacksmith turned to Kalani. He whispered, "She's taking over the trial. I knew it would only be a matter of time."

The public defender approached Zach and smiled wanly. "Well, it looks like I only get one question, so I may as well make it count. Zach, did the Sand Monk at any time ask you to do anything in Sandtopia other than look around and see what this place is like?"

"No. He just wanted to give us an interesting experience."

"Thank you son," said the public defender.

The judge declared, "The prosecution may call its next witness."

"The prosecution calls the holder of the sign, Logarno," announced the prosecutor.

Logarno did not move; he did not want to take the stand.

"Will Logarno please take the stand," the prosecutor urged.

"You will stand up and answer his questions," the Sand Queen shouted angrily. She pointed at the witness stand. "Get up there!"

Reluctantly, Logarno took the witness stand.

The prosecutor approached him. "Logarno, were you the one holding the sign that said: 'Wipe the slate clean, get rid of that evil queen?'"

"Yes."

"Who made it?"

"My granny made it," Logarno replied flippantly. "Who do you think made it, you flunky?"

The Sand Monk grinned.

"So you admit making the sign?" inquired the prosecutor.

"You can take my statement to mean anything you want."

The Sand Queen stood up and wagged a finger at Logarno. "I order you to answer the questions without being cute, you stupid old buffoon!"

The prosecutor continued, "Okay. I'll ask you one last time. Logarno, did you make the sign?"

"Yes. And I'm proud to have done so."

"You're actually proud?"

"That's right, sonny boy." Logarno wagged a finger back at the Sand Queen and squinted. "We don't need her. All that claptrap about her being merciful and indispensable. It's hogwash, if you ask me."

The judge banged his gavel several times, trying to silence Logarno. "Order! We'll have order in this court!"

Logarno shifted his gaze to the judge. "Shut up. I'm going to speak my piece. The truth is, the Sand Queen is a rotten witch. We'd all be much better off if she were six feet under."

The crowd—with the exception of the young sandroids, of course—roared its approval. The Sand Monk smiled broadly.

The Sand Queen was apoplectic. "Logarno," she hissed, "It is *you* who will soon be six feet under."

"So what?" Logarno shot back. "This trial is a complete sham. We all know what fate awaits the Sand Monk. He'll be found guilty and executed. There can be no other outcome. And guess who's next in line? That's right. Me. Along with Pandalese, Eraklena, and Mandalia. We're all headed to the gallows, so I may as well speak my mind while I have the chance—and the audience."

"Shut up! Shut up! Shut up!" shrieked the Sand Queen. She pointed at several lion men. "Seize

Logarno! I find him in contempt of my court. Take him to the Sand Dungeon immediately. I'll deal with him later."

Several lion men rushed the platform and unceremoniously plucked Logarno from the witness stand. As he was being carted off, Logarno shouted repeatedly: "Wipe the slate clean, get rid of that evil queen!"

Kalani, impressed, whispered to the Hooded Blacksmith, "Wow, Logarno was pretty defiant."

"Indeed."

The Sand Queen, still angry, yelled, "I want the Sand Monk! Prosecutor, call the Sand Monk to the witness stand!"

The judge responded, "The prosecution may call the next witness."

"Will the Sand Monk please take the witness stand," announced the prosecutor.

The Sand Monk complied. "Your Honor," he said to the judge, "may I remove this silly hat?"

"Absolutely not," interjected the Sand Queen. "You're a dunce. The hat stays."

"Sustained," ruled the judge.

The Sand Monk grimaced.

The prosecutor began, "Please state your name for the record."

"I'm the Sand Monk."

"And what exactly does that mean?"

"It's the title given to the head priest of Sandtopia's religion. But you already knew that."

The Sand Queen fidgeted.

The prosecutor continued, "If you're the head priest of Sandtopia's religion, why do you have a temple on Earth, in—what was the name of that place?"

"Hawaii," said the Sand Monk.

"Yes, Hawaii. Why do you have a temple there?"

"It's my sanctuary. I can rest there without being hounded by the Sand Queen and her minions. Having a temple there is essential for my mental health."

"Are you trying to tell us that Hawaii is actually a better place to live than Sandtopia?"

"That's what I'm telling you. There's no comparison, really."

"Lies! A pack of lies!" screamed the Sand Queen. "There's no place better to live than Sandtopia. Why? Because of me."

"She's completely lost her marbles," whispered the Hooded Blacksmith to Kalani. Kalani grinned.

The Sand Queen continued, "Hawaii is not better than Sandtopia. Sand Monk, tell us the real reason you have a temple in Hawaii."

"I don't understand."

"Admit it! Your temple in Hawaii serves as a base of operations against me!"

"That's crazy."

"Okay, okay," said the prosecutor. "Let's everybody calm down." He looked at the Sand Monk. "What's the real purpose of your temple in Hawaii?"

"As I said, my temple in Hawaii is a sanctuary," explained the Sand Monk. "When I'm there, I don't have to confront all the troubles that plague Sandtopia."

"But what 'troubles' plague Sandtopia?" asked the prosecutor. "As I mentioned earlier, the Sand Queen has been masterful at keeping order."

"But at what price?" countered the Sand Monk. "I'll tell you. The price is personal freedom. We're not able to criticize the Sand Queen's rule. If she issues a decree that we don't like, there's nothing we can do about it. If we protest, we're immediately arrested and imprisoned."

The prosecutor retorted, "But if we were to allow people to run around and do anything they want, there would be chaos. Chaos in the streets!"

"I didn't say we should allow everyone to run around and do as they please," clarified the Sand Monk. "We still need laws, as well as people to enforce the laws. But we also need an independent court system so people won't be abused." He looked at the Sand Queen. "And, perhaps most important, the ruler of Sandtopia must not be above the law."

"You've got that right!" shouted a man in the crowd.

One of the young sandroids took notice. He rushed over to the man and punched him hard in the face, knocking him out. The Sand Queen was pleased.

The judge banged his gavel several times and shouted, "Order! We'll have order in this court!"

The young sandroid returned to his friends, who congratulated him with high-fives and patted him on the back.

"The ruler of Sandtopia not above the law? This is crazy talk," continued the prosecutor. "Now, let me ask you—"

"Is it crazy?" interrupted the Sand Monk. "I don't think so. It makes perfect sense. In fact, the whole system needs to be reformed. We need to transfer power from the Sand Queen to a Sand Congress. Our laws can still be strict, if we like, but people will no longer be arbitrarily abused when she's out of the picture." He looked at the members of the ruling elite in the second row of seats. "In fact, less power for the Sand Queen would translate into more power for others."

"Shut up, monk!" the Sand Queen hissed. She approached the prosecutor, took off one of her white gloves, and summarily whipped him across the face with it. "You are done."

"Excuse me?" asked the prosecutor, holding a hand to his burning face.

"You heard me. You're done. I'm the prosecuting attorney now." The Sand Queen peered at the judge and smiled slightly. "If that's okay with you."

"But of course."

The Hooded Blacksmith whispered to Kalani, "Here we go."

The Sand Queen pointed at the prosecutor. "Lion men, take him away!"

They seized the prosecutor. As he was being removed from Central Plaza, he blathered obsequiously to the Sand Queen, "Please, your Grace, your Highness. Please. I beseech you to give me one more chance. Surely, I won't let you down. Please!"

She ignored him.

"Please!"

The Sand Queen turned to the Sand Monk. "Monk, I'm in charge now. You *will* answer my questions." As an afterthought, she remarked, "Let me remind you that you're still under oath."

"Yes, yes, I'm aware of that," the Sand Monk said wearily.

The Sand Queen stared at the Sand Monk intently for a few moments before asking, "Isn't it true that you used your temple in Hawaii as a base to hatch your misguided plots against me?"

"I wouldn't put it that way."

"So you admit it?"

"I'll admit that my temple is a place for me to gather my thoughts. To do some deep thinking about how Sandtopia is ruled versus how it should be ruled."

"Oh? Keep talking, monk."

The Sand Monk took a deep breath and raised his voice so more people in the audience could hear his words. "If it's treasonous to think the current system is rotten, that there are better ways to rule Sandtopia, than I suppose I'm guilty as charged."

Numerous people in the crowd gasped. Several fainted.

The Sand Queen smiled. She was pleased that the Sand Monk had just admitted his guilt.

The Sand Monk continued, "Guilty of wanting to build a better society for future generations, one in which absolute power isn't concentrated in the hands of a crazy, evil despot. One in which people—and sandroids—are free to speak their minds, criticize their leaders, and work together to build a lively, spirited democracy."

The crowd roared its approval; the Sand Queen scowled.

Emboldened, and certain that he was headed for the gallows no matter what he said or did, the Sand Monk played to the crowd. "It's with the utmost conviction that I utter the following statement: Wipe the slate clean, get rid of that evil queen! Wipe the slate clean, get rid of that evil queen! Wipe the slate clean, get rid of that—"

This was simply too much for the Sand Queen to bear. "Shut up! Shut up!" she howled.

She looked at the crowd, which was still chanting the Sand Monk's mantra, "Wipe the slate clean, get rid of that evil queen," and removed one of her white gloves. She slapped the Sand Monk several times across the face while hissing, "Look at what you've done! Look what you've done!"

The judge said to the Sand Queen, "Your Highness, may I remind you that the defendant admitted his guilt."

The Sand Queen stopped abusing the Sand Monk. Brightening, she rushed behind the judge's desk, grabbed his gavel, and pounded it several times. "You all heard it," she said, "the Sand Monk admitted his guilt. On the record." After whispering into the judge's ear, she announced, "The judge will now pass sentence."

He banged his gavel. "The court finds the Sand Monk—by his own admission—guilty of the charge of high treason, of plotting to overthrow the merciful and enlightened rule of the Sand Queen."

"What's his sentence?" an exuberant young sandroid shouted.

"Yeah, what's his sentence?" shouted another.

"Death by hanging!" declared the Sand Queen.

The young sandroids cheered.

The rest of the crowd was silent and somber.

"Bring in the gallows!" the Sand Queen shouted exuberantly. "The sentence will be carried out immediately. Immediately, I say!"

A team of lion men pushed a portable wooden gallows into Central Plaza. The judge instructed the jury to disband. The elevated platform on which they had been sitting was hastily taken apart and carted off. Creaking noisily, the gallows was rolled into place.

The executioner emerged, carrying a battleaxe. He was a tall, thin, extremely sinister-looking human with beady black eyes. He clearly relished his job. He climbed onto the gallows, put down his battleaxe, and prepared the rope and noose.

"Because you admitted your guilt freely, I decided to make your death relatively quick," the

Sand Queen said to the Sand Monk. "Wouldn't you agree that death by hanging is preferable to the chopping block? Sometimes it takes six or seven chops for the head to be severed completely."

"Frankly, neither method appeals to me."

"Well, I would have expected you to be more grateful. This just proves my point. You're a deviant halfwit, while I'm extraordinarily merciful."

The Sand Monk glared at her.

The Sand Queen shouted, "Lion men, seize him! Seize the Sand Monk!"

Four lion men plucked the Sand Monk off the witness stand—he did not resist—and carried him to the gallows.

Someone in the crowd shouted, "No, take me instead!"

Another cried, "Take me!"

It was infectious. Scores of people started shouting, "Take me! Take me!"

"Silence!" barked the Sand Queen. "Why won't you all just shut up? We've found the Sand Monk guilty, and it is *he* who will die for his crime. Nobody else."

The Sand Queen strode over to the gallows. "Well, monk, you certainly have a lot of supporters. I'll deal with them later." She looked at the executioner. "Put him in position."

The executioner guided the Sand Monk to the trap door and tied his hands behind his back. After he was in place, the Sand Queen smiled at him. She said smugly, "You lose." She turned to the executioner and held out her hands. "This honor belongs exclusively to me."

The executioner handed the Sand Queen the noose, which she draped around the Sand Monk's neck. "Monk, do you have any last words?"

"You may have won today, but I just planted the seeds of your future destruction."

She stared at him blankly. "You're a stupid, stupid old man."

The Sand Queen removed the Sand Monk's dunce cap and covered his head with a black hood. After returning to her throne, she announced, "Executioner—on my signal, release the trap door and hang the Sand Monk."

The executioner nodded. He stepped behind the Sand Monk, slightly to the side. He grabbed the trap door release-handle, which was sticking up from the platform floor, and grinned sadistically.

Abruptly, there was a commotion at one of the plaza's entry gates. People were being jostled.

"What's going on?" the Sand Queen asked no one in particular. She shouted, "Quell the disturbance immediately! Quell the disturbance immediately! Nothing shall spoil my grand moment!"

"Wait!" hollered a sandroid at the center of the commotion. "Halt the execution! Clear a path!"

"What's the meaning of this?" shouted the Sand Queen. "I demand to be told—" She did not finish her sentence. Twenty sandroids were escorting Glen and Amanda toward her. "Well, well, well, what have we here?"

The sandroids, Glen, and Amanda reached the elevated platform on which the Sand Queen was perched.

With a flourish, Pepros announced, "Your Highness, I humbly offer you two human children. They're not from Sandtopia. They came here through the portal in the Sand Monk's temple in Hawaii."

CHAPTER 12

◆ I ◆

The Sand Queen could not believe her good fortune. She peered at Glen and Amanda and flashed a disingenuous smile. "How nice of you to join us. Your timing couldn't be better. You see, we're about to hang the Sand Monk."

Amanda looked at the figure wearing a hood and gasped.

"Yes. Take a good look, because it's the last time you'll see him alive."

"Amanda!" shouted Kalani. "Glen!"

"Kalani!" shouted Amanda. "You're alive!" She looked at Zach. He smiled at her. "Zach too!"

Kalani got out of her seat, rushed up to Amanda, and hugged her. "How long have you been here?"

"We crossed soon after you guys. We were worried because you didn't return when you were supposed to," explained Amanda.

"Well, isn't that sweet," said the Sand Queen. "You'll have plenty of time to talk later. After the execution. Pepros, find the children seats in the front row. I wouldn't want them to miss anything."

Glen shot Amanda a nervous glance. His eye was still twitching. Pepros escorted them to some open seats.

"Executioner, take your position once again and wait for my signal," commanded the Sand Queen.

The executioner clutched the trap door handle and waited for the Sand Queen's signal. The Sand Queen raised her right arm.

Kalani buried her face onto Zach's shoulder. "I can't watch. It's just so awful."

Kalani heard several objects whiz by. Someone screamed. Kalani quickly raised her head and looked at the Sand Queen. Stunned, she was gaping and pointing at the executioner. He was desperately attempting to remove two arrows that were buried deeply into his neck. Another was sticking out of his chest. Gurgling and stumbling, he fell backwards, off the gallows and onto the dirt ground below.

"What's the meaning of this?" screamed the Sand Queen as she stood up. "I demand to know who did this to my executioner!"

Another arrow—also shot by a menehune archer—whizzed by and buried itself deep into the Sand Queen's face. The force knocked her backwards, causing her to slump back into her throne. She grabbed the arrow and, after considerable effort, pulled it out of her face. It made a nauseating sucking sound.

Immediately, several dacturions surrounded the Sand Queen and pushed her to the ground, covering and protecting her body with theirs. She acquiesced because she did not want any more arrows to pierce her. Although not lethal, or especially painful, they were humiliating.

"Now!" shouted Pepros, at the top of his lungs.

The twenty sandroids accompanying Pepros streamed toward the ten young loyalist sandroids (loyal to the Sand Queen) and pounced on them. Pepros' sandroids each carried short spears whose tips had been coated with a substance called myzlaria, which was poisonous to sandroids. (Only the Sand Queen's chief scientist, a sandroid, knew how to manufacture this substance. The existence of myzlaria was a secret. Only the Sand Queen, the chief scientist, and a few members of the Sand Queen's inner circle knew of its existence. She decided she would use the poison—and thereby reveal its existence—only in the case of a sandroid rebellion against her rule. The Sand Queen did not know her chief scientist was sympathetic to the sandroid rebels and had forwarded some vials of the thick, goopy poison to Pepros.)

Pepros' sandroids began piercing the young loyalist sandroids with their poison-tipped spears. Hysteria broke out among their ranks when they observed that the spear jabs were causing their clear skin to dissolve rapidly, resulting in death (the sand inside of them spilled to ground). Naturally, they tried to flee their assailants. However, throngs of humans in the area—wondering what was happening—impeded their escape. The loyalist sandroids could not get very far; it was not long before they were all dead. The humans who witnessed this cheered.

It quickly dawned on the Sand Queen that the poison might soon be used against her. She became frightened. She instructed one of the dacturions shielding her body to return to the Sand Palace and bring back reinforcements. It flapped its huge wings and rose into the air. Ten arrows immediately struck it. The dacturion emitted a terrible cry and fell to the ground beside the Sand Queen, limp. Other dacturions began falling from the sky as well. Some of them, however, managed to escape back to the Sand Palace.

While the massacre of the young sandroids was taking place, sixty taurgogs approached the main entry to the plaza and pounced on six lion men guarding the gate. A taurgog was a large creature, resembling a cross between a gorilla and a coyote. Its body—the part resembling a gorilla— was enormous, powerful, and covered with black fur. Its head, however, looked like a coyote. Although taurgogs were ungainly, loping around on their knuckles, they had fantastic strength, sharp eyes, and keen ears. Plus, they had a terrific sense of smell. Physically, taurgogs and lion men were closely matched. Although the taurgogs were bigger and stronger, the lion men had sharper claws and teeth.

The six lion men manning the gate were quickly overwhelmed by the crush of yelping taurgogs, who flooded into Central Plaza. The taurgogs, along with the menehune archers, targeted the rest of the lion men. A grand battle ensued.

The Sand Queen, drenched in dacturion blood, peered over the two birds that were shielding her— they had taken numerous arrows and were both dead—to see where the sandroids with the poison were located. She was relieved to see that instead of coming after her, they were preoccupied, battling a group of lion men.

"Okay, assess the situation," said the Sand Queen.

She gazed at the scene. It did not look good. The taurgogs were clearly gaining the upper hand on the lion men, who had clustered together and were slowly retreating toward her. Most of the humans in the crowd had fled, but a significant number—including the Hooded Blacksmith and Jaagdar—were helping the taurgogs in any way possible. Pandalese, Eraklena, Mandalia, and the kids (Glen, Amanda, Zach, and Kalani) were being protected, off to the side, by a group of taurgogs.

The Sand Queen looked at the second row of seats and was shocked by the carnage. Every member of her ruling elite was dead. Numerous menehune arrows had pierced the old ones (shattering their brittle skins), while the younger ones had been jabbed with poison-tipped spears. Heaps of sand—sprinkled with arrows and various articles of clothing and jewelry—was all that was left of them.

The Sand Queen began to panic. "Okay, think," she said to herself. "Think." She peered at the Sand Monk, who was still standing on the gallows, wondering what was going on (he was unable to remove his hood). She sensed an opportunity. The

Sand Queen dashed over to the gallows—two arrows plunged into her chest along the way (which she duly plucked out)—and seized the Sand Monk. (The arrows stopped flying as soon as she reached the Sand Monk, because the menehune archers did not want to kill him inadvertently.)

The Sand Queen removed the Sand Monk's black hood, untied his hands, and gripped his arm tightly. The Sand Monk did not know what to make of all the pandemonium and chaos. After his eyes had adjusted to the light, he noticed the piles of sand on the chairs on which the sandroid ruling elite had just been sitting. He was flabbergasted.

"You're coming with me, monk," the Sand Queen hissed.

The Sand Monk, with all his strength, resisted. Frustrated, the Sand Queen bent over, picked him up, and slung him over her shoulder. She descended the gallows' stairs.

Kalani observed this. Alarmed, she hollered, "Everybody! The Sand Queen's getting away—and she has the Sand Monk!"

Just then, scores of dacturions—reinforcements from the Sand Palace—appeared in the sky above the plaza. They tried to assist the lion men. However, each time the birds dipped below a certain altitude, the menehune archers, shooting from buildings adjacent to the plaza, picked them off with a hail of arrows.

Kalani tugged frantically at Zach's sleeve. "Didn't you hear me?"

"Huh?"

Kalani pointed at the gallows. "Look! The Sand Queen's getting away, and she's got the Sand Monk! What are we going do?"

"We have to follow them," said Zach. "Where's Jaagdar? Where's the Hooded Blacksmith? We'll need their help."

"I don't know," replied Kalani. "There's no time. We need to follow the Sand Queen. Now!"

"What's going on?" asked Glen.

"Yeah, what's going on?" inquired Amanda.

Kalani spoke rapidly. "The Sand Queen's getting away and she has the Sand Monk. We'd better not lose her! Where's the Hooded Blacksmith? Where's Jaagdar?"

"Who?" asked Amanda.

"Arghhh!" exclaimed Kalani.

"There he is!" shouted Zach. "The Hooded Blacksmith!"

"Great," said Kalani. "Get him. I'll follow the Sand Queen, so we don't lose her. Hurry!"

Kalani headed toward the gallows.

"Wait, I'll go with you," Amanda said to Kalani.

"Good."

"Me too," said Glen.

Zach rushed over to the Hooded Blacksmith, who was busy fending off a lion man with a long spear.

"Hey, Mr. Hooded Blacksmith," said Zach, trying to get his attention. "It's Zach."

"I'm a little busy right now kid. Can it wait?"

"The Sand Queen's getting away," Zach explained, "and she has the Sand Monk."

"What? Where is she?"

"She just left the gallows. Kalani's following her."

The Hooded Blacksmith saw an opening and jabbed his spear into the lion man's heart. The lion man howled and collapsed to the ground, dead.

"Okay, kid, let's go," said the Hooded Blacksmith.

"Where's Jaagdar?" asked Zach.

"I don't know," replied the Hooded Blacksmith. "He's around here somewhere. Hopefully he's not dead. You want me to look for him?"

"There's no time!"

"Got it."

Zach and the Hooded Blacksmith raced to the gallows. They climbed the stairs to get a better view. In the distance, they saw the Sand Queen carrying the Sand Monk (she was moving surprisingly fast). They also saw Kalani, Amanda, and Glen racing after her. The Sand Queen unceremoniously dumped the Sand Monk onto the ground and opened a secret trap door, located at the plaza's edge. She forced the Sand Monk down a ladder into an underground tunnel.

The Sand Queen turned around and was beginning to descend the ladder when she spotted the kids racing toward her. An arrow plunged into her face. She grimaced, plucked it out, and made a rude hand gesture toward the kids. Then she descended into the tunnel, closing the trap door behind her.

Glen, Amanda and Kalani reached the trap door. They tried to open it. To their dismay, it would not budge. Zach and the Hooded Blacksmith joined them.

"We can't open the trap door," Kalani explained to the Hooded Blacksmith.

He bent over and tried to open it. "It must be locked."

"What are we going do?" asked Kalani.

"Zach, go back to the central area and try to get a couple of those strange yelping beasts," instructed the Hooded Blacksmith. "They may be strong enough to break the lock. Or, they may be able to break the trap door itself."

"Gotchya," said Zach. He dashed off.

Kalani asked the Hooded Blacksmith, "How's it going back there?"

"Our side is doing well. Whoever planned this attack did an excellent job. Those unusual creatures—"

"They're called taurgogs," interrupted Glen. "The menehune brought them over from another dimension to help out."

"Thank God they did," said the Hooded Blacksmith. "The taurgogs have suffered some losses, but they should be able to defeat the lion men." He paused. "Whoever thought to include the menehune archers was brilliant! They've certainly kept the dacturions at bay. Now, if we can just manage to capture the Sand Queen—" He looked at Glen's eye. "Son, you should have your eye looked at. It's twitching like crazy."

"Thank you," Glen said tartly. He was keenly aware of his problem. His head was pounding and he felt dizzy.

Amanda shot a concerned glance his way.

"What's a trap door and tunnel doing here?" Kalani asked the Hooded Blacksmith. "It's a strange place for such a thing."

"The tunnel probably leads back to the Sand Palace," speculated the Hooded Blacksmith. "We think the Sand Queen has constructed a network of tunnels underneath the city."

"What for?" asked Amanda.

"Spying," explained the Hooded Blacksmith. "Also, it's an efficient way to move her henchman around to terrorize the public. People know a lion man might pop up at any moment."

Zach returned with Pandalese and two taurgogs.

Pandalese, who was having difficulty walking, asked if anybody knew who was behind the attack on the Sand Queen and her minions.

Glen explained, "Jephratus and Zorjin met with a couple sandroids—Pepros and Haljan. Some menehune representatives were there too. They're the ones who brought all the taurgogs."

"Ahh, Jephratus and Zorjin," Pandalese said warmly. He looked around. "Where are they?"

"I think they're with the menehune archers," replied Glen.

"By the way, what are taurgogs?" asked Pandalese. "These peculiar creatures to my left?"

"That's right," answered Glen.

Kalani noticed the healing stone in her amulet, which she was wearing around her neck, was growing warm.

The Hooded Blacksmith addressed the two taurgogs: "See if you guys can open this trap door."

The taurgogs bent over and grabbed the trap door handle. In unison, they pulled hard. The handle snapped off.

"Crap!" exclaimed the Hooded Blacksmith.

"What are we going to do now?" asked Kalani.

One of the taurgogs reared back and smashed his fist onto the trap door. It cracked. The other taurgog joined in. They pounded on the trap door repeatedly. It was not long before they had smashed it to pieces.

"Wow, those are strong creatures," the Hooded Blacksmith remarked.

The taurgogs removed several stray pieces of splintered wood so nobody would be injured. They stepped aside to allow the others to enter the tunnel.

◆ II ◆

The Hooded Blacksmith started to climb down the ladder.

"Wait!" exclaimed Amanda. "Maybe we should get Pepros or Haljan. Their poison may come in handy if we're able to catch the Sand Queen."

"I'd rather not bring any sandroids with us," said the Hooded Blacksmith. "I don't trust them."

"I don't like sandroids any more than you do," Pandalese said to the Hooded Blacksmith, "but you saw how effective that poison was, didn't you?"

"Yes."

"I really think we should try to get some of that poison," insisted Pandalese. "How else can we defeat the Sand Queen should we manage to track her down?"

The Hooded Blacksmith saw his point. "Alright. But just one sandroid. And make sure he still has some poison."

"Okay," said Amanda. "I'll try to find Pepros or Haljan." She dashed off. On her way back to the plaza's center, she came upon a gaggle of rebel sandroids who were busy battling a group of lion men. She asked if they knew Pepros or Haljan's location.

"Pepros is over there, by the elevated platform," said one.

"Yeah, he's about to lead an assault on the dacturions shielding and defending the Sand Queen," stated another. He grinned. "We're gonna get her!"

Amanda thought about explaining the situation to them, but decided there was no time for that. She looked toward the elevated platform and immediately spotted Pepros. She ran toward him.

"Pepros!" Amanda shouted as she approached the elevated platform. "We need your help."

"What are you talking about?" asked Pepros. He gestured toward a group of rebel sandroids. "We're about to get the Sand Queen!"

"That's just it," said Amanda, trying to catch her breath. "She escaped. And to make matters worse, she has the Sand Monk."

Pepros was flabbergasted. "What? That can't be!" He pointed at the dacturions. "She didn't escape. She's being shielded by those dacturions."

"No! No! She slipped away," explained Amanda.

"Are you certain?"

"Absolutely. Glen and I both saw it. The others did too. The Sand Queen grabbed the Sand Monk and ran off into a secret underground tunnel."

"She really has the Sand Monk?"

"Yes! We got some help to chase her down, but we didn't know about the secret tunnel. The Sand Queen entered it before we could stop her."

"Damn!" shouted Pepros. "I didn't even see her slip away. I thought we had her pinned down under those dacturions."

"Figures she'd cut and run instead of fighting," said a nearby human, eavesdropping on the conversation.

"Pepros, we need your help in the tunnels," said Amanda. "Do you still have some poison on your spear?"

"No, but I have some in a pouch in my pocket."

"Good enough. Let's go!"

◆ III ◆

Amanda and Pepros arrived at the entrance to the underground tunnel. The Hooded Blacksmith eyed the sandroid suspiciously.

Pepros looked at the smashed trap door. "Taurgogs?"

Everyone nodded.

The Hooded Blacksmith took over. "Okay, there's no time to waste. I'll go down first. Pepros will follow me. Then the taurgogs. Pandalese will bring up the rear, if he can keep up."

"Hey, wait a minute. What about us?" Kalani inquired.

"This is far too dangerous for kids. You guys are *not* to enter the tunnel," said the Hooded Blacksmith.

"But—" protested Kalani.

"This is non-negotiable. You kids are to stay above ground. Is that clear?"

Kalani frowned. "Yes."

"Send someone to fetch a few taurgogs to protect you, just in case a lion man comes this way," continued the Hooded Blacksmith.

"Fine," said Kalani.

The Hooded Blacksmith, Pepros, and the two taurgogs climbed down into the tunnel (it was a very tight squeeze for the taurgogs). Pandalese descended halfway, but discovered that his leg was too badly injured to make it all the way down.

He emerged from the tunnel, sat down on the ground, and shook his head ruefully. "I really wanted to get her."

"It's okay," said Zach. "Don't worry about it."

Kalani's healing stone started to glow softly.

"Isn't that the healing stone Jasper gave you?" asked Zach.

"Yeah," responded Kalani. She looked at Pandalese. "Can I try it on you?"

Pandalese brightened. "Yes, please!" He pointed toward his leg, which had been cut earlier. It was bleeding again. "Use it there."

"What do I do?" asked Kalani.

"Hold the stone about an inch from my skin and move it slowly up and down my lower leg."

Kalani followed his instructions. The bleeding ceased entirely after the first pass with the warm, glowing crystal. After the second pass, the wounds quickly formed dark scabs. The scabs fell off after the third pass, revealing healed skin. There were no scars.

"That's amazing!" exclaimed Zach.

"You said it!" Kalani smiled as she looked at Pandalese. "How do you feel?"

"Terrific! The pain is gone. Thanks! Now, if you'll excuse me, there's somebody I have to catch."

Pandalese hurried down the ladder and disappeared into the tunnel.

Glen said, "Shall I get a couple taurgogs for protection while we wait here?"

"You'll do no such thing," Kalani said sternly.

"What? Why not?"

"There's no way I'm waiting here while the Sand Queen's down there doing God-knows-what to the Sand Monk."

Glen placed his hands on his hips. "But what about your friend the Hooded Blacksmith? His instructions were quite clear. He wants us to stay put."

The left side of Glen's face twitched violently, several times.

Kalani peered at Glen's eye. "What's with your eye and face, Glen? I don't remember you having a nervous tick before." She mocked him. "Stress getting to you?"

"I don't know," snapped Glen.

"Well, screw the Hooded Blacksmith," said Kalani. "I'm going down into the tunnel. Who's with me?"

"I'm game," said Zach.

"Count me in," added Amanda.

Silence.

"What about you, Glen?" asked Kalani.

Glen paused, weighing his options. "Hmm . . . Well, there's no way I'm waiting out here by myself."

"Good," said Kalani, sounding satisfied. "Let's go."

"Wait!" said Amanda.

"What now?" asked Kalani.

"We should arm ourselves. What if we *do* run into the Sand Queen?"

"Good point." Kalani grabbed Zach's hand. "Come on—let's scavenge for some weapons." She looked at Amanda. "We'll be right back."

Zach and Kalani ran off. Soon, they returned with two spears and a couple of daggers. Armed, the kids descended into the tunnel.

♦ IV ♦

It was not long before the path the kids were following, which was softly illuminated by light bulbs, ended at a "T" intersection. Curiously, there was a door in the wall directly in front of them.

"Which way should we should go?" asked Zach.

Glen sighed. "Here we go again."

Kalani shot him a dirty look. "Maybe we should try the door first."

Amanda answered, "Yeah, I think we should try the—"

The door popped open. A small, cross-eyed, middle-aged man with disheveled hair and a scraggly beard poked his head out.

"Shut up!" he barked. Then he slammed the door shut.

Kalani laughed. "Who—or what—was that?"

"That was really strange," said Zach.

The door popped open again. "I said shut up! Don't you know you're disturbing me?"

"Who are—" Kalani began. The man slammed the door shut again before she could finish her sentence.

"Come on," said Zach, "let's forget about that crackpot. Which way should we go?"

"Maybe he knows something. I say we try to talk to him," suggested Amanda.

"I don't think he wants to talk to us," Glen remarked.

Amanda ignored him and knocked on the door.

The man popped his head out. "Yes? May I ask who you are?" he inquired politely, as if he had not just seen them moments before.

Zach and Kalani exchanged puzzled glances.

"Sir," began Amanda, "did you see or hear anybody come by here earlier?"

The man peered at Amanda and began to laugh hysterically. He shut the door.

"What a peculiar man," commented Amanda. "Should I try again?"

"Go for it," said Kalani.

Amanda knocked on the door. The man opened it slightly and looked out through the crack. "Why won't everyone just leave me alone?" he wailed. "Can't a fool just have his peace and quiet? You're the third cursed group to bother me today. The others—he pointed to his left—weren't nearly as bothersome as you!"

Amanda started to ask, "Sir, if you would just—"

"You came down here to pester me, didn't you? What do you want from me? You must want something." He spat on the ground defiantly. "Well, you won't get it! Do you hear me? You'll get nothing! You've really spoiled my day."

He slammed the door shut.

"That guy's a psycho," remarked Kalani. "Probably spends way too much time down here."

"Did you notice it?" asked Zach.

Kalani asked, "Notice what?"

"He pointed to his left when he mentioned the others passing through here."

"Did he?"

"Yeah, I saw it too," said Glen. "Do you think he was talking about the Sand Queen?"

"Maybe," said Amanda. "It's worth a shot."

"Well, what are we waiting for?" asked Kalani. "Let's go!"

They went in the direction indicated by the crazy man. After five minutes or so of brisk walking, the kids came to a fork.

"Oh no," said Kalani. "Another fork."

"These tunnels are probably full of forks and T intersections. How in the world are we going to track down the Sand Monk with all these forks and T intersections?" Glen asked. He sounded defeated.

"Stop being such a wet blanket, Glen," chided Kalani. "Yeah, it's difficult. But what other choice do we have? Why don't you—"

"Kalani, look!" interrupted Zach. "On the ground, in the tunnel to the right—a scrap of paper."

"Go see if anything's written on it."

"Okay." Zach walked over and picked it up. "Nope. It's blank."

"There's a second one even further inside the tunnel!" exclaimed Amanda. She ran into the tunnel and picked it up. She pointed. "And there's a third one!"

"It must be a trail," commented Kalani.

"Do you think the Sand Monk left it?" asked Zach.

"It's possible," answered Kalani. "Or, it could've been the Hooded Blacksmith, Pandalese or Pepros."

"Well, at any rate, I suggest we follow it," stated Zach.

"No objections here," responded Kalani.

They followed the paper trail. It stopped after the fifth scrap of paper.

"Hey, the trail stopped," remarked Amanda.

"Yeah," said Zach. He scratched his head. "Maybe it'll start again if we come to another fork."

"I hope you're right," said Amanda.

Kalani reasoned, "It makes sense. I mean, how much paper does the trail-leaver even have?"

After several minutes of walking, the path widened noticeably. They came upon a ladder, which led to a trap door in the ceiling above.

"Uh-oh," said Amanda. "I hope the Sand Queen didn't make her getaway here."

Glen said pessimistically, "Yeah, she's probably long gone."

Glen was really getting on Kalani's nerves. She was starting to wish he *had* stayed behind. "Glen—" she started.

"Kalani," interrupted Zach, "I have an idea. I'll climb the ladder to see whether or not the trap door has been bolted shut."

"Oh, I get it," she said. "If it's locked from the inside, then the Sand Queen must still be in the tunnels."

"Exactly," said Zach.

Zach climbed the ladder.

"Well?" asked Kalani.

"It's locked."

"Good. At least that means we're still on the right track."

They walked deeper into the tunnel system and came to a sharp L-shaped turn, leading to the left.

"At least it's not another fork," Amanda commented dryly.

"Yeah—I say we go left," joked Kalani.

They laughed, easing the tension somewhat.

Kalani, in the lead, turned the corner and screamed. Sitting on the ground, slumped against the wall, was a dead lion man.

"This is not good," commented Zach. "I'm sure he's not the only lion man in these tunnels."

"Yeah, but at least it's not the Sand Monk or the Hooded Blacksmith or someone like that," said

Kalani. "Who cares about a dead lion man, anyway?"

They continued walking. Soon, the tunnel widened and they came upon another ladder, which led to another trap door in the ceiling above. Zach climbed the ladder to see if it was locked. It was.

After several minutes, they arrived at another L-turn, this time leading to the right. Zach took the lead.

He rounded the corner. "Uh-oh."

Kalani rounded the turn. "Oh my God!"

Five lion men lay dead on the tunnel floor. This time, however, their bodies were mingled with two dead taurgogs. Based on the numerous claw marks on the tunnel walls (and on the taurgogs' bodies), there had been a titanic struggle.

"This is getting dangerous," Glen said nervously.

"Really?" snapped Kalani.

Glen raised his voice. "Hey, I'm getting a little tired of you and your attitude, Kalani."

"Are you now? Well Glen, the feeling's quite mutual."

"Oh, you just know everything, don't you?"

"Guys, guys, break it up," said Zach, stepping between them. "Now's not the time to argue." He looked at Glen. "If you want to go back and return to the plaza, feel free to do so. But I don't think any of us will join you."

The left side of Glen's face twitched violently. He grabbed his head, which was throbbing. He wanted to sit down. "No, I'll go with you guys."

"Good," said Zach.

Kalani gave Glen a sour look.

◆V◆

The kids pressed on. Soon, the tunnel ended at a large door.

"I hope it's unlocked," commented Zach.

He reached out and turned the handle. Clutching his spear tightly, he slowly pushed the door open and peered inside. "Uh-oh."

"What now?" asked Kalani.

Zach stepped into the room. "You don't want to know."

Kalani, Amanda, and Glen followed him inside. The room was large and empty, except for four dead bodies: two lion men, Pandalese, and the Hooded Blacksmith. There was also a pile of sand, covered by a white robe and a black sash. Next to the robe was a spear.

"Was that Pepros?" asked Kalani, choking back tears.

"It looks that way," said Amanda. She pointed at what was left of Pepros. "That's his robe. It's probably his spear too."

"We have to come back when all this horribleness is over and give them a proper burial," said Kalani, sniffling. She ran over to the Hooded Blacksmith's body and pulled it next to Pandalese's body. She grabbed Pepros' robe and used it to cover the their faces.

Amanda pointed to the ground. "Guys—look."

"Jewelry," commented Glen.

"I know where that's from," said Zach. "The Sand Queen's crown. It must've come off somehow during the fight."

"Are you sure?" inquired Glen.

"I'm positive," responded Zach. "I got a good look at it when she grilled me on the witness stand."

"Then it looks like they found her," said Amanda.

Zach picked up Pepros' spear. "There's still some poison on this." He looked at Kalani. "Check Pepros' robe. Maybe the poison he brought with him is still there."

Kalani searched through the robe. "It's gone."

"The Sand Queen must have it." Zach pounded his fist against the wall. "Damn!"

"And she still has the Sand Monk. So let's get moving," urged Kalani. "There's no time to waste!"

♦VI♦

They walked toward a door at the opposite end of the room. Zach opened it slowly.

"Do you see anything?" whispered Amanda.

Zach turned around. "It leads to another tunnel. I can see a door in the distance."

They approached the second door.

Kalani started to say something, but Zach stopped her by placing his finger on his lips. He whispered, "I can hear someone—or something—inside."

Zach readied his spear. In one quick motion, he clutched the door handle, turned it, and thrust open the door. He sprang into the room, followed quickly by the others.

The Sand Queen whirled around and stared at them. She was standing at the opposite end of the room. It looked like some kind of armory; weapons of all types were hanging on the walls. The Sand Monk, looking drawn and haggard, was sitting behind her in a chair. Fresh welts marked his face.

The Sand Queen quickly sized up the situation. When it was clear to her that the kids had come by themselves, she grew smug. "Well, well, well," she sneered, "what have we here?"

Zach assumed a defensive posture with his spear.

Glen fainted. His eyeglasses spilled onto the floor nearby.

The Sand Queen laughed derisively. She turned to the Sand Monk. "So, monk, these are your valiant rescuers? Your crack troops? You clearly didn't pray hard enough."

The Sand queen returned her attention to Zach. "Listen to me, little boy. I strongly suggest you drop your spear. I wouldn't want to have to—break you."

Zach, trying to sound resolute, said, "I demand you release the Sand Monk. Immediately."

"Yeah, immediately," repeated Kalani.

The Sand Queen threw back her head and laughed haughtily. "And if I don't, what do you think you're going to do about it?"

Zach looked at the tip of his spear.

So did the Sand Queen. She saw the poison. Her expression grew dark. "Where did you get that?" she hissed.

"The spear?" asked Zach.

"No, you imbecile. The substance on the tip."

Zach smiled. "From Pepros, you dark witch."

The Sand Queen sensed danger. She grabbed a sword off the wall. Wielding it menacingly, she glided swiftly toward Zach. When she got within striking distance, she swung the sword toward Zach's left shoulder. He parried the blow with his spear. The Sand Queen pulled the sword back and aimed for his left leg. Again, Zach blocked the sword. The Sand Queen was enraged. She drew her sword back, howled, and swung with all her might at Zach's head. Zach managed to block the sword once again—literally saving his neck—but this time he lost hold of his spear. It crashed down onto the floor. Zach bent over to pick it up.

"Oh no you don't," the Sand Queen said firmly. She held her sword above Zach's neck. "Touch the spear and you die."

Zach knew it was over. The Sand Queen had won. He stood up and looked her in the eye.

"You didn't really think you could beat me, did you? You're just a little boy." She looked at Amanda and Kalani. "Drop your weapons. Now! Or the little boy will get a sword through the heart."

Amanda and Kalani's weapons clanged loudly against the stone floor. They did not know what to do next.

"Turn around. All of you," commanded the Sand Queen.

The kids turned around.

"Up against the wall!"

They complied, pressing their noses against the wall.

"Say your good-byes," the Sand Queen said harshly.

"It's been nice knowing you guys," said Kalani. She sounded petrified. "I'm sorry it had to end this way."

"It's been nice knowing you too," Zach and Amanda said in unison, their voices cracking.

Glen was still on the floor, passed out.

"Sorry Mr. Sand Monk. We tried our best," said Kalani.

"I know you did," responded the Sand Monk. Then, in a deep, commanding tone, he said, "But you should most definitely *not* be sorry."

An arrow whizzed through the air. It plunged deep into the Sand Queen's neck. She shrieked in anger and turned around. The Sand Monk, standing, gazed at her with a devious smile. He was holding a bow that he had just plucked from the armory wall.

"You fool!" she yelled. "Don't you know that arrows can't kill me? Your death will be hideous. I'll see to that."

Dumbfounded, the kids turned around.

The Sand Queen began to moan. She placed her hands on her face, which was starting to melt.

"No!" she howled.

"That's right," said the Sand Monk, still smiling. "Poison."

"How could you do this to me?" The Sand Queen's voice was muffled, like she was choking on sand. She had lost about two feet of height. "You've spoiled everything!"

The Sand Monk approached her. He stooped over and looked her in the right eye, because the left one had already dissolved. "You lose."

"No!" she wailed. "No!"

Silence.

Zach looked down at what was left of the Sand Queen. She was nothing but a pile of grainy sand on a stone floor.

♦VII♦

Kalani raced over to the Sand Monk and embraced him. Zach and Amanda were not far behind.

"Thank God!" exclaimed Kalani, gushing tears of joy. "Thank God!"

The Sand Monk smiled warmly.

"How are you holding up?" asked Zach.

The Sand Monk chuckled and rubbed his face. "Well, my body has certainly seen better days. But my spirit is just fine."

Zach was curious. "How did you get the poison?"

The Sand Monk explained, "The Sand Queen knew she was being followed by a small group. I was slowing her progress—and trying my best to do so, mind you—so she decided to set a trap in the other room. A last stand, if you will. When the Hooded Blacksmith and the others entered the room, the Sand Queen, along with two lion men, ambushed them. It was over pretty quickly. The Sand Queen took care of Pepros, sticking him with his own poison-tipped spear. Pandalese was no match for the lion man who attacked him. After dispatching Pandalese, the lion man joined his friend and the two of them battled the Hooded Blacksmith. You should have seen the Hooded Blacksmith fight! He managed to kill both lion men. Sadly, as he was finishing off the second one, the Sand Queen pounced on him, driving a spear through his chest."

Zach asked, "Afterwards, she brought you into this armory?"

"Indeed," responded the Sand Monk.

"But how did you get the poison?" asked Amanda.

"Oh yes, I almost forgot. After the Sand Queen killed Pepros, she watched her lion men take on the Hooded Blacksmith. She wasn't going to join in unless she had to, I guess. Anyway, her back was turned, so, unbeknownst to her, I rummaged through Pepros' garments, hoping against hope that I might find some extra poison."

"Thank goodness she didn't see you," said Kalani.

The Sand Monk nodded and continued, "I removed the small package of poison from Pepros' pocket and hid it in my own. Obviously, when you guys came in and surprised—and distracted—the Sand Queen, I seized the opportunity to use it."

"I didn't know you were such a good shot," said Zach.

The Sand Monk grinned. "I had some training in my youth."

Amanda looked back at Glen, who was still out cold on the floor. "Mr. Sand Monk," she said, sounding concerned, "please take a look at Glen."

"He can wait," Kalani said dismissively. "Let me heal you with my healing stone."

"No, no, I should take a look at the boy," said the Sand Monk.

He walked over to Glen, kneeled beside him, and placed his hand on his forehead. The Sand Monk whispered a couple of prayers and began to hum an eerie-sounding tune.

Glen woke up. He looked at the Sand Monk and mumbled, "You wouldn't believe the horrible dream I just had."

"Shhhh," said the Sand Monk. "You can tell me all about it later."

Glen tried to stand up, but his legs were still wobbly. He tumbled to the floor.

"Easy now," said the Sand Monk. "Don't try to do too much too soon."

Kalani said, "Mr. Sand Monk, can I heal you now?"

The Sand Monk chuckled. "Do you know how to use that healing stone you've got there?"

"Yes, Pandalese showed me how to use it. It's heating up as we speak."

"Very well," said the Sand Monk. Grimacing, he lay on the floor. "I suggest you move it over my entire body. Pay special attention to my ribs."

Kalani followed his instructions.

After a short while, the Sand Monk sprang to his feet and said, "Wow! I feel like a new man. Well done, Kalani!"

She beamed.

"All those nasty welt marks are gone from your face," observed Amanda.

The Sand Monk made a sour face. "Yes, the Sand Queen was quite fond of whipping people with her white gloves, wasn't she?"

Glen managed stand up. "I guess I wasn't dreaming after all."

"No, you weren't," said the Sand Monk. "Think you can do some walking?"

Glen took a deep breath and exhaled slowly. "Yeah, I think so."

"Splendid!" The Sand Monk looked at the kids. "Shall we leave these musty old tunnels?"

"That's an excellent idea," said Zach.

The Sand Monk draped his arms around Zach and Kalani. With a bounce in his step, he led the four children out of the tunnels.

EPILOGUE

◆I◆

"**S**o, what's going to happen next?" Kalani asked the Sand Monk.

The kids were sitting on the floor of the Sand Monk's Sandtopia temple in front of the sandstone Buddha. They had just returned from an emotional funeral service for Pandalese and the Hooded Blacksmith.

After lighting several sticks of sandalwood incense, the Sand Monk answered Kalani's question. "Well, as you might imagine, news of the Sand Queen's death spread rapidly. To prevent chaos from breaking out, the sandroid rebels seized power and installed Haljan as the new government's interim leader."

Kalani asked, "Haljan's the new leader of Sandtopia? Is he the new Sand King?"

"Oh, heavens no," replied the Sand Monk. "Haljan abolished the monarchy and announced the formation of the First Sand Republic. He called for elections to be held in six months. Moreover, for the first time in history, humans will be given limited representation."

"That's great!" exclaimed Zach.

"It's about time," added Kalani.

"Yes, it's a good thing," the Sand Monk remarked. "We have to remain vigilant, though, because it's very difficult to change attitudes and prejudices. Sandroids will continue to look down on humans for some time, I can assure you. Nonetheless, we'll soldier on."

"Maybe over time Sandtopia really will become a 'sand utopia,'" commented Amanda.

"Yes, my hope is that eventually the island will indeed be worthy of its name. But we still have a lot of work to do. And we must not be complacent. As you saw first-hand, evil exists—"

"Yeah, we saw some pretty tough things here in Sandtopia," interrupted Kalani.

The Sand Monk continued, "Indeed. Remember, you must always have the courage to stand up to evil and injustice—at all times. Even if doing so means questioning or confronting powerful authority figures. Some leaders do not deserve to be in such lofty positions."

"Like the Sand Queen," stated Zach.

"Exactly," said the Sand Monk. "Let me tell you guys something. You are each more powerful than you may realize. I mean, look at what just transpired—four kids, being brave and loyal, helped topple the mighty Sand Queen!"

Kalani smiled. "Well, we did what we could. We had some help, of course!"

"Nevertheless."

"Mr. Sand Monk?" asked Amanda.

"Yes?"

"Before we return to Earth, may I take one more trip to Pure Land? I'd love to show the place to Zach and Kalani."

The Sand Monk observed Amanda intently. "Hmm . . ."

Kalani was curious. "What's Pure Land, Amanda?"

"Oh, Pure Land's just wonderful. That's where we met Valencia and her walking cats. She's quite kind. But she can be a bit bossy at times."

"Walking cats? Doesn't every cat know how to walk?" asked Zach.

"Her cats walk upright on their hind legs," explained Amanda. "Like humans. Valencia even has a cat that plays the piano. Oh, and get this: Glen put his hand right through her!"

"What is she, a ghost or something?" asked Kalani.

"Her vibratory rate's higher than ours," answered Amanda.

"Amanda, have you been smoking something?" asked Kalani. "Because you aren't making any sense." She looked at the Sand Monk. "Do you know what she's talking about?"

"Indeed, I do," said the Sand Monk. "You see, Amanda and Glen stepped through a portal to a place called Pure Land. It's much different from Earth and Sandtopia. The inhabitants of Pure Land vibrate at a much higher rate. That means they're not as solid as humans—or sandroids, for that matter—and therefore don't need food and water to survive. They're kind of like spirits. It's a very pleasant, peaceful place. But it can be dangerous for some humans to go there."

"Why?" asked Zach.

"Look at Glen," answered the Sand Monk. "His troubles are a direct result of having spent time in Pure Land."

"I don't get it," said Kalani.

Amanda responded, "I do."

"You do? Well, please explain!"

"Valencia told us that the shock of experiencing a reality so radically different from Sandtopia and Earth is too much for some people to handle," said Amanda.

"Oh, I get it," said Kalani. "We all know that Glen's closed-minded. He's having trouble dealing with the fact that a place like Pure Land actually exists, and he can't deny its existence because he was actually there."

"Exactly," said the Sand Monk.

"Hey, I'm standing right here," Glen said defensively. The left side of his face twitched. "Anyone else want to take a pot-shot at me?"

The Sand Monk tried to soothe him. "Glen, my intent wasn't to insult you. If Kalani and Zach really want to visit Pure Land, then I'll take them. They can probably handle the experience. In fact, it may be good for them. I would be remiss, however, if I failed to inform them of the potential danger of visiting such a place. As I said, your current symptoms are a direct result of your having visited there."

"So, you're going to let them go?" asked Glen.

The Sand Monk paused. "Yes, I think they can handle it. Especially if I go with them." He quickly added, "But I won't let you join us."

Glen's face twitched violently. "It's a nice place but I don't think I should go back there."

"Indeed." The Sand Monk looked at Glen intently. "I think I should perform another healing on you. Now, I think you have a very special crystal in your pocket."

Glen fingered the crystal given to him by Gavendo. He was stupefied. "How did you know about it?"

The Sand Monk smiled mischievously. "I have my ways. Please give it to me and lie down on the floor, on your back."

Glen complied.

The Sand Monk said a few prayers and started humming an eerie tune, which sounded like a Gregorian chant. He held the crystal several inches above Glen's face. It started to glow.

After a short while, the Sand Monk stopped humming. "Okay Glen, you're good to go. You shouldn't have any more problems."

"Thanks, Mr. Sand Monk," said Glen. "I really appreciate it."

The Sand Monk looked at Zach and Kalani. "Would you like to take a short visit to Pure Land now?"

They nodded their heads vigorously.

"Splendid!"

◆ II ◆

The Sand Monk, Kalani, Amanda and Zach arrived at the sunken path that led to the Pure Land portal. They entered the trench.

"Wow, look at all these inscriptions," commented Kalani.

"Oh yes, there's something I forgot to tell you," remarked the Sand Monk. "We can't stay in Pure Land for very long."

"Why not?" asked Zach.

The Sand Monk answered, "The high vibratory rate means that if we stay too long, our molecules will loosen and our bodies will fall apart. We'll die." The Sand Monk pointed at the markings on the walls. "That's what those inscriptions warn against."

"Good to know," remarked Kalani.

With the Sand Monk in the lead, they arrived at the stained-wood door at the end of the trench. He turned around and asked, "Are you ready?"

The kids nodded.

"Splendid!"

He pushed the door open and walked through, followed closely by Amanda, Zach, and Kalani. They each disappeared into a dazzling, blinding white light.

◆ III ◆

Kalani remarked, "Wow, it's like we're in an ancient Egyptian tomb. There's even a sarcophagus here!"

Amanda said, "Yeah, we call it the Sarcophagus Room."

Kalani stood up. "I notice a difference here. The atmosphere seems lighter than on Earth and Sandtopia."

"Yes, it's less dense," confirmed the Sand Monk.

"Look!" exclaimed Amanda. "There's another small box on the sarcophagus. Last time there were pictures inside. I wonder if there's anything inside this time." She ran up to the box, opened it, and peered inside. She pulled out a single photograph.

"Well?" inquired Zach.

"It's a black and white picture of the pile of sand that used to be the Sand Queen," explained Amanda.

"There's writing on the back," noticed Kalani. "What does it say?"

Amanda flipped the picture over. "It says: 'Well done!'"

"That's kinda neat," said Kalani. "I wonder who wrote it."

Valencia entered the room with a flourish. "I did!"

The Sand Monk beamed. "Valencia! How wonderful to see you again."

"Yes, it's been a while," she said.

"Obviously you've been here before," Zach said to the Sand Monk.

"Many times. It's unusual for me to come here in the body, though. Usually, I come here in my meditations."

Amanda was unable to contain herself. "Valencia, we did it! We saved the Sand Monk!"

Valencia smiled approvingly. "Yes, I know."

Amanda ran up to Valencia and tried to give her a big hug but her arms passed right through her.

Valencia laughed. "Aren't you forgetting something?"

Amanda looked sheepish. "Sorry, I forgot. You're a spirit."

"That's quite alright," said Valencia. She smiled wryly at Amanda. "I see you survived the trip in the sarcophagus."

"Oh no!" exclaimed Amanda. "I forgot I'm going to have to get in that thing again!"

"Don't worry," said Valencia. "I cleaned it. There aren't any more mummy wrappings left inside."

Zach and Kalani exchanged puzzled glances.

Valencia pointed to the next room. "Please, won't you join me in the parlor? I'm sure my cats would love to see you."

They entered the parlor.

"Zach—look!" Kalani pointed at the piano. "There's a cat playing the piano!"

"What? Oh my God, you're right," said Zach. "Amanda, you weren't joking!"

"Of course I wasn't."

The cat at the piano stopped playing and sized up the newcomers. Unimpressed, he scrunched his face and coughed up a hairball. Then, with gusto, he resumed his song.

"Please, sit at my table," said Valencia. "I'll call on Mr. Tribbles to serve some tea." She clapped her hands and shouted, "Mr. Tribbles? Oh Mr. Tribbles? Tea for five, please."

Miss Angel burst into the room, running on her hind legs. Miss Angel's pursuer, a very cross Miss Cassie, followed closely (a ball, thrown earlier by Miss Angel, was stuck on Miss Cassie's head). Miss Angel, who was the faster runner, looked back at Miss Cassie, pointed at her, put her paw to her head, and cackled wildly. In response, Miss Cassie hissed.

"Girls, girls, we'll have none of that!" Valencia said sternly. "Not in front of our guests!"

They circled the room, cackling and hissing, and then left.

"Sorry about that," said Valencia. She shrugged her shoulders. "What can you do?"

"That was strange," commented Zach.

Kalani was speechless.

Mr. Tribbles entered the room, carrying a tray with five teacups, some sugar cubes, and fresh cream. He placed a cup of hot tea in front of each person seated at the table and left. Zach and Kalani were astonished.

Valencia looked at the Sand Monk. "So, what are your plans now that the Sand Queen has been vanquished?"

"I'm hoping to help out with the upcoming elections, to make sure they're fair. This is the first time we've ever had elections on Sandtopia, so there's a lot of work to be done."

"Are you planning to run for office?" asked Kalani.

"Heavens no!" exclaimed the Sand Monk. "I'm not interested in being a politician; I'll be busy enough with my religious duties. I will, however, search for some promising human talent and encourage them to run."

"Who's going to be Sandtopia's next leader?" asked Zach.

"After the general election in six months, the Sand Congress will select a prime minister," replied the Sand Monk. "He or she will be the new leader."

"Who will that be?" asked Amanda.

"It's hard to say," answered the Sand Monk. "I'm sure Haljan will throw his hat into the ring."

"Will you support him?" inquired Kalani.

"Yes, if there aren't any human candidates. There are a few people I would like to see run for office."

"Who?"

"Logarno wants to run. If he's elected to the Sand Congress, I'll put my full support behind him should he choose to run for the post of prime minister."

"Will the sandroids allow a human prime minister?"

"Haljan has announced that sandroids will always comprise the majority of the Sand Congress, even though humans outnumber them in the general population. Therefore, it's highly unlikely that a human will be Sandtopia's first prime minister."

Kalani scowled. "That sucks!"

"I don't like it any better than you," said the Sand Monk, "but we have to take these things slowly. Over time, perhaps, there will be proportional representation. But the sandroids won't allow it right now because they fear a human majority in the Sand Congress. They fear having a human prime minister. Sandroids think—no thanks to the Sand Queen's propaganda—that humans would use this power to settle old scores and persecute them." The Sand Monk turned to

Valencia and asked, "Would it be possible for me to take a stroll with the kids through your garden? It's such a lovely garden."

"Oh please, won't you let us look at your garden?" pleaded Amanda.

Valencia smiled. "What a nice idea."

◆ IV ◆

They walked along a combed gravel path, bordered by polished stones and blooming flowers.

Kalani tugged at Zach's shoulder and pointed at a cluster of flowers. "Look, they're changing colors! Aren't they beautiful?"

"Yeah," Zach responded. He took Kalani's hand and squeezed it gently. She blushed. "The colors are so vibrant."

The Sand Monk smiled. "I wanted you to see how much more striking the colors are in Pure Land. It's due to the higher vibratory nature of the place. I also thought you would like to see flowers that change colors."

"It's wonderful," Amanda gushed. She pointed ahead. "What's that?"

"A stone fountain," explained Valencia. "It's my garden's centerpiece."

They walked to the fountain and sat on its edge.

"I don't want to leave!" declared Kalani. "It's so calm and peaceful and beautiful here."

"Me neither," said Amanda. She looked at the Sand Monk. "Can we stay?"

In the distance, they heard wild cackling and hissing. They watched Miss Angel scurry across a path, followed by Miss Cassie, ball still on head, in hot pursuit.

"Girls!" shouted Valencia. "You had better not mess up my flowers!"

"I know you would like to stay here, Amanda, but it just isn't possible," said the Sand Monk.

"Zach, you want to stay too, don't you?" asked Amanda.

Zach hesitated. "Umm . . . well . . ."

A few birds, warbling beautiful harmonies and melodies, dove down and playfully fluttered around the kids.

Amanda giggled.

"They're saying hello," explained Valencia, smiling.

The Sand Monk turned to Valencia and said, "Thank you so much for showing us your garden." He looked at the smiling kids. "I think it's time for us to leave."

"Yes, I agree," said Valencia.

"No!" said Amanda. "I don't want to go!"

"Amanda!" Valencia said sternly.

Amanda relented, knowing she really did not have a choice. "Alright," she said dejectedly. "We don't have to get in that coffin again, do we?"

Kalani did not like the sound of that. "What?"

Amanda explained, "To get back to Sandtopia we have to climb inside the sarcophagus."

Kalani arched an eyebrow. "You mean we have to lie down inside a used coffin?"

Valencia smiled subtly. "That's right. It's the only way. But don't worry, I cleaned out all the old mummy wrappings and removed the dust."

Kalani felt nauseous. "Ugh!"

◆V◆

They slid open the door to the Sand Monk's Sandtopia temple and entered.

"So, how was it?" asked Glen.

"Oh, it was wonderful!" gushed Kalani.

"Did you get to meet Valencia and her cats?"

"We sure did."

"Let me guess, Amanda didn't want to leave," teased Glen.

Amanda frowned.

"Actually, none of us wanted to leave," said Kalani. "Mr. Sand Monk, thanks again for taking us there for a visit."

"No, thank *you*." The Sand Monk looked at the kids. "Thank you all for your help. You should be very proud of yourselves." He paused. "Now then, I think it's time for us to return to Hawaii."

Kalani chuckled.

"What is it?" asked the Sand Monk.

"I'm trying to figure out how we're going to explain all this to our friends and family!"

"I hadn't even thought about that!" exclaimed Amanda.

"The solution is simple," said the Sand Monk, with a twinkle in his eye.

"I'm listening," said Kalani.

"Tell them the truth," he answered.

Kalani rolled her eyes. "That'll never work. Who's going to believe us?"

The Sand Monk picked up a satchel filled with purple crystals. "Shall we go to the portal?"

Kalani grinned slyly. She grabbed Zach's hand. "Yes, that would be splendid!"